MAPLE SPRINGS

MAPLE SPRINGS

BY

PIERRE C ARSENEAULT

ISBN: 978-1-951122-39-3 (paperback)
ISBN: 978-1-951122-52-2 (ebook)
LCCN: 2022941201

Artemesia Publishing
9 Mockingbird Hill Rd
Tijeras, New Mexico 87059
www.apbooks.net
info@artemesiapublishing.com

Content Notice: This book contains descriptions of enslavement, tor-
ture, and kidnapping that may be disturbing to some people.

Follow Pierre at:
www.pcatoons.com
www.mysteriousink.ca

DEDICATION

This book is dedicated to all those who are afraid of the
dark yet brave it anyway.
This one's for you.

PROLOGUE

DAMPENED BY the night's light rain, Lucinda Mayweather's dress clung to her as she stood shivering in the dark doorway of the small barn. She crouched, feeling at her feet in search for the kerosene lantern she had recently extinguished. Finding the lantern, she quickly lit it and shone it before her, seeing only the solid back wall of the barn. The small earthy scented empty building used to keep hay in the winters was sealed tight expect for the open door behind her, yet the strange looking pale man who had been there moments ago was nowhere to be seen.

It is as if he has magically disappeared into the darkness, thought Lucinda.

She still didn't know what sort of person the strange looking pale man was, but she didn't care. He had come to her with promises of power and strength, enhancing her natural abilities to take all the things that she wanted. In exchange she would use her gifts to get him what he fiercely craved.

It seemed simple as all she had to do was use skills she possessed to fulfill her side of the bargain, a smiling Lucinda thought. The deal had been struck and if he really could do the things he promised, she would finally get everything she ever wanted and more. That was all that mattered.

1

Lucinda held the lantern high, lighting her way in the rain, humming a heavenly melody in a soft voice as she made her way back to her lover's house. She needed to gather her things and leave before he woke. She would take his horse, leaving him his new Model T, which she despised. She had to leave and quickly as the people of the tiny hamlet were becoming suspicious and she couldn't have that. Especially not now that she would be able to get whatever she wanted.

CHAPTER I

THE NOONDAY sun glaring on the police cruiser's windshield, Officer Cortez' almost didn't see Sandy Newman as she stepped off the sidewalk and into traffic.

"What the hell?" Officer Cortez shouted as she slammed the brakes, stopped the car, and got out, heart racing wildly from the near miss.

She pulled Sandy Newman out of the street and onto the sidewalk. From what she could tell, Sandy had lurched into the street to flag down her police cruiser.

Now Sandy rambled incoherently at first, or at least it had seemed so to Officer Cortez, who was still reeling from the near miss. After catching her breath, Officer Cortez composed herself but in the heat of the moment, her years of experience was replaced by bitterness and impatience.

"Calm down, ma'am and start from the beginning," Officer Cortez said in the least condescending tone she could muster to the mature lady before her. She pulled a small notepad and pen from her breast pocket, dabbed the tip of the pen to her tongue and readied herself to take notes.

"Sandy. My name is Sandy, not ma'am."

"Fine, Sandy," Cortez replied, trying not to display her annoyance with something like an eye roll. She had to remain professional. "This is your flower shop, isn't it?" Officer Cortez asked wanting to confirm what she already knew. The sign above the storefront she faced read The Flower Shop, one of the least original business names Cortez had ever come across; she would later tell coworkers.

"Yes," Sandy blurted while fidgeting, clearly still frazzled by whatever had inspired her to place herself in front of a moving vehicle.

"Okay. Take a deep breath and tell me again what happened."

"Well I was coming back from the printer," Sandy said gesturing in the direction of Repeat Printers. "I was ordering wedding invitations. My niece is getting married, you know."

"Sandy, get to the point," Officer Cortez said impatiently while trying to appear understanding.

"Well, this big mangy mutt came running at me. Scared the shit out of me," Sandy stated while dabbing at the perspiration on her brow.

"You flagged me down for a dog?" Officer Cortez asked incredulously.

"A stray dog."

Officer Cortez couldn't hide the disbelief on her face. Sandy Newman, owner of The Flower Shop, had flagged her down for a dog. She jotted down a note about a stray dog.

A wide-eyed Sandy blurted the next part. "It had an arm in its mouth."

"A what?" Officer Cortez's face scrunched as she looked up from her notepad.

"An arm," Sandy stated while nodding as if this was proof of what she had seen. "It was dead."

"The dog?"

"The arm. I mean it was like old dead. Not like fresh dead."

"I'm sorry, what?" Officer Cortez asked, lowering the

notepad. This required her full attention.

"It was all rotten and I think a few fingers where missing," Sandy said while shuddering. "Maybe the dog ate the fingers?"

"Look, Sandy. I'm sure it was just a branch," Cortez said dismissively while tucking the notepad and pen back into her pocket.

"It was an arm."

"A dead arm?" Cortez grinned. "Did you see which way the culprit went?"

A flustered Sandy pointed down toward the printing shop. "Down that way. Toward the printers."

"I'll look into it," Officer Cortez said in what she thought was a very convincing tone of voice. "But it's probably just a branch."

Sandy, obviously angry, pivoted and marched into her flower shop.

"Imagine that," Cortez mumbled. "A severed arm and its dead too," she said with a chuckled as she walked down the sidewalk. Half a block away, a large black cat casually strolled before Cortez. It sat on the sidewalk and made eye contact. Confused, Cortez stopped in her tracks and wondered why the cat seemed familiar to her.

She glanced back to see if Sandy was watching. She wasn't. Cortez turned again but the cat was gone.

"That was weird," Cortez said as she scanned the area for signs of a stray dog.

***

Later that night, near the Maple Springs Park entrance, teenager Robyn Skidmoore stood under a flickering streetlamp amidst fluttering shadows. A gentle breeze messed her short dark hair while also rustling the leaves on the trees adding to the creepy darkness. The flickering of the lamp suddenly stopped. Its illumination now faint, it cast weak shadows on this warm June evening. Shadows Robyn blended into, except for the light glinting off her studded belt. Her pale appearance enhanced by black pants and black Led Zeppelin T-shirt. In one hand, she held a shiny chrome staple gun and a black folder.

Robyn looked around nervously, recalling the old rumors of monsters and evil creatures lurking in Maple Springs Park. The gooseflesh on her arms that had been previously put there by the hoot of an owl was dissipating. But darkness made her imagination run wild as she glanced at the tree line not far from the cement curb at the edge of the road beside her. Shadows seemed to sway in the gentle breeze. The darkness made her anxiety bubble to the surface. Thick clouds covered the crescent moon and caused the shadows to blend with the deep black of night blurring where comfort ended and darkness began. Robyn's irrational fear of the dark, which had plagued her childhood, often returned in such moments. But it had never truly been the dark that scared her as much as what she imagined could be lurking in it.

Robyn took a deep breath and focused on the task at hand, calming her nyctophobia.

The lamppost was metal and so she couldn't use the staple gun. She would use the roll of packing tape she wore around her thin wrist like an oversized bracelet. In dealing with her anxiety, she had almost forgotten about it as it blended with her other bracelets. Tucking the staple gun into her studded belt, she pulled a page from the black folder and paused.

The page showed a picture of Sun-Yun, a young girl of Korean descent with shoulder length dark hair, a stunning smile and happiness in her eyes. And Robyn's best friend. It was a selfie taken in the very park that Robyn was next too right now, during happier times. Robyn had tried not to believe the rumors about a monster in the park, but how else to explain the disappearances? A tear ran down Robyn's cheek as she checked if the poster had any spelling errors. She felt stupid for compulsively worrying about spelling. It was another one of her many quirks that her best friend would have teased her about. The word **MISSING** was written in a large black bold font at the top of the page followed by the question; have you seen this girl? The poster had Robyn's cell phone number on the bottom.

Sun-Yun Kim had been missing for over a week and it seemed like the townsfolk had brushed it off. After Robyn's persistence, the police spoke to Sun-Yun's parents and then insisted all was well.

How could they brush off their daughter being gone this long? They'd said that Sun-Yun had gone to visit family, but when Robyn had said the Sun-Yun wouldn't leave without telling her, texting her, her parents had said Sun-Yun didn't like Robyn anymore.

Robyn knew that was a lie. They'd been best friends since the first grade, even though all the other kids had shunned Robyn and made fun of her. Robyn hadn't fit in even back then. But Sun-Yun had sat with her at lunch. They had shared sandwiches on the very first day; Robyn's peanut butter and jelly, Sun-Yun's ham and green cabbage. Robyn was different but that had never mattered to Sun-Yun, even all those years ago. But now, with her childhood friend missing, those happy memories brought sadness instead.

Robyn palmed away a tear and proceeded to use the packing tape to hang the poster she had made. The poster up, she put the roll of tape back on her wrist and tucked the folder under her arm.

As she turned to walk away, a heavenly scent of lavender wafted to her, carried on the gentle breeze. Robyn lifted her chin and smelled at the air as if trying to capture all of the strangely intoxicating scent. The clicking sound of shoes on the sidewalk startled Robyn and she did something she would have never done as a child. She ran to the edge of the dark woods and hid in the shadows, not wanting to be seen out alone after dark.

The sudden quiet was overwhelming, the only sound her own breathing. In the quiet, even the crickets were waiting to see who was coming. Hard chills suddenly rocked Robyn's body as the realization of being in the complete dark engulfed her.

Robyn bit her lower lip hard, struggling not to scream as her fear of the dark gripped her. But in that moment, the scent of lavender intensified and this time it seemed overpowering. She felt her anxiety wash away as all she could think of was the scent and where it was coming from.

As the clicking of the shoes on the concrete came closer Robyn could now hear an angelic voice humming softly, a heavenly melody that had a soothing effect on Robyn. Her fear of the dark abated and a relaxed feeling overcame her. She contemplated stepping out from the shadows to greet the figure which appeared in the distance. Unsure why she would feel this way, Robyn shook the fog from her mind and decided to remain hidden as she watched the stranger approach.

Robyn couldn't help but sense a familiarity as she watched a beautiful mature woman with long, wavy blonde hair casually stroll into view. She had high cheekbones, a strong jaw line. She walked down the sidewalk as if all was right in her world. A pang of jealousy coursed through Robyn as she watched the carefree woman walk toward where she had been mere moments before. The woman wore a long flowing beige skirt which had lacy ruffles at the bottom, with what looked like a light blue shirt as a top. The sleeves were rolled up to her forearms and the shirt's hem was tied at the waist with a large knot of blue fabric. She wore large gold hoop earrings that shone in the faint darkness as she strolled casually to the lamppost. The melody the enchanting woman hummed sounded strange yet welcoming. *She looks like a fortune teller from a carnival*, thought Robyn.

"Stevie Nicks," Robyn whispered before she realized she had said this aloud. She placed a hand over her own mouth as her eyes grew wide hoping the woman hadn't heard her. Stevie Nicks is what Robyn recalled her father saying about the women standing under the faint light of the lamppost. He had said she reminded him of the singer from Fleetwood Mac, only prettier if that was possible. A fact that her mother said was preposterous as Stevie was much-much prettier than this strange woman could ever be. Her mother had clearly been jealous.

The blonde who looked like a fortune teller reached out a hand and gently touched the picture on the poster as if caressing the young girl's cheek. The smell of lavender again felt overpowering as Robyn took her own hand away from her mouth and sniffed the air, breathing deeply. A renewed calming feeling swept over her as she watched the woman gently tear the poster off the lamppost. She examined it carefully before crumpling it into a ball and tossing it on the grass between the tree line and the cement curb. As the crumpled poster came to a stop, anger swelled up inside Robyn. The woman had cast Sun-Yun's poster aside as if she didn't care what had happened to her. She was like all the others, who didn't care about any of the other missing people of Maple Springs. Robyn started to rise, she wanted to throw the crumpled poster in the woman's face. How dare she dismiss Sun-Yun like that! But every thought of confronting the woman was stifled as the blonde turned and stared in Robyn's direction.

Her serene appearance had been replaced by a stern expression as the woman glared in Robyn's direction with such intensity that gooseflesh appeared on Robyn's arms for a second time that night.

Unsure why, Robyn knew the woman wasn't looking at her but past her. Something else had caught her attention and that made Robyn want to scream. She bit her lower lip even harder as she watched, fear of the unknown tugging at her very soul. The women turned and began walking again although with less carelessness and more determination. As if now, she had somewhere to be, she walked off leaving the crumpled poster on the grass.

A large drop of rain hit Robyn's cheek as she stepped from under the canopy of trees that had concealed her. She wiped it away as she realized she was now shivering in fright. She looked at her shaking hands as she tried to steady herself. A sudden loud cracking noise came from the woods behind her, reigniting her fear of the unknown. She darted to the glow of the faint streetlamp and turned to see if whatever had made the sound had followed her. More drops of rain came as she realized the calming soft scent of lavender was now gone, replaced by her previous uneasy feeling. She stared into the dark woods in the same direction she thought the enchanting woman was probably looking and saw nothing at first. Then high in the trees a glitter of something caught her eye. Maybe ten feet off the ground two reddish lights sat in the tree. Unsure of what she was really seeing, she was about to dismiss them when they flickered out, then came back on. Like someone, something, had blinked. A bout of panic set in.

"Monsters aren't real!" Robyn shouted in frustration.

The glowing red lights faded away as the rain began. Unsure if what she had seen was her imagination playing tricks on her, Robyn turned and ran for home, propelled by a little extra zest as she couldn't get the idea that something had been watching her out of her thoughts.

***

A light crackling of brush came from where the girl had hidden, and a small dark silhouette appeared in the shadows. The small figure remained hidden as a large lumbering shape with glowing red eyes emerged from the brush yet clung to the shadows. The large creature took a long stride, reached a weirdly beast-like arm covered in stiff hairs into the faint glow of the streetlamp, scooped up the crumpled poster from the ground and quickly stepped back into the darkness of the trees. The small figure stepped backwards following the much larger thing vanishing into the dark park where it had previously concealed itself.

Moments later, in the stillness, the lamppost light began flickering again for a few moments and then burned out, letting the darkness win this night.

***

Having come in using the back door, Robyn crept up the stairs in the faint glow of nightlights. She had been caught in the sudden downpour just a few blocks from home, so now she left a trail of wet footprints and water droplets behind her. She walked as softly as she could, not wanting to wake her parents as she had no desire to explain being out this late. Her parents wouldn't understand. They had already begun talking about how Sun-Yun Kim had gone back to South Korea. A fact that was ridiculous because Sun-Yun wasn't born in South Korea. She was born right in Maple Springs, in the back of her father's store because her mother had waited too long before going to the hospital. Her parents were originally from South Korea before immigrating. But that didn't stop people from saying that her best friend had gone back home, even when she argued and tried to explain that Maple Springs was her home. Robyn's mother had even said something about visiting family and had brushed it off during their last discussion. So even they wouldn't understand why she had made posters and had to put them up all over town. Someone had to know something, and she had to know what had happened to her best friend. Robyn simply couldn't accept the idea that her friend had vanished like the others.

Rumors were that others had disappeared as well. She'd heard these rumors since she could remember; tall tales of a Boogieman who lived in Maple Springs Park or the one that came in the dark and stole people away. As a child, she never believed those stories, but they did make the dark a place she avoided at all costs. But now, years later when people started vanishing again, she couldn't get a straight answer from anyone about any of it. Robyn had pieced together through rumor and gossip that at least six others had vanished over the last few years. A few people said it wasn't that many; she was worried that it was more. Some talked about it being for a long time and some denied it all. Nobody seemed to know how many had really gone missing and the struggling Maple Springs Gazette's website was no help at all.

When she'd asked the local veterinarian, Robert Emerson, what happened to his wife, he shrugged and mumbled something about how she had finally gotten up the courage to leave him—something about her not being able to cope with all the animal hair. But when Robyn said he was crazy and that others were missing too, including her best friend, he brushed her off like many of the others had done before him. And when Robert wasn't looking, Robyn put a poster up on the bulletin board of the veterinary clinic anyway.

Now, in the glow of the hallway's nightlight, creeping past her parent's closed bedroom door, she noticed the door of her brother's bedroom was ajar. Gently pushing it open and peering inside, she saw her little brother sleeping under a thick blanket. She crept into the dark room and stepped on one of the many action figures strewn about. She muttered a curse under her breath and dried her hand as much as she could before flicking on the nightlight above his dresser. She glanced back and saw dozens of action figures strewn about, some carelessly and some in carefully calculated positions. But now that she could see, Robyn carefully avoided the other action figures as she made her way to the door. At last count her little brother Duncan, whom she sometimes lovingly referred to as Skidmark, had over a hundred various sized action figures, his favorites being the cheap Chinese knockoffs of monsters and robots. He liked those best because they didn't have stories. He could use his imagination and come up with his own stories for them. His current favorite was in bed with him as he slept; a hybrid of a muscular horned ape with goat hooves and large monstrous fangs. She recalled Duncan was still working on the story for this one as he couldn't make up his mind whether it was good or evil.

Robyn often pretended she hated her little brother but that wasn't the case. She had loved him from the day her parents brought him home from the hospital. Perhaps even before that. But now the nine-year-old had become a friendless annoying brat. Robyn closed the door behind her and froze as she heard Duncan stir. Listening intensely, she heard nothing else and so went to her own room to get out of her wet clothes. The rain had ruined all her posters, but she wasn't too worried as she could make more at her father's printing shop where she worked part time. She would have to do it when he wasn't there so he wouldn't say something stupid about her best friend going back to Korea again. She tossed her wet clothes in the hamper. Something she knew her mother hated but she did anyway.

Minutes later, Robyn was in bed, passed out from exhaustion while her parents slept soundly in their room. The nightlight in the upstairs hallway flickered but remained lit. The glow from underneath her brother's bedroom door flickered and went out. From underneath the same door, a red glow grew softly until it lit the floor of the hallway. The glow remained for a brief while and then faded away as quick as it had appeared leaving the hallway softly lit by the nightlight in the hall outlet.

CHAPTER 2

THE LONG beige skirt and blue shirt clung to the rain dampened Lucinda Mayweather as she walked along Main Street to the house with the white picket fence she called home. For years since coming to the Maple Springs area she had tried to remain under the radar. But people had always been drawn to her and she might as well use her charms and abilities to her benefit. So, she decided to relocate to a more prominent place in town where she would be able to get better access to more influential townsfolk. This home on Main Street was perfect except it had previously been occupied by Leonard Legault, a legendary recluse with very little use for people. Lucinda had heard the rumors early on of how Leonard had had a way of getting under people's skin quite easily. And since the man was an enthusiastic taxidermist, the irony of people saying this was not lost on Lucinda Mayweather.

Rumors were that Leonard had money hidden in his home. Earnings he had squirreled away as an accountant for organized crime. But if you inquired many would tell you those were unfounded rumors. And since Leonard didn't hunt, he had to purchase the carcasses from locals for his hobby of making statues with dead things. But now people didn't bring him dead animals anymore as Leonard was sick. Bedridden. And Lucinda had moved in to help care for the aging recluse. Nobody really knew how long she had been at Leonard's house. That was just as conflicting as the rest of the "facts" people knew, ever since Lucinda Mayweather came to town.

But now she walked with purpose, marching up the walkway of the blue and white trimmed, large two-story Victorian house. She walked past one of Leonard's creations, a stuffed deer posed on the front lawn. She stopped on the stoop next to a large stuffed grey squirrel perched on the veranda's railing and glanced at the way she had come, half expecting to see someone or something following her. She had sensed something strange but didn't know what. Something hidden in the woods of Maple Springs Park and whatever it was had been watching her. And while she sensed its presence, she couldn't tell what it was and this bothered her as she would normally have ways of sensing these things.

Satisfied that noting had followed her after all; she entered through the unlocked front door and was greeted with faint illumination and a muffled scream. The scream stopped and was replaced by faint sobs for help.

The house was softly lit as always with many antique fixtures, the thick dark curtains prevented any outside light from invading the home. Every square foot of Leonard's home had a decoration of sorts or something ornate to fill any potential voids. Antiquities, strange art and his works of taxidermy filled every corner, every space and every inch.

A stuffed owl, old and worn with age, sat near the front door and Lucinda gave it an affectionate pat. She unbuttoned the damp blue shirt, untied the knot at her waist and removed the garment revealing a torn silk camisole. Lucinda shuddered at the thought of how the blue shirt wasn't what she had been wearing when she left the house just hours ago. Her lover had been a tad overzealous in removing her blouse, tearing it in the process. And while she had loved the frilly white blouse she had worn, her lover had more than made up for ruining it with his passionate lovemaking. Lucinda smiled as she hung the shirt on the rack of a large stuffed moose in the wide hallway. In the simple ruined camisole with her long skirt flowing, she walked past a stuffed coyote, running her fingers over the fur on its back.

Lucinda walked past a stuffed crow perched on a lit antique light fixture and stopped before a wide, old wooden door. As a fresh hoarse scream began, she slid the deadbolts open revealing a staircase descending into the dark basement. The damp smell of mildew mixed with the cloying sweetness of lavender wafted up the stairs as warm air caressed her skin. Lucinda smiled as she flicked on the light. The scream stopped abruptly as Lucinda descended into the abnormally warm basement. Antique imitation torch sconces cast a faint glow throwing as much shadows as it did light yet still illuminating the large room. The basement was littered with dried flowers, plus cloves of hanging garlic and hundreds, perhaps thousands, of dusty jars on wooden shelving that covered most of the walls. Where there weren't shelves, there were cabinets, leaving very little empty wall space anywhere. The jars contained strange looking liquids and jellies of various colors. Some contained Leonard's garden preserves while many contained dried herbs, plants and spices of sorts. A large jar contained various sized eyeballs that looked all too real. Another contained thousands of teeth, from different animals, though a few looked suspiciously human. A large wooden table with multicolored stains on its surface, sat in the center of the room. More shelves and cabinets had been built under the table, and these held a variety of tools and more jars.

"Hush, girl," Lucinda Mayweather said as she walked thought the room to the old metal cell against the back wall.

The young Korean girl from the poster sniffed at the air as she relaxed her grip on the metal bars. Sun-Yun Kim closed her eyes and pushed her face between bars and inhaled deeply, a sudden strong scent of vanilla filled her sinuses.

"I thought you would never come back," Sun-Yun mumbled as she became suddenly docile. She opened her eyes. "I was afraid."

"Don't be afraid, my child," Lucinda replied in a soothing tone.

"I'm sorry," Sun-Yun replied with much sincerity.

"I know," Lucinda whispered. "But I'm here now."

"Is it that time again?" Sun-Yun asked.

"Yes, my child. It's that time again."

"He scares me," Sun-Yun replied with downcast eyes, as if ashamed to be speaking ill of the one that Lucinda called on. "The man with the cold skin, there's something wrong with him."

"It's okay, my child," Lucinda replied. "He won't hurt you. But you have to do this for me, okay."

"Yes. For you...I understand."

"Do you, my sweet child? That's good." Lucinda reached through the bars and caressed Sun-Yun's hair making the young girl smile ever so slightly.

The ornate antique imitation torch sconce near the corner of the room flickered and went dark. Behind Lucinda, a man cloaked in darkness stepped out of the shadows. It was as if the shadows clung to him, refusing to let go, as he walked toward the cell that contained the young girl. Shadows dissipated and revealed a pale skinned man with graying hair. He wore a strange looking suit that might have been the height of fashion in the late 1800's. His top hat matched the open breasted black suit, exposing a yellowing white ruffled shirt. The shadow man smiled, showing yellow, pointy teeth as he walked past Lucinda, stroking her cheek with a yellow fingernail as he did. Lucinda shivered at his touch. The shadow man walked through the bars of the cell as if they didn't exist.

"I was waiting for you," he croaked in a hoarse voice. "It's been a while since you called to me."

"I'm trying to make this one last," Lucinda replied. "People aren't as easily swayed anymore."

"Poor you," the shadow man said sarcastically, a thin smile exposing his yellow pointy teeth.

Sun-Yun grasped at the bars of the cell fiercely as she locked eyes with Lucinda, as if now begging for protection. Lucinda reached through the bars and grasped the young girl's chin in her hand and returned her gaze. She gently shushed Sun-Yun as she watched a tear run down the girl's cheek.

"I thought maybe you had finally changed your mind about our arrangement," the shadow man said with a coy smile.

"Never," Lucinda replied as she watched the shadow man brace himself behind Sun-Yun and place his cold hands on each side of the young girl's head. His long fingers touched at the front of the girl's face and his smile widened as he made eye contact with Lucinda.

Sun-Yun's eyes rolled upwards into her head, leaving only whites to be seen as her body stiffened. Her grip tightened on the bars, her knuckles whitened as she convulsed before the tenseness faded and her body relaxed. Her mouth opened and drool ran down her chin and dripped down her front to land on her filthy t-shirt.

The shadow man's smile widened even more as Lucinda turned and walked away, leaving him to his feeding. She paused in the stairwell to glance at him before leaving the room and locking the basement door behind her.

***

Breakfast at the Skidmoore house always included a heaping helping of chaos. Gloria Skidmoore was already doing her first load of laundry of the day while griping about a certain someone putting wet clothes in the hamper, again. Tim Skidmoore was making his son his favorite blueberry pancakes; unsuccessfully trying to make fancy shapes which end up looking like Rorschach blotches. Nine-year-old Duncan sat at the kitchen table drawing a picture of his favorite action figure as it stood guard near the edge of his page. Robyn starred at her phone while eating dry toast and brewing a pot of coffee while griping about getting a Keurig like everyone else on the planet.

"Well everyone else can help fill up the landfills with their one serving coffee pods but not in this house," Tim remarked as he flipped a pancake that was supposed to look like a giraffe but had an abstract look to it at this point, as if it was illustrated by a four-year-old.

"Unlike those people, we care about the environment," Gloria added.

"All I said was that if we had one, I wouldn't have to wait so long for a stupid coffee," Robyn replied. "Besides... nobody complains about the single serve creamers or the sugar packets. Or those millions of little stir sticks people throw out after just one use."

"Actually, those stir sticks are being banned in a lot of places, along with straws," Gloria said from behind the laundry hamper.

"Cofffeeeeeee..... braiiiins.... Err... I mean, coffeeeee," Duncan mocked doing his best zombie impersonation as he scribbled away on his drawing.

"Shut up, turd-brain," Robyn replied setting down her phone to finally pour herself a cup.

"Robyn?" her father said.

"What? He's being a shit head and I haven't had my coffee yet because of this stupid antique machine you guys insist on using."

"A shit head... ha!!" Duncan muttered with his typical immature grin.

Robyn's phone binged, singling a missed call. A quick glance told her Thomas McDougal had called yet again. He probably just wanted to make fun of her. Those jocks types were like that and she dreaded talking to him. *I'll call him back later*, she thought, *after coffee*, while taking her first sip of much needed patience inducing nectar.

"Duncan, be good," Gloria added as she disappeared into the laundry room.

Tim flopped a pancake onto a plate and placed it front of his son, "Giraffe?"

"Roadkill giraffe," Duncan replied with a scrunched nose as he reached for the ketchup.

Tim smiled at his son's joke as he spoke. "You're going to leave that thing here like we talked, Duncan."

"Do I have to?" Duncan asked in the whiney voice his sister despised.

"Mrs. Litney at daycare asked that you leave it home," Gloria added as she emerged from the laundry room. "She said it scared some of the younger kids." She was referring to Duncan's favorite action figure, the hybrid muscular horned ape with goat hooves and large monstrous fangs.

"Why do I even have to go to daycare anyway," Duncan complained.

"Because Dad has a business to run, Robyn is doing deliveries for him this summer and the last time I took you to work with me was a disaster," Gloria said in frustration as she poured herself a coffee. She often brought this up, never letting the boy forget his Home Alone style rampage in the back room of the Thrifty Dollar Store she managed.

"And you're still too young and immature to be alone," Robyn added with a smile she hid behind her steaming cup. She glanced at her father and saw a look that meant; *don't goad your brother*. Something she ignored, not wanting to argue about her best friend going back to Korea. A conversation that would be incredibly depressing.

Robyn's phone rang again and this time she answered.

"Not now," she barked and ended the call. Thomas McDougal could wait to try and be funny.

CHAPTER 3

*H*OW CAN *you love someone so fiercely yet hate them with every fiber of your being*, wondered Robyn as she drove off in the Repeat Printing company van; her first delivery of the day in the back.

Her stupid little brother had farted the whole way to daycare and tried to blame it on her. The stench was so bad she felt like vomiting while her father shot her that glance of his via the rearview mirror. She wanted to punch him but the last time she did that, her mother grounded her for two weeks and Robyn felt she was too old to be grounded. At eighteen, she wasn't a little kid anymore, but Duncan had a way of pushing her buttons. He had been such a sweet kid when he was little but once he started school, he'd changed and became a little brat. So, it took all her willpower not to tattle on him when she saw he had his favorite action figure tucked away in his backpack as he was getting dropped off at daycare. The same stupid action figure Mom told him he couldn't bring with him. The temptation to tattle was huge, just to pay him back for getting her grounded that last time. But now she had other things to worry about and all she wanted was some quiet time to think about her next move and telling on Duncan would have the opposite effect.

She would take a little detour after her first delivery. Grab another coffee and head to the park to do some serious thinking. But first, her delivery to Robert Emerson's vet practice. Apparently, Robert had decided to run for city council and had ordered leaflets from her father's printing shop. And after answering a barrage of questions about other printed things Robert would need for his upcoming campaign as he signed for his delivery, Robyn froze on her way past the vet's bulletin board. Amidst the posters of dogs and cats lost or needing homes, the one she looked for was gone. The poster of her missing friend was no longer there. Anger rose in the young girl as she glanced back toward Robert who was busy obsessing over his recently printed leaflets. Outrage welled up inside her for the man she had felt pity for so recently. Robert's wife Nancy was among those who'd mysteriously vanished even if now he went about as if nothing was wrong. But at this very moment, nothing but anger swelled in her.

She thought briefly about putting up another poster but what was the point? Robert would probably throw it away again, like before when she'd seen one crumpled in his wastebasket. Her anger now subsided as she wondered if maybe someone other than Robert had taken this poster down. Perhaps someone with good intentions had wanted to make copies or had information and wanted to call her? Perhaps, but a part of her felt that it was more than likely Robert took the poster down and discarded it without a second thought. Hate festered inside her for whoever took down the poster and for now that would be Robert.

Plus, she was almost out of posters and would need to print more. Something she intended on doing while her father took a real lunch break. Something he hadn't been able to do in years. Printing wasn't the lucrative enterprise it once was. Business was good but not good enough to hire full time staff. A few part timers were all he could afford. And this summer, that part time staff consisted mostly of Robyn.

I'll print another batch of posters while he is eating his ham and cheese sandwiches in Maple Springs Park, thought Robyn while absentmindedly chewing at her cuticles as she left the vet clinic. *I wish I could take a real lunch break*, she thought. *Maybe I would have time to check the park and see if the dark forces that are rumored to be there do exist.*

And I'll call Thomas McDougal. After a brief bout of texting, he had seemed sincere when he told her he wanted to talk to her about Sun-Yun's disappearance.

***

Duncan stood transfixed under one of the many ornate lampposts on the edge of Maple Springs Park; his T-shirt damp with perspiration from having run all the way there from Mrs. Litney's daycare. In his right hand dangling at his side was his favorite action figure. The same action figure that had again, gotten him in trouble with Mrs. Litney. Although he tried hard to keep it hidden from the strict daycare operator and the other kids, Mandy Taylor had seen it and started crying. And after some pressing questions from Mrs. Litney, Duncan eventually confessing to being told by his parents that he couldn't bring action figures; especially this one, to the daycare anymore. And when she told him she was going to have to call his parents, Duncan panicked. Sneaking out the side door, he ran. With no destination in mind, he wasn't running to anything in particular but rather away from the trouble he was in with Mrs. Litney.

But now standing under a streetlamp on Bishop Street which ran along one side of Maple Springs Park, he was transfixed by a poster taped to the steel post. He recognized the girl in the picture as Sun-Yun, his sister's best friend. The one some of the older boys called Some-Yum for the fact that she was pretty hot, he had heard them say. Also, he knew the poster was printed at his father's printing shop since it had a small telltale watermark on the bottom right-hand corner of the page. That and he recognized his sister's phone number. His mother had made him memorize it, just in case he ever needed it.

Duncan noticed his sister coming down the sidewalk. He swallowed nervously and tightened his grip on his plastic action figure. Without hesitating, Duncan dashed into the thick brush at the edge of the park, the branches snagging at his clothes. He hid in the brush and watched as his sister walked past him, a black folder tucked under her arm and a roll of packing tape on her wrist amidst the dangling bracelets she wore.

He knew he would get yelled at once his mother got a hold of him. His father would try and calm her down with his, 'let him be a kid' talk. And he would add his; 'it's just a toy after all' speech. And while mom would agree that it was just a toy, she would remind them both that the other kids at daycare were much younger than Duncan. She would again tell them that kids like Mandy Taylor were too young and wouldn't understand that the scary looking doll Duncan loved to play with was just a plastic toy. And Duncan would again get frustrated at his mother, reminding her that action figures were not dolls. Plus, Mandy was only crying for attention, he would tell them yet again. And since Duncan knew what he had coming, he was not in a hurry to get home anytime soon. Besides, his mother was at work, his father would be printing orders in the morning and his sister certainly didn't want to have her kid brother following her around all day. And at this point, there was no way he would go back to daycare, not after being gone this long. Mrs. Litney would be hoping mad at him and had probably already called his mother anyway.

Duncan held his action figure up in front of him, looking it over as he smiled and said, "Like grandma says, there's no time like the present."

He glanced toward the sidewalk, his sister nowhere in sight. He decided to cut through the park, something his sister would never do but Duncan wasn't a scaredy-cat like she was. If she saw him, she'd think he was either fearless or stupid. Duncan never considered that venturing through the woods of Maple Springs Park wasn't something anybody in town would do anymore. Not even in broad daylight. Those that noticed would point out the lack of birds and squirrels, then rapidly change the subject as a chill ran down their spine. But Duncan wasn't afraid.

Being careful not to be seen, he emerged out of the brush and walked down the sidewalk as if nothing in the world was out of place. As if he should be there, on Main Street, alone. A nine-year-old, walking down the sidewalk until he reached old Leonard Legault's house, the blue and white trimmed large Victorian house where *she* now lived. That pretty blonde lady who smelled like his grandmother's special oatmeal cookies, and not the ones she kept in the jar and fed everyone either. The special ones she made when he was alone with her. The ones she used her magic ingredient in. Rum. And just enough to give it that taste she loved, she would tell him. She only ever let him have a few, during those special visits. The pretty blonde woman smelled like that.

Duncan realized he was standing by the white picket fence, smelling at the air as he detected a slight aroma of his grandma's oatmeal rum cookies. He shook his head to clear the fog in his mind as he remembered why he had come here in the first place.

"There's no time like the present," he repeated to himself as he shifted his gaze to one of Leonard's creations, a stuffed deer posed on the front lawn.

He glanced about to make sure he wasn't being watched before retrieving something he had hidden near the corner of the picket fence on a previous reconnaissance mission. He set his action figure down and pulled a sealed plastic baggie from under a shrub and retrieved a Zippo lighter and a small canister of lighter fluid before stuffing the baggie into his pocket. He wasn't supposed to play with it. He had promised his parents when they gave him his late grandfather's Zippo lighter. He swore he would never ever play with it. He knew fire wasn't something you played with. He was smart enough to know that. But this wasn't play. This was work, he thought as put the lighter in a pocket.

He'd stolen the canister of lighter fluid from the house a week before and had hidden it, along with the Zippo, under the bush. Looking around again to make sure he still wasn't seen, he scrambled over the picket fence and hid behind Leonard Legault's deer on the front lawn. He peeked under its belly at the house to see if he could catch a glimpse of Lucinda Mayweather. The scent was faint, but he smelled the cookies and that told him she was home.

Being careful not to get any on himself, he cracked open the tip of the yellow canister of lighter fluid and took a step back. He glanced around and at the house and saw that the coast was clear. He squirted lighter fluid liberally onto the stuffed deer, getting it all over it while being careful not to douse himself as well. Once satisfied he had sprayed enough, he squirted some down the deer's leg and made a thin trail to the bush at the corner of the picket fence. He picked up his action figure, smiled at it before pulling the lighter from his pocket and kneeling on the ground next to the fuel. After three tries, the old Zippo lit. Duncan touched the flame to the trail of lighter fluid and marveled at how quickly the fire traveled across the lawn and up the deer's leg. Most of the deer was quickly engulfed in flames much higher than Duncan had imagined. Panic swelled in the young boy as he got to his feet, leapt over the fence and bolted across the street.

He ran as fast as he could until he was safely hidden between two neighboring homes, safely behind a smelly plastic garbage can. He watched the stuffed deer burn for what must have been a good minute before one of the neighbors ran over with a fire extinguisher and struggled to put out the blaze.

Fearing he'd be discovered, he cut through a back yard and headed to the next street, eventually making his way back to Main Street, knowing full well he would have to go to one of his parents' place of work and the choice was easy. Dad wouldn't be quite as upset as mom and he might even let his son play on the computer while he got work done.

Duncan felt the Zippo lighter through his pants pocket as he walked. Can't lose that, he thought, or mom and dad will kill me. He tossed his demonic looking action figure into the air and caught it.

"You're like Loki," he said to it referring to the Norse God of Mischief. "A trickster, yeah... that's it."

He smiled as he walked on, happy with himself.

CHAPTER 4

STANDING IN the dimly lit basement, Lucinda had been watching the shadow man, his long cold fingers splayed over Sun-Yun's face with his palms covering the girl's ears. It fascinated Lucinda that he could only do this to the willing; take from them the essence that bound their soul to the fleshy bodies they inhabited. There was a time, in the beginning, that she felt remorse for the ones being sacrificed, made to part with their bodies so she could live, but that was then and this is now. The only real part she was concerned about now was that the shadow man gave her what she wanted; her part of the bargain, letting her keep her own essence in exchange for someone else's.

Lucinda watched the young Korean girl who was kneeling at the edge of the cage, her eyes blank and her mouth agape with both hands wrapped around the bars. Sun-Yun was doing as she was told. Lucinda was troubled by the small streaks of white already appearing in the young girl's hair. She was a fool to think because the girl was young, that she would have a lot to give. Lucinda was using too much energy to keep things as she wanted and so needing too much from the girl in return. She was oblivious to this and at this pace, Sun-Yun wouldn't last more than a few weeks, maybe a month at the most. What was left of her bonding essence was depleting much faster than anticipated.

This meant Lucinda would have to find herself a new volunteer to feed the shadow man or he would take away the gifts he had given her. She would need a new volunteer soon.

A loud noise roused Lucinda from her deep thoughts. Something was happening and it must be nearby for it to be audible in the basement. Sound didn't penetrate this old house easily, which was one of the many reasons she had chosen it. The sound she now recognized as a siren, most likely from a fire truck she thought. She glanced at the shadow man, his yellow toothed smile wide, his gaze fixed on the young girl as he drained some of her essence, each time taking only what Lucinda allowed. The young girl's blank stare assured her that all was fine and that she could go check on the commotion outside.

Lucinda locked the basement door behind her and quickly went outside to the veranda. She stopped next to the large stuffed grey squirrel perched on the railing and saw thin black smoke billowing from the front lawn. The few neighbors not at work that morning had gathered around the picket fence to watch. The stuffed deer Leonard Legault had perched near the middle of his lawn was blackened and still giving off sooty black smoke. Her neighbor Dwight McGarvey stood nearby clutching the fire extinguisher he had used to douse the flames. The firemen gathered around the smoldering deer as they chatted amongst themselves. A police car, lights flashing but sirens off pulled up and parked slanted in the street before the house.

The handsome police office stepped out his car in a panic, as if he had still not realized that the fire had been contained. Officer John Fitzpatrick glanced at the house looking for its resident. He spotted Lucinda as she walked off the veranda and down the walkway toward the burnt deer. Officer Fitzpatrick rushed to her, placing his hand on her arm to get her attention but she paid him no heed.

"What happened? Are you okay?" Officer Fitzpatrick blurted, his voice filled with concern as he fixated on her stunning blue eyes.

"Not now," Lucinda replied as she brushed his hand away and continued on to greet the firemen. She smiled wide as she spoke in a soft voice.

"Thank you all so much for your concern but as you can see, the fire's out now," Lucinda said as she placed her hand on the arm of one of the firemen. She locked eyes with him as he froze and returned her gaze.

"I'm sorry, ma'am," he said while clearly mesmerized by her. He breathed deeply. She smelled like his late wife's perfume. "That perfume... my wife used to... I'm sorry, could you repeat that?" He asked.

"I said, the fire's out and I'm sure you brave men have other, more important duties to attend to instead of a deer fricassee," Lucinda said with a sly smirk.

"What happened?" Dwight asked as he watched Lucinda carefully. He'd been enamored with her ever since she moved next door, something he had not exactly kept a secret. She was the most beautiful woman he had ever seen, he often said to anyone who would listen. And she always smelled like sweet and sour sauce. "How did a stuffed deer catch on fire?"

Lucinda fixed her gaze on Dwight who didn't stand a chance against her charms.

"Wires," Lucinda replied without hesitation. "Bad wiring is what it was. Leonard had that deer wired so that it would move its head up and down."

She saw Dwight frown at the thought. For a brief moment, she could tell he knew this wasn't true but coming from the beautiful Lucinda Mayweather, he would believe it and she knew it. If it came from her, how could it not be true? I mean if anyone should know it would be Lucinda. She had worked her charms on Dwight and watched his expression change as of course she would know this. Lucinda had molded Dwight to believe anything she told him. She knew that by now he had altered his thoughts to the fact that Leonard must have told her all about it, shown her, in fact.

"Yeah," Dwight said. "Wires. I remember the deer used to move its head."

She knew a part of him would know this wasn't true. He'd lived next to Leonard for sixteen years and had never once seen the deer or any other of Leonard's creations move. She knew that, but her gaze made Dwight melt and now felt compelled to agree with her. Dwight would later think back and have no idea why he found himself agreeing with Lucinda Mayweather.

"Wires," Dwight muttered.

"Ma'am," the fireman said. "If it's wires, then maybe we should check the house to make sure..."

"Hush, no," Lucinda replied. "No need. That's already taken care of."

"Taken care of?" the fireman replied, befuddled as his crew watched, waiting for instructions.

A few of the neighbors returned to their homes now that there was no show to watch, while others watched Lucinda's every move, enamored by her presence.

The handsome officer's facial expression filled with concern as he stood a few feet behind Lucinda as if waiting to see if she needed him.

Speaking softly, Lucinda stated, "Yes, it is."

"I suppose it is," the fireman replied. "All taken care of," he added. "Let's go guys; back to the station."

"Go home, everyone," Officer Fitzpatrick said as if he

had suddenly remembered he had a backbone. "Go home," he repeated to the few remaining onlookers.

Lucinda watched as the firemen took their leave as did the rest of the neighbors. What was left of what used to be a deer no longer smoldered.

Officer Fitzpatrick stood next to Lucinda as she faced the blackened deer.

Once she was satisfied that no one would hear her, she spoke to him again.

"John," Lucinda said. She knew calling Officer Fitzpatrick by his first name made him putty in her hands. She glanced around to make sure Dwight had also gone home before she continued. "Find out who did this for me."

"But... the wires?" Officer Fitzpatrick asked. "You said..."

"Never mind that," Lucinda said as her patience grew thin. John Fitzpatrick wasn't a stupid man but his ability to resist her charms was completely nonexistent. It was as if he became a bit childlike whenever he was around her. Until she told him she wanted him to make love to her that was. Then his animalistic urges got the better of him and he was all man. He was a great lover when she told him to be.

"I need you to find out who set fire to my deer."

"Don't you mean Leonard's deer?"

"Don't be stupid, John. Now find out who did this but don't tell anyone you're looking into this for me."

"The wires?"

"Yes, John. We want them to think it was the wires. But find out the truth for me," Lucinda said as she walked away from him, walking toward the house.

"You want me to come inside and..."

"Go," Lucinda blurted. "But save yourself for me tonight."

"Yes, ma'am," Officer Fitzpatrick replied excitedly as he nervously fiddled with his gun belt.

***

Officer John Fitzpatrick watched the woman he desired disappear into Leonard's—no, her house. Once she was out of sight, he looked about the neighborhood. All was quiet again as it should be on a Monday morning. The excitement caused by the burning deer replaced by a languid normalcy. But when he glanced at Dwight's house, he noticed the shades in the living room window moving slightly.

Dwight had been watching them talk. And Officer Fitzpatrick couldn't help but wonder if he'd been watching both of them or just Lucinda. Jealousy wrapped its hands around John's mind in a subtle caress, giving him the gentlest of nudges as he debated knocking on Dwight's door. Although Lucinda had said not to let anyone know he was going to be looking for who did this to Leonard's deer.

No, it was her deer she said, although that didn't matter now. The only thing that mattered was that he please Lucinda, in all the ways she desired being pleased.

John's heart raced as he wiped perspiration from his brow at the mere thought of being with Lucinda.

CHAPTER 5

DUNCAN SAT at his father's desk in the back of the printing shop, playing classic minesweeper on the old desktop computer. His father wouldn't permit him unsupervised access to the internet and all the other games were lame. At least that's what he told his father each time he got to play on the antique computer. His sister had teased him all through the lunch hour about how mom was going to chew him out when they got home. How Mrs. Litney had called her and told her about his scary doll and Mandy Taylor's reaction to it every time she saw it. And it wouldn't matter how much Duncan was convinced Mandy did it for attention, it would always come down to mom threatening to take his action figures away if he didn't start listening. A threat she had never gone through with, yet, but Duncan feared he might have pushed his luck this time. This time mom hadn't suggested he keep it in his backpack or out of sight. Instead she had insisted he not bring it at all. He knew he was in trouble. He knew being grounded wasn't an option. Not with the families' hectic summer schedule, so mom might just have to make good on her threat, if he wasn't more careful from now on. And he had debated telling on his sister about the posters she was printing about her friend who had gone back to Korea. He had seen her print more while dad was away on lunch. But this wouldn't get him out of trouble and Duncan knew this little piece of information might just come in handy later on.

He glanced at his action figure of the hybrid horned ape with goat hooves before slowly leaning sideways, peeking at his father from behind the computer monitor. After having cleared the third paper jam in a row; his father was watching his printer carefully. Satisfied his father was preoccupied, he opened a browser and typed as quietly as possible.

"Hilarious pranks," he typed and hit enter. Lists of April Fools pranks came up first. Some sites offered compilations of pranks on video. One site was titled "Harmless and Hilarious Pranks."

That won't do, he thought. He cleared the browser and typed in a new search.

"Nasty evil pranks."

A website offering nasty brutal pranks was the first in the list of many to come up. One of the videos on the top site showed someone drawing spiders on a roll of toilet paper and rolling it back up. Duncan burst out laughing, forgetting he was trying to remain under the radar.

"What are you up to, son?" his father asked.

Duncan deleted the search history, closed the browser and opened a new game of classic Spider Solitaire while he smiled wide to himself.

"Son?" his father asked as he collected his print job.

In a scramble to not disclose what really made him laugh, he said the first thing that came to mind as he glanced at his action figure.

"I'm sorry, dad. I was just thinking about Mandy crying again. I know she does it just to get me in trouble with Mrs. Litney."

"She's five, son."

"Four," Duncan replied. "I think," he muttered after.

***

A sullen Duncan, elbow firmly planted on the dinner table with his cheek resting in his left hand, used a spoon to move his peas around on his plate. He could tell Robyn itched to check the text she had just gotten but didn't dare look at her phone while at the dinner table. She knew better than to bring any attention her way right now. The last thing either of them wanted was to be grounded. Not that the Skidmoores were big believers in grounding as that was saved for larger offences but best not to tempt fate. Not while their parents were in discipline mode.

Duncan had wolfed down the Shepard's Pie but picked out all the peas. He had never hidden the fact that he hated peas but everyone else loved them. So, mom always added peas to an otherwise delicious meal.

"I don't understand your infatuation with that doll," Gloria said as she did what she considered scolding to her son. Her version of scolding would seem tame to most parents.

"It's an action figure," Duncan said with a lot less zeal than his usual reply when someone called his toys dolls. His parents knew it irritated him. But from experience, he knew better than to lose his temper while his mother was giving him one of her lectures. Plus, his action figure was standing on the table next to his firmly planted elbow.

He scooped some of the peas into his mouth and swallowed them whole as fast as he could to avoid tasting them. *Mom is upset enough as is*, he thought.

"And you can't just run off like that," his mother said. "Mrs. Litney has enough to worry about without you disappearing on her."

Tim scooped up Shepard's Pie, dipped it in ketchup and chewed slowly while listening. He had scolded Duncan while at the printing shop, so he was quiet now.

Duncan watched Robyn poked her cell phone and tried to read her text nonchalantly so no one would notice.

From across the table, mom shot her a dirty look.

"Oh my God!" Robyn blurted as she scooped up her phone. "Leonard's deer on his front lawn caught on fire today," she blurted.

Tim paused with his fork sticking out of his mouth and muttered a single word, "Whu?"

A few clicks later and she was on Facebook using the fake account she used to avoid being bullied by some of the meaner kids she had gone to school with. She flashed her parents the phone with a picture of the blackened deer. Duncan looked but didn't appear as excited as he might have under normal circumstances. Something he hoped his parents would attribute to the scolding he had been getting.

Tim swallowed his food, "How?"

After a quick scan of the comments on the picture, Robyn said, "Some are saying it was electrical, but others are saying lightning."

"Lightning?" Gloria said in disbelief.

Duncan scooped up more peas, pinched his nose and swallowed them whole.

"Dwight McGarvey says his neighbor found a can of lighter fluid next to his garbage cans," Robyn read from another comment.

Duncan, who had been drinking his milk, choked and spat milk on the table as he remembered putting the lighter back in its proper place but not the canister of lighter fluid. Covering his face with his napkin, he saw his chance and dashed off to the bathroom. In his haste he forgot his favorite action figure on the kitchen table.

***

Naked, covered only by the thin black silk blanket she had made her lover purchase; Lucinda reached over John Fitzpatrick's lean body for a small container on the nightstand. She opened its lid, inhaling deeply the scent escaping from the tiny jar.

"I'm sorry," John said. "I know I can do better," he added meekly referring to his short fuse in this night's love making.

"Oh, you're not done," Lucinda said.

John ran a hand through her hair as he pondered professing his love for the most beautiful woman he had ever laid eyes on. Her beauty was intoxicating. Her high cheekbones, perfect jaw line, thin pointed nose and piercing eyes always turned heads. That and her long flowing, wavy blonde hair combined with a curvaceous body; men were drawn to her like moths to a flame. In reality, Lucinda knew that John's lust was due to a bit of magic and her natural beauty. Her charms and the special ingredients that she added to her baked goods helped snare and hold the men she used, but all the magic in the world couldn't keep the fat off her ass. So, she vigorously exercised and watched her diet. A long life wouldn't be worth it if she didn't get to make love to any man she wanted to. And right now, she wanted John Fitzpatrick, for many reason.

"But I..." John began before Lucinda interrupted him.

"But first, did you find out who burned my deer?"

"You mean Leonard's deer?"

"Whatever," Lucinda replied impatiently.

"No. Not yet. But we did get a canister of lighter fluid from Dwight McGarvey."

"And what did that tell you?"

"Nothing yet, but I can't have someone check it for fingerprints without someone asking questions. And you said to not tell anyone."

"I suppose you're right about that," Lucinda said as she ran a hand down John's chest and trailed it down his hard stomach.

"You told everyone bad wires caused the fire."

"I did," Lucinda replied.

"I need a way to get someone to run the lighter fluid for prints."

"What if there was another fire?" Lucinda asked.

"A fire?"

"Yes, that's it. You get another canister of lighter fluid, set something on fire somewhere and then you can say our can was found nearby and tag it as potential evidence in the arson investigation."

"What if someone sees me getting lighter fluid," John replied. "They might know it was me who set this new fire."

"Don't worry about that," Lucinda replied as she crawled up to kiss him. "I'll get you the lighter fluid and you'll set something on fire for me, won't you?"

"I'm already on fire for you," John replied. "I..."

Lucinda planted a passionate kiss on the young officer before John could profess his love for her yet again.

Lucinda pulled away, straddled John's torso and cracked open her small jar again. This time she dabbed her fingers in the contents and ran the jelly over her lips.

John, mesmerized with the woman, ran a hand over her hip and up her side stopping at her breast which he cupped in his hand. He looked up at her with longing as he spoke.

"I want to make love to you again, but I need a little time for it to work again," John said.

Lucinda leaned in and kissed him passionately, smearing gel over John's mouth as she did this. John tried to push her away at first when he felt the sting of the stuff on her lips, but Lucinda wrapped her arms around his neck and head and continued the kiss. Soon John felt lightheaded, swooning in her embrace. He felt the room spin for a moment as he struggled to breathe. He had begun thinking he would pass out when the strange sensation faded and he began to realize what was happening. What Lucinda called his Johnson was rock hard again and the room was again filled with the scent of sex as she had climbed on top of him and was using him to pleasure herself. The dizziness having all but left him, he reached up and ran his hands over her body as he locked eyes with the woman he couldn't get enough of. A sudden urge to take over the situation welled up in him as he sat up, wrapped his arms around her and flipped her over onto her back without ever breaking their embrace. He grasped handfuls of her long blonde hair and began making passionate love to her the way she had told him to the first time they had laid together. Lucinda's charms were at work again, but John Fitzpatrick didn't mind at all. The fire would wait until tomorrow night.

CHAPTER 6

A **DAY LATER**, at 3:17 AM, under the cover of darkness and by the light of the moon, Duncan Skidmoore crouched next to the picket fence on the edge of Leonard Legault's property. No lights were on inside or outside, now or ever. The house felt abandoned even though this was the place where Lucinda Mayweather resided now and took care of the bedridden Leonard. That's what most people said. Duncan had good reason to suspect that perhaps there was more to it than creepy old Leonard Legault being sick. Duncan understood Lucinda wasn't an ordinary woman. He knew she was special. He had seen it with his own eyes, with a little help, of course.

Duncan turned and looked back at the way he had come. He had snuck up from behind Dwight McGarvey's house across the street. The outside light on the side of Dwight's house, freshly broken from a few moments ago, now dangled on an electrical wire. He looked next to the house where a large silhouette blended into the shadows. Two red glowing eyes burned brightly below the silhouette of large ram-like curled horns. The tall imposing figure stood stock still in the cover of darkness, blending in the shadows betrayed only by the glow of its eyes. Duncan held a hand out and waved it downwards, signaling to the large thing in the shadows. The red glow of its eyes dimmed to a barely noticeable shimmer. Duncan turned back to Lucinda's house, satisfied all was quiet; he crept over the fence, past the blackened deer and hid in the shadows next to the house. He looked up and felt his skin crawl as just above him, mounted on the side of the house was a large grey squirrel, posed in a state of panic as if it was ready to bolt away.

Duncan crept past another stuffed grey squirrel perched on the deck railing with the intention of peeking through a window on the covered porch. The curtains shut tight; he saw nothing but more darkness. He crept to another window that had a large stuffed black raven perched on the sill and found more darkness. Stepping off the veranda, he crept past a sun faded, stuffed raccoon clutching a pinecone perched on the lawn, making his way to the side of the house where he noticed a faint glow from a basement window. Kneeling next to the window, he tried to peek inside and found that instead of curtains; this one looked streaked and blackened. It must be painted on the inside as the outside felt smooth. Duncan pressed his face to the glass and cupped his hands on the sides, trying to peer inside. Unsure of what he was seeing through the streaks, he thought it looked like metal bars on the inside of the glass. *But why are the lights on in the cellar*, he wondered. Duncan felt the grass around him until he found what he was looking for under the edge of a bush; a small rock that filled the palm of his hand. It would do he thought as he turned back toward the small basement window only to come face to face with another of Leonard's creations. He couldn't believe he'd missed this one as it was staring him right in the face. A large black cat, sitting near the window he had been peering through a moment before.

He steadied his nerve enough to ready himself to throw the rock into the window when the cat arched its back and hissed at him.

"Shit!" the nine-year-old uttered, a curse that would have earned him a scolding from his mother had she heard him.

The cat stepped between him and the window and moaned, making Duncan's skin crawl. But before he could try scare away the large black cat, a clattering noise caught his attention. The trashcan from Dwight's house was metal. Although it was much louder than he had hoped, that was the signal. Someone was coming. That was when he heard the clicking of shoes on the sidewalk and melodic humming. Duncan hid behind a small shrub on the edge of the property, a shrub that badly needed pruning. He lifted his nose and smelled a fragrance of oatmeal rum cookies.

She was near.

Panic rose in the young boy. He crept up to the blackened deer and saw Lucinda walking with casual strides down the sidewalk. She was humming the most beautiful melody. Duncan found himself mesmerized, watching her as she walked toward him.

A loud clattering as a metal trash can landed in the street woke him from his trance, startling Lucinda as well.

A light came on inside Dwight's house.

He watched Lucinda who had stopped walking and was looking at the crumpled metal trashcan in the middle of the street. In a panic, Duncan threw the rock he had over Lucinda's head and toward a neighbor's house. The rock hit a car, setting off its alarm which began blaring loudly. Nearby he heard a dog baying. With her back turned to him and the cover of the car alarm, Duncan saw his chance and quietly ran across the street toward where he had come from and hid among the shadows.

I'll have to snoop some other time, he thought as he waited for Lucinda to go inside.

***

At 3:17 AM the night was at its darkest. Robyn carried her father's favorite flashlight, the one he bought at a flea market for ten dollars. She didn't know why she recalled that dumb fact while trying to calm her mind. On a normal night, the park creeped her out but tonight felt even more dreadfully eerie as she couldn't hear a sound. Not a cricket peeped, nor frog croaked. It was as if they too waited on bated breath to see what lurked in the darkness. And while Robyn's fear of the dark wasn't as bad as it had once been, wandering in Maple Springs Park in the middle of the night wasn't something she wanted to do without her father's treasured flashlight. Or without company either, if she could avoid it.

Thomas McDougal was someone Robyn would have never even said hello to before with his perfectly quaffed hair and chiseled good looks. He was nearly two years younger than Robyn, one of the high school jock types always wearing his letter jacket, and he had an air of arrogance around him that was like a bug zapper, pulling kids in to be near him, then shocking them when they got too close. But his calls and texts had been insistent and when she finally broke down and took his call, he had shared his own story; the one about his grandfather who'd disappeared a couple of years ago. Robyn had never wanted to be near Thomas, let alone be seen with him, but she was now seeing a different side of him. The side that still missed his grandfather. She could sympathize with that.

"My parents insist that my grandfather moved to Florida. Its bullshit and I know it," Thomas muttered.

Robyn listened, still in disbelief that he wasn't the asshole she had expected him to be.

"He hates the heat. He gets rashes when it's too hot." Thomas stated. "He'd never move away. He loves going fishing too much. Even if he did, he wouldn't not tell me."

Thomas choked back emotion before continuing.

"He'd call. I know he would," Thomas said wiping away a tear.

Robyn could believe that if his grandfather had moved away, he would have kept in touch like Thomas said. Or she wanted to believe it. Thomas made his grandfather sound wonderful. Unless that was him being delusional. Remembering his grandfather how he wanted him to be. Some people do that, especially kids. But one thing was clear to Robyn, Thomas, who it turns out wasn't as much of a dick as she thought he was, loved his grandfather and refused to believe the stories everyone fed him. In this sense, he was a lot like her and this she understood.

"There's something about this park," Robyn said. "I know it."

"Could be," Thomas replied, agreeing with her. "My grandfather used to come here a lot to walk his dog. He lived about two blocks away."

"The last time I spoke to Sun-Yun, we made plans to meet here at the park," Robyn said as she flicked the flash-light to a bright, narrow beam and scanned the woods as they walked. "I never saw her again."

"I never believed them when they said she went back to Korea," Thomas said. "She's not from Korea."

"I know," Robyn replied. "Her parents are, not her. I don't understand why everyone says that about her. It doesn't make any sense."

"It doesn't make a lick of sense," Thomas agreed.

"A what?"

"Nothing. Just something my grandfather used to say."

"Thanks for coming to meet me here, at the park," Robyn said.

"Thank you for asking me to come," Thomas replied.

"For trusting me... oh and I like your idea. I think it might help jog people's memories and put an end to the bullshit stories."

"I'm not sure it'll end the bullshit, but I just want answers. And I want to find my friend," Robyn said. She was losing hope that Sun-Yun would be found alive.

After spending over an hour after dark talking and putting up posters, they'd agreed to meet up later, to look for clues. And after sneaking out of her house and meeting Thomas at the print shop they'd wandered aimlessly through the park, hoping to find clues to the mysterious vanishings. Robyn felt less scared than she had the other night when she'd been here putting up the poster about Sun-Yun. She told herself it was because she had her father's flashlight this time, not because Thomas was with her, even if he wasn't a total dick.

"I gotta go," Thomas said as they neared the edge of Maple Springs Park; emerging into the glow of a streetlamp. "My parents will kill me if they noticed I snuck out at this hour."

"Don't forget to send me the picture," Robyn said as she began leaving in the opposite direction.

"I won't," Thomas replied. "Trust me, I won't."

"I'll text ya later," Robyn said as she turned and walked away.

Now alone, Robyn walked in the street parallel to the park. Now that Thomas had left, her anxiety and paranoia about the woods in Maple Springs Park returned. Her feeling that the woods contained an evil presence came back and she knew this kind of thinking was idiotic. This type of thing only existed in fiction and so she had to be stupid to think the park was haunted. Also, to think there was something to that Lucinda Mayweather woman everyone seemed to love. Something strange was going on in Maple

Springs and it was probably the cause of the disappearance of her best friend. But being a grounded person, at least she thought of herself in that a way, thoughts of such things made her wonder about her own sanity.

Was she losing her mind? Did losing her best friend do this to her?

No, she thought. *I'm not crazy.* Her best friend had vanished and a few days later, everyone acted as if it had never happened. But if she wasn't losing her mind, then a good part of this stupid little town was. This was the thought going through her mind when a sudden crackling from the woods of Maple Springs Park startled her. Robyn froze in her tracks, she wanted to scream but her throat suddenly felt dry and unable to comply.

About thirty feet in front of her, by the light of a lamppost, a boy emerged from the park and ran into the street. She quickly realized the boy was her little brother Duncan and he looked frightened. Robyn started to yell but couldn't as her dry throat cut out on her. And Duncan never saw her as he bolted across the street and disappeared into a backyard. But before Robyn could try and grasp what had just occurred, a much louder crackling rustling sound came, followed by a rhythmic thumping. Before she could react, a large monstrous creature burst out of the same wooded area her brother had come from. The tall creature briefly illuminated by the streetlamp was a muscular goat horned ape with goat hooves and large monstrous fangs. With glowing red eyes, it ran at a gallop and never slowed or paid any attention to her as it crossed the street and followed the path her brother had taken mere seconds ago.

A chill coursed over Robyn as she tried to wrap her mind around what she had just witnessed. She knew she should chase after the thing chasing her brother as he was in obvious danger, but her legs failed to move.

What was that? she wondered?

Then everything around her spun and dimmed. Robyn felt everything move and sway as she came close to fainting. A strong aroma of lavender suddenly roused her back to consciousness as she staggered. Still unsteady on her feet, but her mind clearing up, she turned to see a barefoot Lucinda Mayweather clutching at her dress, panting from a trek in the woods. Lucinda looked angry, and out of breath. She glared at Robyn who stood in the street under the light of the moon. Lucinda felt the ground where the monstrous creature had left a hoof print, raised her hand to her face and inhaled deep. She smelled her hand a couple of times before spitting on the ground and walking back into the park, the way she had come.

The asphalt beneath Robyn felt as if it had solidified again as her head stopped swimming, her anxiety subsiding. She took a few steps then all went black.

***

At 3:39 AM, Officer John Fitzpatrick wore dark colored pants, a black jacket and a baseball cap pulled down. He had a small canvas bag slung over his shoulder as he walked down Main Street. A uniform wouldn't exactly be appropriate attire for this evening's task. A task he was doing out of sheer desperation. He needed to keep Lucinda happy, or she would find herself a new lover. He knew this to be true because she told him she would. Lucinda never hid what she wanted. She never gave casual hints. She spoke her mind and did it with authority. And John was powerless against her charms.

He had carefully thought out his plan before heading to his destination this evening. Stillwater's Bar and Grill was the perfect location. The old building had a large parking lot and near the back, along the fence sat two dumpsters. Exactly the type of situation he needed for the task at hand. John looked about to make sure nobody was around and that all was quiet. He turned his attention to Stillwater's Bar and Grill, making sure that all was as quiet there as well.

With gloved hands, John dug out a canister of lighter fluid from the small bag he had brought with him, cracked it open and flipped open the lid of one of the dumpsters. John poured generous amounts of lighter fluid into one of the dumpsters, spraying all over the garbage inside while being careful not to get any on himself. When the canister was emptied, John tossed it inside the dumpster along with the fuel-soaked contents of the giant metal garbage container. From the same bag, he fished out a second container of lighter fluid, but this one was near empty and was wrapped in a plastic bag of its own. John carefully unraveled it, and gently placed the canister next to the second dumpster, far enough away to avoid catching fire. He took one last look around before pulling a small, battered cardboard box containing wooden matches and with a single match, set the dumpster ablaze.

He glanced about to see if anyone had seen the sudden illumination. Satisfied that he had yet to be discovered, he scooped up a piece of crumbled asphalt at the edge of the parking lot and threw it hard through a side window of Stillwater's Bar and Grill, setting off the alarm. On the second floor of the building, a light came on in what John assume was Stanley Stillwater's bedroom. John didn't wait to see if he was right. He ran hard and fast back the way he had come and didn't stop running until his sides were splitting from pain.

***

Robyn awoke in a panic, scrambling to her feet and getting her bearings. She had been laying in the street. Why, she wondered at first? Then the memory of what she had seen came in the same instant as the pain in her right knee.

A flash of memory of a giant monstrous thing, chasing her brother. She bent at the waist, clasped her tender knees and breathed deeply, trying hard not to succumb to her anxiety yet again.

Ignoring the pain, she ran for home. Her panic subsided slightly when she saw movement in her brother's bedroom window. She crept up the stairs as quietly as she could under the circumstances. She had expected to find the creature gorging on her brother's flesh. But instead, opening the door to her brother's bedroom she found him lying in bed, fast asleep.

"How?" she whispered.

She stepped into the bedroom and saw Duncan's favorite action figure, upright on the nightstand. Duncan probably put it like this as if it was standing guard. Her brother was weird when it came to his toys. But even in the dimly lit room, in the glow of the nightlight she could see it was of the large monstrous creature she'd seen crossing the road. A giant creature, ten or twelve feet in height and running at full gallop chasing after her brother. She had seen all this with her own eyes. But now her brother slept in his bed as if nothing had happened.

Had she imagined it?

Her sore knee reminded her that passing out in the street, really did happen. And she clearly remembered seeing the creature before she passed out. She took a step forward toward the nightstand but froze in her tracks as the action figure's eyes began to glow a dull red. She felt gooseflesh on her arms. That's when she noticed Duncan was now sitting bolt upright in bed, his eyes still closed but his head was turned toward her as if watching her. Robyn pivoted and ran out of the bedroom, slamming the door shut behind her and didn't stop until she was in her own bedroom with the door locked and the lights on.

A pale-skinned figure in a top hat, hidden in the corner shadows of Duncan's room, stirred slightly and then was gone again.

Duncan lay down, still sleeping but the eyes of the half ape part goat action figure remained a dull shimmering red.

With her bedroom lights on, Robyn thought sleep would never come but exhaustion soon found her and so did the nightmares of monsters chasing her little brother while she watched, helpless to stop it. She would wake in the morning, confused about where the dreams began and reality had ended.

CHAPTER 7

WRAPPED IN the only warmth she had, an old filthy blue comforter; Sun-Yun felt utterly defeated as she sat alone in the dark cage leaning in the corner sobbing softly, fondling the thin leather bracelet with the small heart charm her best friend had gifted her long ago. The antique imitation torch sconces cast a faint glow in the room but not enough for Sun-Yun. She had seen him emerge from the darkest of shadows where during better lighting of daytime, she saw nothing but concrete. This scared her the most. How was this possible? What kind of man was he? Was he a man at all?

Lucinda had finally shown her kindness the previous night and given her the dusty blue comforter after Sun-Yun had begged her for some comfort. Anything. But Lucinda hadn't forgotten what Sun-Yun had done to the small mattress she'd had in the beginning. Sun-Yun had tried to convince Lucinda that spilling the bucket containing her feces and urine was an accident. But Lucinda Mayweather had a way to see through her lies. She also had a way of coaxing people to tell her things, and while Sun-Yun had resisted at first, that hadn't lasted very long. She had confessed her feelings of abandonment to Lucinda, the one she now loved. Having been left alone for a long time, she had felt resentment, but had crumbled before Lucinda, the moment she had returned.

Lucinda knew that most people these days don't know what real hunger is. Not people from Maple Springs anyway. A small town like this doesn't even have homeless people. Perhaps if it had, the missing might go unnoticed for a long time. But small towns offered creature comforts that big cities didn't. And Lucinda's charms were much more useful in small quaint little communities like Maple Springs. And small-town folk, well-fed small-town folk didn't know what real hunger was. A day without food or water had left Sun-Yun thinking she was near death. And her resistance crumbled quickly. Although rebelling came in small doses in between visits as Lucinda's charms wore off. But soon after being placed in captivity, Sun-Yun had begun to feel genuine love for her jailor. Something that confused her at first, but she quickly forgot when the man from the shadows first emerged from the darkness.

Sun-Yun had barely slept in days. She assumed it was morning due to the amount of daylight coming through the barred window near the top of the wall. During the day, she could see the glass had been blackened but it looked streaked. It was hard to tell as the window was out of reach. She assumed the blacked-out window had been painted sloppily, which had left the streaks. And the little amount of light the streaks allowed through made Sun-Yun believe that the sun was rising and soon it would be daytime. How many days had passed, she wondered? She knew she had gone hungry the first day. Then the mattress incidence was on the second day. Her fury had helped her resist her captor's charms but being a bit naïve, she had no way of knowing this.

Sun-Yun stared at the metal dish that contained a dried piece of crust from the chicken potpie Lucinda had brought her the previous evening before leaving her alone again. Sun-Yun's eyes shut on their own from sheer exhaustion. When she opened them again, she focused on the large plastic water bottle next to the plate. It was near empty, and Sun-Yun was thirsty again. Her throat was still raw from the last time she tried screaming for help. She couldn't remember how long ago that was anymore as her eyes closed against her will yet again.

She had no way of knowing how long she slept but when she opened her eyes she saw him, crouched before her. His top hat tilted slightly with his thin arms between his spread legs, long thin fingers touching the floor. His pale skin made him look dead and yet she smelled his rotten breath through his yellow pointy teeth. He smiled wide as her heart began to race and the room began to sway.

"Lucinda?" the young girl said softly.

"Oh, she's not here," he replied. "It's just you and me," he added while smiling.

"No!" Sun-Yun said sharply through a dry crackling throat. "No more," she whimpered.

His smile vanished as he looked at her with curiosity.

"You're killing me, aren't you?" Sun-Yun asked, her voice crackling.

"I'm not taking anything you're not giving me willingly," he said, his smile returning as he examined the premature white hairs and the deep crow's feet starting to appear on the young girl's eyes.

He left out the part where he couldn't take her essence from her without her giving it willingly. She didn't need to know that part.

"I did it for her," Sun-Yun croaked. "I did it for Lucinda." Exhausted, Sun-Yun closed her eyes and leaned her head against the wall.

"I know," he replied. "You love her. They all do."

She opened her eyes but didn't move.

"Who's they?" Sun-Yun's voice was barely audible.

"The ones who came before you," he replied. "You're not the first one she's taken for me."

"You lie. She brought me here because she loves me."

"I know it's hard to accept. Because if there were others, that means you're not that special now, does it?"

"That's not true. She wouldn't lie to me."

"Ask her about the old man. Ask her about Ezra Mc-Dougal. Or the little girl named Elizabeth Woodworth; everyone caller her Lizzy but she hated being called that. Ask her about them. About how long they gave her."

"What do you mean, how long?" Sun-Yun inquired as she lifted her head from the wall. "Gave her what?"

"Just ask her," he said as he stood up straight.

"I remember hearing about Ezra. He's Thomas's Grandfather," Sun-Yun muttered. "Robyn hates Thomas and his friends."

"Does she?" he asked. "That's good to know."

Sun-Yun wouldn't remember falling asleep but when she awoke, he was gone.

Had he really been there, she wondered? Had she dreamt of him?

She couldn't help but feel that he hadn't done anything to her because Lucinda hadn't been there. As if he needed some sort of permission. Lucinda's blessing.

She was right about this but had no way of knowing for sure. But had she dreamt of the shadow man or had he really come to her?

She stretched forward, feeling her stiff limbs ache as she grabbed the water bottle and clutched it to her chest. She had every intention of quenching her thirst, but sleep came first.

She had vivid dreams of others being in the cage with her. A white-haired old man with his pants hiked up and navy-blue suspenders stood with his hands in his pockets as he shifted his dentures around in his mouth; back and forth, back and forth. And a young blonde girl with pigtails and knee-high socks that looked old fashioned. But the young girl and the old man said nothing. They simply stood in the cage, waiting. Sun-Yun knew deep down inside, they waited for Lucinda Mayweather. They waited just like she did now.

***

From the back seat of the family car, Duncan had protested during the entire drive to daycare while Robyn, in the front seat simply stared at what lay at her feet. His mother had made him empty out his backpack and had confiscated his favorite action figure before dropping her son off. The action figure she'd placed at Robyn's feet while telling her son that he would get it back after daycare. She grilled her son about behaving as Mrs. Litney was fed up. She reminded him that she had to beg the daycare owner for one more chance and that she wasn't about to let her son mess that up. Not for his infatuation with this stupid toy. If he could get through the day without getting into trouble again, his mother had promised she would give it back.

But now with Duncan dropped off at the daycare and Gloria dropped off at the Thrifty Dollar Store, Robyn sat in the front seat with the action figure facedown at her feet. She flipped it over with her foot and stared at it. The monster she thought she had seen chasing her brother looked exactly like this stupid plastic thing and it gave her the creeps.

"I called Robert yesterday and asked if he could help you unload the boxes, so you won't have to lug them all by yourself," Tim said as he drove.

"What?" Robyn asked. She hadn't understood what her father had just said.

"The boxes... for Robert." Tim said.

"What about them?" Robyn asked.

"The corrugated plastic signs that Robert ordered are in," Tim replied. "Or did you forget? I told him we would deliver them first thing this morning."

"Yeah, okay," Robyn replied as she poked the action figure at her feet again, looking for a button or somewhere to insert batteries that would explain the red glowing eyes she had seen.

"I asked Robert if he could help you unload the boxes," Tim repeated.

"Dad, they're corrugated plastic. They weight a lot less than the brochures I delivered to him last time."

"I suppose, but there's like twelve big boxes of these."

"I'll be fine," Robyn replied. "I can manage."

"Plus, the wires too; those wire brackets to stick the signs in the lawns. There's a couple of boxes of those, too."

"I said I'll be fine."

"Those are heavy so be careful."

"Are you going to vote for him?" Robyn asked.

"Robert? I haven't decided yet."

"I overheard you and mom talking about him this morning."

"We went to school with Robert, your mother and I. We've known Robert for a very long time. He always ran for everything in school, class president and whatnot so this didn't surprise me." Tim pulled the car into the parking space behind his printing shop. "Although after his wife left him, I didn't think he'd be up to it, but I guess I was wrong."

"I can't believe Duncan actually left his doll behind," Robyn said.

"Action figure!" Tim said in his best impersonation of his son. "I know, although mom wanted to throw it away to teach him a lesson."

Robyn replied with a, is she crazy look that made Tim smile.

"That's what I told her too. Plus, she'd just end up having to get him a new one from work anyway."

Robyn carefully exited the car, making sure not to step on the demonic looking toy which she was beginning to hate with a passion. She shut her car door and looked inside the car, expecting the action figure to be standing up or gone even. But there it sat, right where she'd left it. Damn thing gave her the creeps now and she couldn't say anything about it, or she would get in trouble for being out in the middle of the night. She couldn't afford that as there was too much to do. Plus, her parents wouldn't understand. They would remind her that Sun-Yun had gone back to Korea and she would get in trouble which would impede her search for her missing friend.

***

Meanwhile Duncan somehow managed to spend the entire day at daycare without angering Mrs. Litney; something that would go unnoticed to most as it felt like a normal day to them. To Duncan, it felt like he was missing out on something; like he was supposed to be doing something but wasn't able to. He knew he had work to do but he couldn't let himself get grounded, or worse, have his mother commit to this morning's threat of confiscating all his action figures. He couldn't allow that to happen. Not now. He wouldn't like it if he got grounded. He'd be mad and Duncan didn't like to make him mad.

CHAPTER 8

LATER THAT evening, in his bedroom lit only by the glow of a small desk lamp and the screen of his laptop, Thomas McDougal sat at his computer desk chatting with his newfound friend. They only met because they had a common interest in the current mysterious goings-on of Maple Springs. Had Robyn not been bold enough to put up posters in the search for her missing best friend, they would have likely never spoken to each other. As people who travel in completely different social circles, they were opposites in every way. But losing loved ones can bring strangers together. Even strangers who had previously disliked each other without knowing the person they judged mostly based on appearance.

"Hey," he typed into the social media chat. "Did you get the picture I texted you earlier?"

Robyn replied, "Yeah, I need one more picture to finish the poster. I'm searching Facebook."

"Which one?"

"Elizabeth Woodworth. She was in daycare last summer with my brother. He called her Tizzy-Lizzy. She vanished and was never seen again."

"She was the last one to go missing, wasn't she? Before Sun-Yun."

"Yes :'-(2 months after Robert's wife."

"Right," Thomas replied, who like Robyn, remembered the missing for what they were; missing. Unlike the other people in town who had crazy stories about their disappearances or simply refused to talk about it.

"I've been searching for pictures of Lizzy but I've not found any. It's like she never existed."

"Weird," Thomas typed. "Not on her parent's page?"

"I looked and nada."

"My parents know the Woodworth's I don't remember them talking about her."

"It's like they erased her," Robyn typed. "It's like they forgot her."

"Does your brother remember her? If he was in daycare with her?"

"You're a genius!!!"

"Why?" Thomas typed and had to wait several minutes before he got a reply.

"Got it!"

"What?"

"A pic of Lizzy," Robyn wrote. "The daycare has a Facebook page. It has group pics of kids with Elizabeth in them."

"Cool!"

"It was your idea," Robyn typed. "Now I can finish the poster. I'll print it as soon as I can."

"Cool," Thomas replied. "I'll help you put them up."

"Thanks," Robyn wrote. "Are you sure? It'll be late at night again."

"I'm sure."

"Like very late."

"I know."

"Like 3AM late."

"You want help or not?"

"lol... sure. Thanks. I appreciate the company while wandering in the dead of night."

"Poor choice of words?" Thomas replied.

"True. Sorry." Robyn replied.

"It's ok. I gotta get some sleep," Thomas wrote.

"Gnight," Robyn typed. Thomas stared at the chat box for a moment then saw, "Thomas..."

"What?" he replied, hurriedly.

"You're not a complete dork after all :-)" Robyn wrote.

"Thanks. And you too," Thomas replied and logged off.

***

Lucinda lay naked on her back, on the silk sheet covered bed while John Fitzpatrick lay at her side with his head resting on her stomach, the smell of sex heavy in the air. An exhausted John ran a hand gently over one of Lucinda's firm thighs and trailed a finger gently over her hip and ran a circle around her navel.

"Stop that," Lucinda said softly. "You're going to get me started again."

"Would that be so bad?" John inquired.

Lucinda ran fingers through John's hair as she spoke. "No, but no seconds tonight."

John planted soft kisses on Lucinda's stomach before laying his head down again.

"You're so beautiful," John whispered. "What's your secret?"

"Exercise, sexercise and a little bit of magic," Lucinda replied with a sly grin as she gripped John's hair gently in her grasp and pulled it tight. "Did you find out who torched my deer?"

"Not yet. But I'm working on it."

"The dumpster fire worked well."

"Yes. I torched it like we talked about and made sure they would find the fuel can with the prints on it."

"Did you get the results yet?"

"Not yet," John replied sheepishly, hoping he wouldn't upset his lover. "I'm just a patrolman. I don't have the authority to speed it up. Officer Cortez is the closest thing we have to a detective at our little police force and is going to look into it tomorrow."

"Perhaps I'm sleeping with the wrong man," Lucinda replied. "Is this Cortez handsome?"

"She," John replied with jealousy in his voice. The thought of Lucinda replacing him so easily didn't sit well with him. She only played this card when she felt he wasn't performing as well as she liked, and he knew it. But he couldn't help but be bothered by it anyway. "She is ranking officer on the force. We're too small a town to have full time detectives. They come in when needed on real cases."

"She's going to call you when she's got a name?"

"No as I can't ask her to without her asking questions," John replied. "But I'll get her to tell me, don't you worry."

"Oh, I'm not worried about that," Lucinda replied as she ran her hand through her lover's hair.

***

Lucinda wasn't worried because she knew she couldn't leave this to someone like John. He didn't realize what Lucinda had to lose. She couldn't afford to have another witch hunt. She knew the stories handed down of the old witch hunts in the 15th century. But most people didn't know about the ones that happened after that. Witches became much better at hiding who they were and what they could do. And the good ones focused their magic on charms to get what they wanted, or simply to convince people to leave them alone. She recalled having to charm her way out of witch hunts in the 1940's and again in the 1960's. Long ago, she had made a deal with what she thought may be a devil. A devil that would help her have what she wanted the most; to remain youthful and beautiful forever. A woman both gifted and cursed with the kind of beauty that men lusted for and women admired. They admired her because of her magical charms as otherwise they would have despised her simply because she could turn heads without lifting a finger. Lucinda was strikingly beautiful, with high cheekbones, a strong jaw line and piercing blue eyes. And hair like golden silk with natural waves and curls that simply never quit. She would never admit it to anyone but her beautiful hair was a work of magic. Simple magic taught to her a long time ago. But now she would have to keep the shadow man fed or he wouldn't stop others like him from taking bits of her essence, draining her until her soul was freed from her earthly form. Instead, she would have him take essence from others in her place, keeping the bargain they had made. In exchange, he would keep her from aging. But the shadow man couldn't just take from another for her. They would have to give freely, and this would be taxing for Lucinda. But using the charms she had learned over the years she could always convince the weak willed to do this for her. But the more she used her charms and magic, the more she felt drained. The more drained she felt, the more essence she would need to feed to the shadow man to keep age at bay, or worse, death.

She had been told that death waited for no man. This she now knew wasn't true because death was waiting for her. But lovers like John made being beautiful and desirable impossible to give up. But now the poster of the girl she had in her basement were being put up all over town and Lucinda thought the person doing this was able to resist her charms. How much could they resist? And was this the same person who'd torched the deer? She needed to know and soon. She was having to expend too much energy in keeping everything quiet. And unlike the old days, one couldn't simply apply a potion to the town's well water, or in a modern town's water supply. People now had water coolers and bought bottled water. Things had to be done the hard way. Thankfully she could easily charm the local bakery staff to use special ingredients Lucinda provided in their breads, baked goods, and pies. But not everyone bought from the bakery. Lulling an entire town was much easier in the old days, thought Lucinda as she looked at John as he snored softly, his head still on her stomach.

Lucinda eased her way out from under John and got out of bed. She had to feed the shadow man tonight. She could feel it. He would smile showing his yellow pointy teeth to her when he did. Sometimes she felt he was mocking her, but she couldn't let herself be bothered by that. She needed what only he could give her almost as much as he wanted what he took from them.

CHAPTER 9

OFFICER JOHN Fitzpatrick awoke to an empty bed. Lucinda was gone and all that remained was the memory of the lovely smell of fresh strawberries that filled the air when she was near him. And like every other evening, when Lucinda came to call on him for his prowess in the bedroom, she would wear him out and leave while he slept. He knew she was using him, but he didn't care. John was in love with the woman he had met just four months prior at the gym, and getting to have sex every night. In the beginning, she would often criticize his abilities, telling him he was a selfish lover. How he was only concerned with his own pleasures. This had bothered John greatly as all he wanted to do was to please the woman he had become infatuated with. But soon, she was coaching him, guiding him along to becoming the lover she desired. John had become infatuated and only wanted to please her and they both knew it.

Now John, while in civilian clothes, drove his truck slowly past Lucinda Mayweather's house. On his way to the station to start his shift, he couldn't help himself, taking a detour with the sole purpose of driving by her house. This wasn't the first time John had done this, each time with a burning hope of catching a glimpse of her. Just a small glimpse that would get him through his day. And also to keep an eye on things to make sure other men weren't going to steal her away from him. This is what he looked for each time he drove by her house. But this time he saw something completely unexpected.

Standing next to the white picket fence were two men who looked to be arguing.

John felt panic well up inside him as he wondered if these men were fighting over his Lucinda. He slowed his truck as he approached, hoping not to attract attention so he could see what was happening. He recognized the man facing him as Lucinda's neighbor Dwight McGarvey. Dwight was clearly agitated and held two grocery bags in one arm while gesturing wildly as he spoke to the man before him. John glanced at Leonard's old house and back to the men before realizing what he had just seen. He stopped his truck in the road, near the pair of men. The men paid him no mind as he looked on in disbelief.

The lawn of Lucinda Mayweather's home was covered with what looked like plastic signs on wire stands. There must have been thirty, maybe more, purple signs with a man's picture and text in big letters.

Vote for
Robert Emerson
Councilor at Large

John now recognized the balding, mustached man arguing with Dwight as the same man whose picture was on the lawn signs. Local vet, Robert Emerson was running for town council and must have thought it was a great idea to cover Lucinda's front lawn with the signs. Something Dwight didn't seem to agree with, judging by the intensity of the conversation the two men were having.

John looked around and didn't see Lucinda anywhere. The police officer in him wanted to go over, talk to the men and assess the situation but not being in uniform made him wonder what the men would think. Would they wonder why he was concerned about Lucinda Mayweather? If they asked questions about why he was there, this could piss off Lucinda and he couldn't have that. He couldn't risk her being upset with him.

He would hurry to the station, get in his uniform and swing by in his cruiser. Then he wouldn't need to worry about them wondering why he had stopped to see what was going on. The men would assume he did so because he was a cop and saw something that looked odd, which would be exactly what it was anyway. Only this would be much easier to explain to Lucinda, if this got back to her. That was the most important part, thought John as he drove off toward the station.

***

"I'm telling you, I have no idea who put those signs on Leonard's lawn but it wasn't me... *or* my guy," Robert blurted. His insistence seemed to be finally getting through Dwight's thick skull.

"Lucinda's lawn... and if you didn't put these signs up, then who did?" Dwight barked.

"I have no idea," Robert replied meekly as he scratched his balding head and wondered who did. He dug out a cell phone, dialed and put the phone to his ear.

"Hey, um... I need a favor. You know Leonard Legault's house? Can you meet me there? Now... if you're not too busy that is." Robert muttered something and ended the call.

"You should have asked him if it was him," Dwight said.

"I don't have to ask him," Robert replied. "I know it wasn't him, okay."

"How can you be so certain he..."

"Look, I paid this guy well to do this for me and I know he's not an idiot, okay," Robert replied in frustration. "He knows he's gotta ask permission to put up signs on people's property. A sign... not like thirty."

"Just make sure you get those damn things off her lawn before she gets back," Dwight replied as he adjusted the grocery bags and marched up Lucinda's sidewalk walking past the blackened deer as he went up the steps to the veranda.

Robert watched as Dwight walked into the house as if he lived there. Robert turned his attention to the signs he had recently purchased at Repeat Printing. He sighed and began plucking the signs and making neat piles near the fence in preparation to be picked up and redistributed.

***

Dwight closed the door behind him and stood still in the dimly lit house listening intently. The house was somber and quiet as expected. Perhaps too quiet. He knew Lucinda wasn't home. When he had seen her outside, she had barked at him to call Robert, which he did as he watched her leave, marching off carrying a large plastic container, fuming with rage as she stomped along. Seeing Lucinda angry scared him. He knew there was something special about her, so he always tried hard to remain on her good side. Plus, he had an arrangement with Lucinda that was too good to be true. He remembered how easily she had read him the second time they had spoken. Now Dwight did as he was told, bringing Lucinda the groceries she asked for, in exchange for a special favor now and again.

A shiver ran up Dwight's back. Leonard's home creeped him out. The glow of the antique sconces eerily illuminated all of Leonard's stuffed animals, making them look like creatures from a bad horror movie. He took a deep breath and tread quietly, hugging the side of the hallway on the opposite side of the giant moose that he swore he'd seen it move the first time he'd delivered Lucinda's groceries. In the dim light, the damned thing looked angry, he had told Lucinda. She'd had to remind him that all the critters, big or small, were dead. Stuffed with foam, she had told him. But that didn't stop Dwight from being completely spooked by them all.

In the kitchen, he set the grocery bags on the kitchen counter, warily eying the large red-headed pileated woodpecker that was perched to the very top of one of the cupboard doors. He gave a guarded glance at the top of the fridge where a stuffed raccoon seemed to loom, making sure it wasn't moving. He placed his hands flat on the counter and closed his eyes, slowly counting to ten before turning his attention to the groceries. He placed the fresh vegetables on the counter in a neat pile. He pulled a small bottle of vanilla extract from the bag and read the label again to make sure it was what she had asked for. Next to that he placed cake flour, yeast and a large bag of chocolate chips. While watching the raccoon, he put the carton of skimmed milk in the fridge. Dwight pulled the hand-written grocery list from his pocket; he read it again as he glanced at the recently placed items on the cupboards.

"Lucinda?"

Dwight's knees got weak, and his heart raced as he heard the timid voice calling out.

"Why won't you come see me? Have I done something wrong?" The voice continued in a faint, plaintive tone.

Chills ran down Dwight's spine and he gripped the counter as he listened to the voice which seemed to come from behind him.

"Please, Lucinda?" the voice said meekly, as if it lacked the strength to call out any louder.

Dwight turned slowly toward the kitchen cupboards expecting to see someone or something standing there but there was no one. He felt a bead of sweat on his forehead as his heart raced, and his mouth felt dry. He stiffened as he saw a grey and black squirrel posed as if to leap from the top of a cabinet.

"Lucinda..."

Dwight jumped. He knew if he heard the voice again, he would pass out. He couldn't allow that to happen, not in this creepy house full of dead things. He clamped his hands over his ears and walked quickly to the front door.

"Lucinda..." Dwight didn't hear the voice as it trailed off, like it couldn't manage another word.

Dwight reached for the door handle and then remembered his payment for the groceries. He glanced back and saw it sitting on the mantle, next to a stuffed ferret. He badly wanted out of this creepy house, but he also didn't want to have to come back either. He stepped quickly, scooped up the pair of patent leather stiletto shoes from the mantle and went out the front door. He stopped outside with his back to the door as he tried to calm himself. His head spun, his heart still raced, and his palms felt clammy and cold.

At the fence he could see Robert Emerson watching him. Robert clutched some of the plastic signs that had recently covered Lucinda's lawn. On the other side of the fence was a burly looking bearded man in overalls and a baseball cap who also watched him. This had to be the man putting up the signs for Robert.

"Are you alright?" Robert asked.

"You look awful pale, mister," said the man in the overalls.

"I'm fine," Dwight muttered as he clutched the shoes to his chest, attempting to hide them. He strode down the walkway, crossed the street and didn't stop until he was in his house with the door closed behind him. He flicked on the lights, even though the room was already brightly illuminated by the daylight shining through the thin curtains. With his back to the door, Dwight breathed deeply still clutching the shoes to his chest. He exhaled slowly, while pondering if he had imagined the voice calling out to Lucinda.

Dwight didn't know about the basement vent beneath the edge of the kitchen cupboards, let alone the young girl locked in the basement directly underneath said vent. He knew Lucinda had secrets but never dared ask. He had already thought the house was haunted and now assumed he was right.

Dwight shivered as a chill ran up his spine. He took another deep breath, trying to calm himself but now he smelled the patent leather shoes clutched to his chest. He grasped the shoes in both hands and held them up to his face and inhaled deeply, smelling the leather and the woman he had grown to lust after. She must have seen me looking at her feet, thought Dwight for the millionth time since Lucinda Mayweather gave him that first pair of shoes and asked him for a favor, all at the same time. She had read him like a book. A cheap book of erotic desire as he caressed the shoes and his mind pictured Lucinda's slim, and very sexy feet.

**

Officer John Fitzpatrick had a plan. Get to the station, get into uniform, hop in his cruiser and head straight over to Lucinda Mayweather's house and find out just what in the hell was going on between Dwight and Robert. That and why the hell had Lucinda let Robert plaster his signs all over her lawn?

Was she seeing Robert too? He wondered about this as he strapped on his duty belt. What if she was? John would have to take care of that before it became a problem. This was going through his mind as he marched down the hallway and heard Officer Cortez's loud laughter coming from what had to be the break room. Officer Cortez wasn't the laughing type, but when she got going, she was loud and obnoxious. He tried to stick to his plan but her boisterous laugh echoed through the hall which made it impossible for John to ignore.

Before John entered the break room, he knew Lucinda was there, as he could smell fresh strawberries. He never understood why she smelled that way, but it always made him happy. He'd asked her once if she wore strawberry scented perfume. Lucinda had laughed and pinched his cheek like he was an innocent child asking a silly question. But what he saw in the break room made his heart flutter and his mouth dry up.

Lucinda Mayweather sat at the break room table across from Officer Cortez. Between them, on the table, sat a large plastic container half filled with muffins. Cortez had the biggest smile John had ever seen on her. For the first year he knew Cortez, he didn't think she could smile and yet here she was, grinning and laughing with Lucinda. But the part that had made John nervous wasn't the smile, or the laugh, but the canister of lighter fluid which sat on the table next to the container of muffins. It wasn't just any canister of lighter fluid either. The evidence bag it had been in sat underneath it as if the canister was a mere paperweight for the plastic bag.

"John," Cortez blurted. She had never called him by his first name until now. "Have you met Miss Mayweather?"

"Oh, call me Lucinda," Lucinda said as she gave a wide smile, glancing back and forth between Cortez and John.

"We've met," John replied as he struggled to speak through a dry throat while he glanced at the muffins. He remembered the first times he met Lucinda, how not long after; she had fed him muffins and cookies. "My special recipe", she had said. He'd asked her what made it special, and she'd replied, "It's a secret." The cop part of him had suspected there was something in those muffins then and there would be something in these now.

"Small world," Cortez said. "Turns out Miss Mayweather... I mean Lucinda here is a friend of Stanley Stillwater."

Lucinda smiled at John in a way that calmed him slightly, as if he knew he wasn't in trouble. *But what the hell is the canister doing on the break room table?* he thought.

"Lucinda wanted to know if we had caught the person who broke the window at Stillwater's Bar and Grill."

John found himself speechless. A part of him wanted to be angry but he was afraid Lucinda would get mad at him in return, if he got angry with her. She knew he was working on getting this information from Cortez. But he had to be subtle as to not arouse suspicion.

"Turns out it was some guy," Lucinda said. "A man, right?" she added while looking at Cortez.

"The prints on the can belonged to some kid," Cortez said as she pointed at a muffin as if asking Lucinda if she could have another.

"A kid?" John asked. "You know this how? Are his prints in the system?"

"He was part of a school program a few years ago," Cortez replied. "But he's not the one who broke the window and set the dumpster on fire."

"No?" John asked.

"A security camera from up the street shows a man in

black," Cortez said.

"But they don't know who it is," Lucinda added while looking at John. She had what John saw as a serious "don't screw this up" look on her face.

"The camera was too far away," Cortez added before taking a bite of muffin.

"But it was the boy's prints on the can," Lucinda said, still looking at John.

"The boy's prints," John repeated.

"Duncan Skidmoore's," Cortez mumbled through a mouthful of muffin.

"Interesting," Lucinda added.

John wasn't the most attentive when it came to Lucinda but what he saw now he assumed was her trying to signal to him that he should leave. Bewildered at what had just happened, John decided it best to follow Lucinda's lead and leave to not risk saying the wrong thing.

"It was nice meeting you," John said to Lucinda. He had already forgotten he had told Cortez they'd already met. But Cortez seemed too interested in eating her muffin and talking to her charming new friend to notice.

John took a step backwards, not wanting to take his eyes of the pair of ladies before he turned and left. As he headed down the hall again, he recalled the scene at Lucinda's house. He remembered Dwight and Robert standing by the fence, arguing from the looks of it. It was probably too late now but he would swing by, just in case.

CHAPTER 10

THE NEW Thrifty Dollar Store cashier with the shiny nose ring and the heavy eye shadow held up the phone as she spoke. "Gloria! It's for you." She set the phone down on the counter as Gloria made her way behind the cash to answer the call.

"Hello?" Gloria answered.

"Gloria? It's Mrs. Litney."

"What's he done now?" Gloria replied coldly assuming her son had caused mischief for the millionth time.

"Nothing," Mrs. Litney replied. "Actually, he's been really well behaved the last few days, but that's not why I'm calling."

"Oh!" Gloria replied in surprise. "What's the matter?"

"Well to be honest, I'm concerned about his health."

"Go on."

"Well, he never used to want to nap before. Said it was for babies and he wasn't a baby."

"Yeah," Gloria replied, biting at a fingernail while anxiously waiting for Mrs. Litney to get to the point.

"Well today I found him napping before it was even time to nap."

"Really?" Gloria didn't vocalize it but agreed this was peculiar behavior.

"I mean I figured he was tired, and he looked fine, so I didn't worry at the time but after the other kids were done napping, he was still sleeping."

"What are you saying?" Gloria asked.

"He must have slept four hours," Mrs. Litney added.

"Oh... okay."

"He looks fine now, a little groggy maybe. I just thought you should know."

"Okay," Gloria replied, not knowing what else to say.

"I'll keep an eye on him, but I thought you should do the same," Mrs. Litney added.

"Thank you for letting me know."

"I gotta get back to the kids now," Mrs. Litney said before she ended the call.

Gloria hung up the phone and dialed a new number.

"Repeat Printing... Repeat Printing," Tim said.

Gloria cringed and recalled their conversation about how Tim actually thought repeating the company name was a clever way to answer the phone.

"Tim," Gloria wasted no time getting to the point. "Did Duncan seem okay to you this morning?"

"Yeah, why?" Tim asked.

"Mrs. Litney said he slept most of the day."

"I see," Tim replied.

"I'm worried."

"I was expecting him to have gotten into trouble or something," Tim replied.

"I know... it's not like him to sleep while at daycare."

"Maybe he's catching the flu or something," Tim replied, concern in his voice. "We'll keep an eye on him; take him to a doctor if he looks sick. Maybe take his temperature when we get home."

"Okay," Gloria said as Tim hung up the phone. Not long after ending the call, Gloria regretted calling Tim at all, before they'd gotten home. She knew he would worry all day now. *But it's not like I couldn't* not *tell him, could I?*

she thought.

"He's either too rambunctious or too quiet," Gloria said aloud to no one in particular. "You can't win."

"What was that?" the nose ring wearing cashier inquired.

"Oh nothing… just… just never mind."

***

Once she finally had all the pictures she needed, it took Robyn a couple of hours to complete her poster and get it ready for printing. This is what she had told Thomas, adding that it was an agonizing two days to finally get some time alone at the printing shop to get them printed and stashed in the delivery van where she could retrieve them without her father knowing.

Thomas McDougal became emotional when Robyn showed him the printed posters. In the past few days, he had confessed to Robyn that this was the first time since his grandfather's disappearance that someone shared his opinion of this not being normal. That his grandfather, a man who had lived his entire life in Maple Springs, would have simply left without packing anything or saying goodbye just wasn't possible. It was the first time someone actually cared that he had vanished.

He had blushed when he said it turned out that the only one who cared was the girl he remembered as a senior at high school; one of those too cool for school types. Robyn had blushed when he had said she wasn't as cold as they all said she was and that she actually had a heart. He had said he was amazed that she cared enough to help not only him but all these missing people.

And the creepy part was they'd both said exactly the same thing in unison as he looked at the printed poster.

"Why those random seven?" they wondered aloud.

"Weird," Thomas added as he wiped away a tear. "They've nothing in common."

"Nothing except all being from Maple Springs," Robyn replied as she looked around to see if anyone else was out at half past midnight on a weeknight.

"True," Thomas replied with shaking hands as he held the poster to catch the light from the overhead streetlamp. "I hadn't thought of that part."

They both had been focused on the randomness of the seven people on the poster. His grandfather, Robyn's best friend, the little girl everyone had called Lizzy and Robert Emerson's wife Nancy. There were three more that he hadn't really known, not until his grandfather had disappeared. Like everyone else in town, he had been quite oblivious to the vanishings of Maple Springs. So when Tiffany Doucette simply stopped showing up for work at the Thrifty Dollar Store, people just shrugged it off saying she had finally met some guy on that dating website she was always on and had left town to be with him. George Wallaby, the towns' only used car salesman was rumored to owe money to the mob for gambling depts. People said that they had taken him to Leonard where they had him stuffed and mounted and what was left of him was now standing in the back room of some mob boss's office, the location of which seemed to change each time the story was told. Ritchie Wood, the last victim, was rumored to be playing in the minor leagues somewhere, trying to make it as a pro baseball player. That was the reason people gave for him just up and leaving one night, many years ago.

Thomas and Robyn had spent the last two days discussing this very topic. Which lead them both to wonder the same thing about these random seven.

This was something they agreed on. There was no real link between them unless you considered the fact that they all lived in Maple Springs and all 'magically' disappeared.

"I used to be terrified of the dark," Robyn said to Thomas who was tapping a poster to a lamppost.

"Used to be?" Thomas replied as he broke off a piece of tape and plastered it over a small tear in the poster.

"I'm much better now," Robyn replied sheepishly. "When I was ten, I wouldn't even go outside at night and slept with my bedroom lights on. Sometimes my dad would turn them off while I slept and if I woke up during the night, I'd freak out."

"That's hard to believe," Thomas replied. "I mean before we met, you were wandering around town in the middle of the night putting up posters. Alone."

Robyn blushed and looked away as they walked down the street. They stopped at an abstract street art display which looked like a man made of scrap metal. He held a sign that had a place where people put up posters to advertise events, things for sale and other random things.

"When I figured out it was you putting up those posters, I thought it made sense. You always seemed fearless when we were in school."

"Yeah," Robyn replied as she dug out a poster for Thomas to put up on the art display. "Fearless. Same kid who slept with all her lights on until I was twelve."

"We didn't know that," Thomas replied as he grabbed the staple gun for this poster. The backing on the sign of the abstract metal man was wood. It was battered and rough from being stuck with pins and staples over time. Thomas looked the board over for an empty space big enough for the poster.

Robyn reached past Thomas and tore down a poster of a young girl who was looking for work as a babysitter. She crumpled it up and tossed it at a nearby garbage can.

The ball of paper bounced off the rim and landed on the sidewalk.

Thomas looked at her as if about to ask why but she answered before he could.

"There were no more little tear off numbers on it anyway," she shrugged. "Besides this is much more important than Tiffany what's-her-face making a few bucks looking after little Chucky."

Thomas put up the poster of the missing of Maple Springs.

"Do you believe in monsters?" Robyn asked.

"What? Do you mean literally or figuratively?"

Robyn cringed at the word literally. She hated that word, but she didn't say anything. Her mind was on other things. Robyn wanted to tell Thomas about the night she saw that monster chasing her brother. She wanted to tell someone, but she hadn't told anyone yet. She didn't feel there was anyone she could tell. She was afraid to as it didn't seem real and if it was, that was a terrifying thought. If it was real, her brother should have been torn apart, maybe even been eaten by this monster. Yet when she found him, he was sleeping soundly without a scratch on him. This confused her. Plus, the monster had looked exactly like that stupid doll of his so she assumed she had imagined it, maybe it had been just a dream.

"I know it sounds stupid but all the rumors of monsters in the park," Robyn said.

"My friend Vincent said he saw something in the park one night," Thomas replied. "A monster... but every time he tells the story, the facts change. He's full of shit. I know he's just making it up to get attention."

"I think my dad knows about the posters," Robyn said.

"What makes you say that?" Thomas asked.

"I don't know," Robyn replied as they walked down

the street looking for a place to put more posters up. "I just get the feeling he knows. He's probably seen one and saw the watermark. I don't know why I just didn't remove it. Kinda stupid of me."

She glanced around at the darkness as if looking for something hidden in it. All she saw were the memories of her childhood fears trying to claw their way back to the surface of her anxieties.

CHAPTER II

AT TEN BEFORE midnight, Tim had woken for the third time since going to bed. He had been, and still was, worried about his son. According to Mrs. Litney Duncan was tired a lot of late. He had not only stopped resisting nap time, he had been sneaking off to sleep in secret. She'd found him in the coat closet last time, curled on the floor with a couple of old coats as blankets and a teddy bear as a pillow. So when Tim woke for the third time with that on his mind, he simply had to get up and check on his son. And when he had, in the dimly lit bedroom he had been pleasantly surprised to find the boy, fast asleep, blankets a mess and action figures strewn all over the bed. Tim hadn't bothered removing any of the toys from the bed for fear of waking his son. The boy had clearly been playing when he fell asleep. So when he had found his son sleeping, Tim had done what any father would have done in this case, checked on his other child. But what he had found was an empty bed where his daughter should have been.

That was when he had remembered seeing his daughter's secret files on the computer at work earlier that day. The folders contained random stuff he had remembered her printing for her room, like retro posters and album covers. But the one that had come to mind was the poster he had seen, the poster of some of the former residents of Maple Springs. He had heard crazy conspiracy theories about how monsters had eaten them or they had been abducted or murdered, or both. The rumors were often something outlandish. He knew that Ezra McDougal had moved to Florida. He knew that Ritchie Wood had gone off to play minor league baseball in pursuit of the major leagues. George Wallaby had been killed by the mob and was probably sleeping with the fishes, although some said he had been taxidermied. Tiffany had run off to be with some guy she met online. Robert's wife had left him and rumor was she was living with an ex-con or something. Sun-Yun had gone back to Korea. The little girl, he didn't remember at all. So he had been pretty upset when he'd seen that his own daughter was feeding these conspiracy theories. He had every intention of confronting her about it the next morning when they were alone at the shop. But when he found her room empty, he had put two and two together and knew exactly where she would be.

Now standing in the dark of night, near the corner of the drug store, he watched his daughter flirt with some boy as they put up the damn posters all over town. *Little fucker is probably brainwashing her*, thought Tim as he walked quietly down the sidewalk. He wondered if he was the one filling her head with conspiracies, not wanting to blame his own child. He kept in the shadows near the buildings as he watched his daughter and the boy walk off down the street after having put up another poster. When they weren't looking his way, he snuck behind the metal artwork of the man holding the sign. He glanced at the variety of posters on the board and recognized a few of the posters as stuff he had printed. Not only did he remember printing them but his company name was watermarked on the bottom left-hand corner of the poster. He gave everyone who let him put that watermark on their poster a small discount off the print job. It was great advertising, when it was something you wanted your company name on. But what he considered a bullshit conspiracy poster wasn't something he wanted his company to be associated with.

He peered past the iron man, looking down the street; and he couldn't see his daughter or that boy she was with. He glanced around as if he expected to see someone watching him from nearby. In the darkness he saw no one. He pulled the poster off the board and looked it over before folding it into a small square and stuffing it into his back pocket. Something he would forget and later would be confused at the clump of paper his wife would find in the wash, no longer recalling what it had been to begin with.

He turned around and marched toward home. *I'll deal with this tomorrow*, he thought, not realizing yet that he would forget the paper in his pocket.

***

Lucinda Mayweather stood in the shadows next to the pharmacy as she watched Tim Skidmoore remove a poster off the iron man sidewalk art display. She watched him as he looked about, probably looking to see if anyone was watching him. He looked in her general direction but she could tell he hadn't seen her. What was Tim, the father of that boy who burned her deer, doing out at this hour of night? And what was that poster he tore down and pocketed? She was tempted to go ask him, using her persuasive charms to get him to tell her everything. But she knew that he would not have all the answers to her questions.

Lucinda felt as if she was spreading her influence too thin of late. It was making her use too much energy to keep everything as it should be. The shadow man gave her what she needed in return for what he needed. But to keep this up, she had to give him more than she wanted. Or rather Sun-Yun was giving him more of her essence than Lucinda wanted. At this pace she would need a new volunteer to feed the shadow man so he would continue letting her keep the essence that gave her youth and boosted her abilities. But that would mean convincing the town's folks that yet another disappearance was nothing to fret over which would in turn take up more of her energy, spreading herself thinner still.

As for Tim, she would have to go visit his printing shop and bring him some muffins so they could have a chat and see what was bothering the father of the little arsonist. By the time she would be done with him, all would be right in his world again and he would have forgotten all his troubles (and the poster in his pants pocket), Lucinda knew as she watched Tim march toward her hiding spot.

He walked with purpose until he got near her and then he slowed. He glanced around as if confused. He sniffed at the air and closed his eyes. Lucinda knew she gave off a smell to people who felt her influence, some more than others. John always raved about how she smelled like fresh strawberries. Tim shook off the scent as he staggered forward, as if he had just remembered that he was on his way somewhere before he got distracted. Lucinda, standing next to a brick wall, looked up at the side of the building. Above the drugstore sign, she could see a busted security camera that pointed downwards where she stood.

"Perfect," she whispered as she heard a shuffling noise coming from behind her. Lucinda spun around, her blonde hair and large hoop earrings swaying as she turned quickly to face the large imposing figure that stood in the darkness at the other end of the alley.

A large, muscular horned ape with goat hooves and

large monstrous fangs stood there. The creature's eyes glowed red as Lucinda fearlessly took a step toward it. She marveled at the sheer size of the creature which stood about ten feet tall, maybe taller. Lucinda took another step toward the imposing beast, peering at it as if trying to discern what it really was. She saw the large creature's glowing eyes but above those, between its horns she saw a faint red light on something that looked square and out of place on such a colossal monstrosity.

"What are you?" she barked at it.

The demonic looking creature stepped back and put an arm up as if shielding itself from the small blonde woman before it. Lucinda stepped forward once more. The creature spun around and ran away.

***

Duncan sat on his bed in the glow of a nightlight, his iPad on his lap as he watched the scene unfold via the Go-Pro camera he had strapped on the giant toy's head. He was amazed at how fearless she had been, facing off with a ten foot tall, fanged, horned ape. That was incredible to the nine year old boy. Duncan caught movement from the corner of his eye. Near the closet, between the dresser and the wall, from the darkest of shadows cast by the faint glow of the nightlight and the iPad, something moved.

Duncan smiled as he vocalized his previous thoughts and said, "That was incredible!"

The shadow in the corner bulged as if stretched before it tore and revealed a gray haired, pale-skinned man who smiled as he emerged. The shadows ran off him like an elasticized liquid and returned to the corner where they belonged. His smile revealed his yellow pointy teeth. He wore a top hat and clothes that were strange to the nine year old who never listened in history classes.

"She is quite something, isn't she?" the shadow man said as his smile widened even more.

"I'll say," Duncan replied as he gripped his iPad in both hands and watched in disbelief. "I thought for sure she'd be scarred of a ten foot tall monster."

"A plastic monster," the shadow man said as he crept closer to the boy and peered at the screen the boy was mesmerized by.

"She doesn't know that," Duncan blurted.

"True," the shadow man replied.

Duncan watched the footage from the GoPro as the creature ran at full speed, now headed down the street where he lived. The shadow man went to the window and looked outside over the hip-roof at the street below. He extended a long-fingered-hand toward the window as the lock slid open and the window rose without touching it. The plastic monster with glowing red eyes burst into sight, running up the street. The creature pivoted, ran down the front lawn and leapt into the air at the hip-roof. As it soared through the air, the plastic monster shrunk in flight back to its original size, the smaller version of itself quietly landing on the hip-roof. With the GoPro still at its normal size tangled on a horn, the lopsided action figure marched to the window where the shadow man reached out for it, grasped it and brought it inside.

"She sure doesn't spook easily," Duncan said.

"Perhaps not," the shadow man replied. "But she is easily infuriated," he added with a smile.

The shadow man looked at the small plastic toy in his hand, the eyes of which now pulsed with a red glow. Duncan laughed as he climbed out of bed and took the toy from the shadow man. He untangled the GoPro from the action figure and placed the camera on the top of his dresser.

Duncan stiffened when he heard the back door of the

quiet house open and close. Action figure still in hand, he bounded into bed, hid the iPad under the blankets and tucked himself quickly under them as well, pretending to be fast asleep. He opened one eye to see the room emptied and the shadow man gone, probably back into the shadows where he always came from. Mere seconds later, when his bedroom door quietly opened, Duncan was breathing deeply, giving his usual best performance of an innocent boy in deep slumber. Although soon, he wouldn't be acting anymore as sleep came calling, bringing with it dark dreams of the beautiful blonde woman with large hoop earrings. In his dream, she embraced the top hat wearing shadow man and they danced together like in the old black and white movie his grandmother loved.

***

"You need to conserve your strengths," the shadow man said to Lucinda. He stood behind Sun-Yun, in the cage of the dimly lit basement in what used to be Leonard Legault's house. He ran his long bony fingers through the young girl's brittle grey hair as he smiled. "This poor girl won't last long at the rate you're feeding me."

Sun-Yun sat on the floor wrapped in a blanket, leaning against the bars, her strength depleted and yet she allowed the man from the shadows to take more of her fortitude away.

"I know that!" Lucinda barked. "But the people of this stupid little town are becoming impossible. Nosy people who won't mind their own business," Lucinda said as she touched at the corner of her eye. She felt the crow's feet which had started appearing the previous night. She had also found a few white hairs and this simply wasn't acceptable. John hadn't noticed and had still fawned over her, but he was also under her spell. Her charms worked incredibly well on him.

"I can reverse those," the shadow man said. "But be careful. If you let them get too bad, they'll become irreversible, even for me," he added, obviously goading her.

"Feed!" Lucinda said with a voice filled with rage as she pointed at the shadow man.

"Please," Sun-Yun said in a barely audible whisper. "I only want to please you," she added in a quivering voice as she looked at Lucinda while hot tears streamed down her cold cheeks.

"I know," Lucinda spoke softly. "And I love you for it," she said with sincerity. What Lucinda really loved was the sacrifice the girl was willing to make for her.

Sun-Yun smiled weakly as the shadow man placed his cold hands on each side of her head. Once Sun-Yun's eyes went blank and she began convulsing, Lucinda spun on her heals and marched up the basement staircase. The shadow man smiled wide as he took the essence from the young girl with the grey hair, in exchange giving Lucinda back the essence and power she desired more than anything.

CHAPTER 12

AT A LITTLE past seven in the morning, nobody saw the newer model Lincoln Town Car pull up in front of Leonard Legault's house. Nobody noticed as the sharp-dressed man exited from the vehicle and stood in the middle of the street. Despite the expensive suit and a matching fedora, he still looked rough, more like a boxer than a banker. On the left side of his face ran a large scar that looked like somebody had tried to push it through a cheese grater. He pulled a half-smoked, fat cigar out of his breast pocket with a thick fingered hand and placed it in his mouth, moving it around as if trying to get comfortable. He stuffed his hands into his pockets and looked around the neighborhood. Sure no one was watching; he turned his attention to the eccentric house before him.

"What the hell?" he muttered as he looked at the blackened deer on the front lawn. He walked past the picket fence and down the sidewalk, pausing to get a better look at the deer which looked like it had been roasted in an oven. He took the cigar from his mouth and exhaled as if it had been lit. He climbed the porch steps, clamped the cigar between his teeth, and stopped at a large stuffed grey squirrel perched on the wood deck railing. He ran his hand along the side of the squirrel, finding the slit in the fur and pulled a key from the makeshift pocket. He used the key to unlock the door but found it already unlocked and so pushed it open. He took another imaginary drag from his unlit cigar and pocketed the key before stepping through the doorway into the dimly lit house. He entered with an air of familiarity, closing the door behind him.

The first thing he saw was a lacy white bra hanging off the moose antler. His eyes narrowed in confusion. "What the hell?" he muttered again. He turned his attention to the second floor as he walked up the stairs past a couple of Leonard's creations, a large black cat, sitting on the stairs and a large hawk perched on the handrail. On the landing at the top of the stairs, he paused to look at a long black skirt that hung off antlers of a wall mounted deer head. This struck him as strange and out of place for Leonard's house. In the bedroom and bathroom, he found more women's clothing hung up as if they had been put out to dry after being washed. Against a bedroom wall was an antique vanity strewn with jewelry, make up and a large hair brush with long blonde hairs stuck in it. A string of pearls hung from one of the dim antique imitation torch sconces which barely lit the room. He spun around, exited the bedroom and entered the office across the hall. Its walls and shelves were covered in more of Leonard's dead things, old books, and various antiquities. A large hawk sat on a tall perch, its head turned toward the door as if keeping watch. A wooden desk held an old computer and stacks of file folders and paperwork that looked like they hadn't moved in a long while. The dust in this room spoke volumes as he examined the cluttered office.

Exiting the office, he went down the stairs walking past the single creature that decorated the staircase, a large hawk perched on the handrail, and stopped before the basement door. He slid the deadbolts open revealing the musty yet sweet smelling basement staircase. He casually strode down the dark stairs while looking around the dimly lit basement. It was as he remembered, dried flowers, cloves of garlic hanging, and jars on wood shelves. He walked past the jars with the eyeballs and teeth and paused at a series of jars with a dark liquid in them. From the dust on the shelf, he could tell a few of Leonard's special jars had been moved, perhaps tampered with. He turned his attention to the large wood table in the center of the room. Everything seemed normal enough. At least that's what he thought until he heard a rustling sound coming from the metal cage in the corner.

"Water," said a barely audible hoarse voice.

The man in the suit looked into the cage and saw a small figure curled in a thick, dirty blue blanket sitting on a small mattress on the floor. A small, dirty hand opened the blanket to expose a tired looking, gray-haired, Asian woman. She swallowed as if trying to muster enough strength to speak again. This, he thought looked painful.

"Water... please," she managed to say through a dry crackling throat.

"What the hell?" the man in the suit muttered.

The weak looking woman in the blanket reached out, pointing with a trembling hand.

"Water."

The man looked around, saw the blanket woman was pointing at a jug that sat on the floor, out of reach for anyone locked in the cage. He shrugged, picked up the jug and opened it. He smelled the contents, pulling away quickly as if he had expected it to be something bad. Unsure, he smelled it again and was reassured it was simply water. He placed the cap on it again, squeezed the jug through the bars of the cage, crumpling it in the process and tossed it at the woman. The jug hit the blanket and landed next to the woman. With trembling arms, she picked up the jug and struggled with the cap. The man in the suit took an imaginary drag from his unlit cigar as he watched the woman remove the cap on the jug. She rested the jug against her, lifted it to her mouth and struggled to drink. She gulped greedily at the water before setting the jug down, splashing water on the mattress in the process.

"Thank you," the grey haired woman muttered.

The man in the suit said nothing.

"He's killing me. I'm dying," the woman in the blanket said softly. "But it's for Lucinda." With trembling hands, she took another drink of water before placing the cap back on the jug.

"Leonard's killing you?"

"No. The man, from the shadows. He comes from the darkness," the woman said with a crackling voice.

"For Lucy?"

"For Lucinda," the blanket woman added.

"Lucinda. Gotcha."

With a quick backwards glance, the man in the suit climbed the stairs and closed the basement door. He glanced at the stuffed coyote in the hallway and at the moose with the bra hanging from its antler. He walked out the front door and down the sidewalk, stopping next to the blackened deer. He took an imaginary drag from his unlit cigar and pulled a phone from his pocket. He speed dialed and placed the phone to his ear.

"Boss, something weird is going on here."

He listened intently as the person on the call spoke.

"Yeah. He ain't home. There's women's things in the house."

He listened.

"Yeah, boss... that ain't like Leonard to have a woman over to his house."

He listened again as he took a drag on his unlit cigar.

"No, boss... I ain't smokin. I quit, remember?"

He listened some more.

"Nah, boss. I don't think it's the cops. But something weird's goin-on-here."

He listened still.

"Sure, boss. Find Leonard. Gotcha."

He ended the call and pocketed the phone while he took an imaginary drag on his unlit cigar. He looked down as he felt something press against his leg and saw a large black cat. The cat walked past one leg as it rubbed up against the other before it stopped and sniffed at his legs.

"How'd you get out here?" he wondered aloud, recalling seeing this cat on the staircase. "I didn't think Leonard liked pussy. Your kind either... at least not alive, anyway."

***

Dwight worked from home, making, managing and hosting websites. This is the reason why, when the car door slammed and woke him, he had gotten up to see who was stirring about at this hour in the morning in such a quiet neighborhood. When he looked outside, he saw a fancy looking Lincoln in front of Lucinda's house. He picked the crud out of his eyes while he yawned. The car was out of place in this neighborhood. From his vantage point, he couldn't see the license plate. Dwight squirmed as he watched through his living room window, peeking through the blinds. He had to pee. After a few minutes, on his way back from emptying his bladder, gut instinct told him to grab the cordless phone and his little black book, just in case. Parting the blinds slightly to not attract attention, he saw what he had waited for. The owner of the car was standing next to the blackened deer while talking on the phone and smoking a cigar.

"Faaaacckkk!" Dwight said as he thumbed through the book, found the number he wanted and dialed.

"Who's this?" Officer John Fitzpatrick replied.

"John, it's me Dwight McGarvey. I live next door to—"

"I know who you are," John blurted. "How did you get this number?"

"Lucinda gave it to me."

"She gave *you* my cell number?" John asked.

"Yes," Dwight replied. "Just in case."

"Just in case, what?"

"In case something came up," Dwight blurted. He felt like calling John a dumb-ass but refrained from doing so.

"Why the fuck are you calling me?"

"Fingers is back," Dwight replied.

"What? Am I supposed to know what that means?"

"Fingers. You know... Tony the cannoli, sleeps with da-fishes, mob guy."

"Listen, Dwight. If you're fucking with me because you want to take Lucinda from me, I'll k—"

"NO... you're not listening. That guy people offensively call Cannoli, the mob guy; more commonly known as Fingers on account he breaks a lot of fingers... he's here, at Leonard's house, snooping around."

"Who?"

"I don't know his real name but everyone calls him Fingers. He's at the house."

"He's there, right now?"

Dwight watched as Fingers drove away.

"He just left, heading into town."

"What was he driving?"

"Lincoln Town Car, I think."

"Call me if he comes back," John replied, ending the call before Dwight could say anything else.

***

Officer John Fitzpatrick sat in his cruiser, befuddled,

staring at his phone. Dwight had never called him. And what Dwight told him sounded like something made up, too strange to be true. *He has to be fucking with me*, he thought. That's when his radio blared and duty called. A quick interaction with dispatch had him on route to a three car collision on the outskirts of town, something that would keep him busy for most of the morning. It was early afternoon before he remembered that morning's call. He pulled his cell phone from his pocket and called the one person that might know where she was.

"Stillwater's!" he heard Stanley shout into the phone over blaring country music. Stillwater's Bar and Grill had an old jukebox full of country music hooked to a pretty impressive set of speakers. John recognized the old Bobby Bare song *Dropkick Me Jesus* playing in the background.

"Stanley. It's John. Is Lucinda there? At the bar?"

"Lucinda? Hell yeah," Stanley replied.

"Listen, Stanley. This is important."

"What? You gotta speak up, John. Lucinda's got the music turned up loud in here."

"Don't let her leave. I'm coming over."

"What? Don't let who leave?" Stanley asked.

"Lucinda," John repeated.

"Me?" Stanley said as he cupped his other ear. "I can't leave. I own the place. What are you talking about?"

John ended the call without realizing Stanley had asked a question, started his cruiser and headed toward Stillwater's Bar and Grill. He was worried. If Dwight was telling the truth then Lucinda would be in trouble if she crossed paths with this Fingers character, if he was real.

On his way to the bar, John's thoughts returned to the incident that had happened not long after he'd met Lucinda Mayweather at the gym. She had visited Stillwater's Bar and Grill and many of the regulars had become smitten with Lucinda. Naturally, a fight had broken out, and the entire Maples Springs police officers on duty at the time—all four of them, including John—had responded to an old-fashioned bar brawl.

The scene had been the most amazing thing John had seen as a police officer. All the men looked like they had wanted to kill each other and it had taken considerable effort to get them to break up the fight. And yet, not a single one of the patrons pressed charges or even held a grudge. The next night, they were right back at Stillwater's drinking together as if nothing had happened. The only reminder of the fight being the bandages and bruises they all sported.

As John turned the cruiser he remembered that it had been at Stillwater's where he'd first heard that Lucinda had learned about the reclusive taxidermist who lived alone with all of his stuffed creations. John had heard the rumors spread at the bar that Leonard had a secret stashes of cash in his home and that he was protected by the mob. Supposedly, Leonard had fallen sick, become bedridden, and Lucinda had graciously agreed to care for him, though John knew better. Leonard wasn't sick. Something had happened to him.

But he didn't care about Leonard. All John wanted was to feel Lucinda Mayweather's passionate embrace. Which is why he had to find Lucinda before this Fingers character did. He flicked on the cruiser's lights and stepped on the accelerator.

When he arrived at Stillwater's Lucinda was already gone. Nobody seemed to know where she had gone to. John asked Stanley Stillwater if he knew about this Fingers character and Stanley was all too happy to share the gossip. As John listened it sounded like a lot of wild speculation, but he listened just the same.

CHAPTER 13

ROBYN SAT in the Repeat Printing delivery van, across the street from Mrs. Litney's daycare. Both parents had secretly asked her to check on her little brother. Both parents asking, without letting the other know they were doing so, as not to worry the other. Under normal circumstances, Robyn would have thought this was pretty funny and would have made fun of her parents. But ever since she saw her brother being chased by some sort of demonic creature, even though she still was unsure it wasn't a dream, she had been worried as well. And her father had seemed out of sorts that morning. As if something was bothering him. He had started to say something to her but had stopped himself. Too scared to ask, she had changed the subject. There was simply too much crazy shit going on. And her brother, he had been acting a little strange as well. And according to her parents, he had been behaving himself at daycare. This alone would be strange for her rebellious little brother. But his constant napping was out of character. That morning he had fallen asleep at the kitchen table. Robyn had seen her mother nudge her father so he would see the boy, with an elbow resting on the table and his head resting in one hand, fork in the other while he snored softly.

This is what was racing through Robyn's mind as she started to get out of the van but froze before she had opened the door. The blonde woman in a long, blue, flowing skirt and shirt was marching up the walkway to Mrs. Litney's daycare. Confused, she watched the woman she remembered as Lucinda, walk into the daycare. Robyn tried to remember details about this woman she knew little about. She tried to recall anything about her having children of her own. Robyn stepped out of the van and was about to cross the street when her phone rang. She pulled it from her pocket and saw a number she didn't recognize. Answering the call, she spoke hesitantly.

"Hello?"

"You the one who put up those stupid posters all over town?"

"Yes," Robyn replied. "Do you know anything that will help me find the missing people?"

"Missing? I don't know what you heard but ain't nobody missing in these parts."

"Who is this?"

"Listen here, you!" the caller said as they proceeded to curse up a storm as Robyn pulled the phone away from her ear as she waited for the caller to calm down so she could try and figure out who it was. It sounded like a woman yet the voice was a bit deep. She couldn't be sure. Plus they might not tell her anything but if she knew who the person was, perhaps that could help enlighten her in some way. Why would this person take the time to call her to refute what the poster claimed?

Robyn would listen for a moment, waiting for a chance to give her side of the argument, but gave up and ended the call to go find her brother.

***

"You smew wike bwubewie jam," the tiny, little girl said while smiling at Lucinda Mayweather.

Duncan, who hadn't yet seen Lucinda, smelled the familiar scent of his grandmother's special oatmeal cookies. *She's here*, he thought as he recalled the shadow man telling him about Lucinda's special smells. How people would often smell their favorite smells around Lucinda.

"Can I help you?" Mrs. Litney asked the beautiful mature blonde woman.

"That boy over there, is that the Skidmoore boy? Is that Duncan?"

Mrs. Litney hesitated and looked around in confusion. A sudden powerful smell of Fireball Whiskey hit her, a smell most others refer to as cinnamon. Mrs. Litney hadn't had Fireball Whiskey in over ten years. The scent hit her like a brick. She needed a meeting and fast. Otherwise she might cave to the sudden craving. Something she had worked so hard not to do for so many years.

"I'm sorry," Mrs. Litney said with a smile that looked forced. "What can I help you with?"

As Duncan turned his attention to the entrance, he saw Mandy smiling as she held up a doll for Lucinda to see.

"That boy," Lucinda said as she looked directly at him. "Is that Duncan Skidmoore?"

"Why yes," Mrs. Litney answered as she glanced about at her charges. Mrs. Litney's head swam. She felt dizzy. Mrs. Litney watched Lucinda who was staring at Duncan.

Lucinda examined the boy and saw nothing special about him. She had a way of sensing abilities in people and felt nothing from the boy that would make him unique or gifted in mystical arts in any way. He was an ordinary boy she thought, as she turned and walked out just as suddenly as she had entered the daycare.

***

Duncan breathed deeply, as if he had been holding his breath all along. Mrs. Litney turned her attention to Mandy as she burst into sudden hysterics.

Since nobody was watching, Duncan went into the coat closet he had often napped in and covered himself with a tattered blanket. Once in the complete darkness, he spoke.

"She knows," Duncan said.

"It's okay," Duncan heard. The voice came from the darkness. "Don't worry," the shadow man soothed.

Duncan was startled when he heard the closet door opened suddenly and the blanket was quickly pulled off him. Standing before him was his sister, Robyn.

"What are you doing?" Robyn asked abruptly.

Behind Robyn stood Mrs. Litney who still had a perplexed look on her face while she held little Mandy in her arms, consoling the little girl.

CHAPTER 14

IN THE LATE afternoon, a frail, gray-haired Sun-Yun sat curled up in her dirty comforter on the floor of the cage, starring at the plate of food before her with glazed eyes. This was the hungriest she had ever felt in her entire life. The now cold pizza pockets Lucinda had left her might help satiate the ravenous hunger she felt constantly now but she doubted it. A part of her desperately wanted to find out but she lacked the strength to move. She couldn't will her arms to rise to the occasion, reach out and scoop up the food before her. She had nothing left. Not even to feed herself. A warm tear ran down her cold cheek. She was dying and she knew it. But she didn't feel sadness. Instead she felt the satisfaction of having given all that she could to the one she loved more than life itself. She had given her all to Lucinda and didn't regret a single thing about it. She didn't have the strength or willpower to do so. Lucinda had taken them as well, without Sun-Yun's knowledge.

Her water jug was near empty which was good, thought Sun-Yun. She didn't have the strength to pick up a full one. After a long pause, she tried to reach for it and in her mind she did. It took her a moment to realize that while she told herself to, her arms hadn't move. If she could drink a little, quench her thirst, perhaps it would give her the strength to eat. She would try harder, thought

Sun-Yun. She couldn't possibly give up now as she would never get to be with Lucinda again if she did. She wanted to see her, one more time.

She took a deep breath with the intention of quenching her thirst, but her exhale would be her last. The food would remain uneaten.

***

Marching down the street, on her way home, Lucinda felt a sudden pang in her stomach and her skin began to crawl. She was gone. The girl she used to feed the shadow man was dead. Lucinda doubled over in pain, the stomach cancer returning with a fever and her melanoma made her skin crawl. Death wanted her and her body wanted to die. It had wanted to die for a very long time. Human bodies are not meant to live this long, but Lucinda didn't care what nature had intended. She'd made a deal and was going to get what she deserved.

She breathed deeply, feeling pain in her lungs as she did. She needed a new volunteer to feed the shadow man and quick. Waiting was no longer an option. Not anymore. She used to have more time between "volunteers" but as the years passed, the urgency grew. If she took too long, then the damage would be irreversible. That's what the shadow man always told her and she didn't want to find out if this was true. As the pain in her stomach subsided a little, she felt her joints stiffen. She began walking slowly with a labored intensity. This time she had something much more urgent than a pesky young boy to deal with.

***

The antique imitation torch sconces in the corner of the basement flickered and then went out. The shadow in the now dark corner of the cage seemed to grow and from it emerged what Lucinda sometimes called the shadow man. He had used many names throughout the ages as feeble minds couldn't grasp what he really was. He had to tell them various things to keep them from the brink of insanity. He could tell them he was an angel of death but in reality, it was more like he was an agent of death, making sure the essence was collected from the dead so their souls could leave their fleshy prison. But people were too weak minded for that kind of horror.

He stood in the corner and smiled wide, examining the dead and depleted girl in the cage, dead much earlier than fate had planned for her.

Lucinda will be reminded of why she needs me, he thought. She would feel her body deteriorating rapidly, her beauty fading and her life draining as her essence quickly ebbed away. She would panic. She would find him someone else for him to feed on so he would take their essence instead, returning hers. She would feed him like he had trained her to. Find him a willing subject to give its essence in trade for her to keep her own so she could live in their stead. It was an arrangement that he could make without breaking any of Death's rules since the subjects gave willingly. He smiled wide as he blended back into the shadows he had come from.

CHAPTER 15

"I THINK I'M losing my mind," Robyn said, avoiding eye contact with Thomas. The sun was setting as they strolled down a path in Maple Springs Park. A gentle breeze rustled the trees around them as they walked. "I think something is going on with my brother."

"What makes you say that?" Thomas asked.

"And my parents too," Robyn replied. "My dad knows I printed the posters. I mean sure, the company watermark was on them and so it's a bit obvious, but I wanted him to see that. Maybe it would help him understand that this is not normal. Seven people don't just disappear with no explanation."

"Yeah but he believes the bullshit stories. You said so yourself."

"My mom too. But I guess I thought if he… if people saw all seven of them on the poster together. It… it might help them to wake up."

"It might help them remember to not forget," Thomas replied.

"Right," Robyn said as she stopped on the trail, near a small building which housed equipment used by park custodians and had public bathrooms as well.

"I don't get it," Robyn said. She looked at the poster they had put up a few nights prior. It had been partially covered in colorful graffiti, which covered the wall.

"I knew we should have brought posters," Thomas said, whishing he could put up a new one over the defaced one.

"I've gotten about six calls so far about the posters."

"Really?" Thomas said with an air of disbelief.

"I told you about the first few."

"The woman who yelled at you... yeah, you told me about her."

"And the man who called me a stupid bitch. Said he knew who I was and that I better quit it or he would kill me."

"You should call the cops," Thomas said as they started down the path again.

"And say what? You know those people you're not looking for, which are really missing but nobody cares about? Yeah well someone is harassing me because I'm looking for them on my own."

"Good point," Thomas replied. "I'm not sure what to think. I mean why would people call you just to be mean. I guess I don't get it."

"I don't either," Robyn stated. "How can people be such dicks?"

"What were you saying about your brother earlier? You said you were worried about him."

"I'm not sure I saw what I think I saw," Robyn stated. She could tell she was confusing Thomas as he didn't know what she was referring to. "But he's been acting strange lately, more than usual."

Before she could elaborate, Robyn's phone rang. She glanced at the screen and saw "Unknown". She glanced at Thomas and answered the call placing it on speakerphone.

"Hello," she said with apprehension in her voice.

They heard a rustling sound, as if the caller was struggling with the phone.

"You little bitch," the caller said before the call abruptly ended.

"That was a woman," Thomas said.

"I don't know," Robyn replied. "I wish I knew as they've called several times."

The phone rang again, startling Robyn who almost dropped her phone. She looked at Thomas as if she was making sure he was paying attention as she put the phone on speaker again.

"No... don't!" Thomas said but it was too late.

"Hello?" Robyn said.

"Who is this?" the voice of a man asked as the screen again displayed the word "Unknown".

"Who are you?" Robyn inquired.

"Listen, you the one with the posters?" the man asked.

"What do you want?" Thomas asked.

"You're not the one who's been calling me, are you?" Robyn inquired as she shot a confused gaze at Thomas.

"Look, I don't know about those folks on the poster but I'm looking for Leonard."

"Who are you?" Robyn asked for a second time.

"Leonard Legault?"

"Who?" Thomas asked.

"The creepy bastard with the deer on his lawn... have you seen him?" the man asked impatiently.

"Leonard Legault... the guy with the stuffed animals all over his house," Robyn added knowing that Thomas would have to know about the house if not the old recluse who lived there.

Thomas's face went blank before he muttered something.

"Dr. Frankenstein's house?" Thomas whispered, referring to the nickname some of the kids had used on account of the creatures he stitched back together.

"I tell you what. I'll keep my eye out for the people on your poster if you keep an eye out for Leonard, okay?" the man said.

Robyn didn't know what to think as the call ended. It was the first time anybody had called and believing her that people were missing.

"You think he's saying what I think he's saying?" Robyn asked.

"What?"

"That there are more people missing than we know about… and that Leonard Legault is one of them?"

Robyn's phone chimed as a text came in. The message was brief.

Call me at this number if you find Leonard.

A second text came through with a phone number.

***

After sunset, John drove his truck to Leonard's house, a place he'd only been too a few times despite his relationship with Lucinda. The phone call from her had surprised him. Lucinda hated using phones and so for her to call him meant she needed something really important. He'd been summoned by phone two other times before, and always for the same reason. Something he confirmed when he pulled up in front of Leonard's house. By the front door on the veranda leaned a short-handled spade. She needed him to bury someone. Again. The thought tugged at the very fabric that once was Officer John Fitzpatrick, the man of law. And while he'd taken bribes and looked the other way a few times—always on really petty stuff—he had never covered up the sort of thing she would be asking him to cover up tonight. Again. His stomach twisted and his mouth went dry at the thought. He wanted to tell her he couldn't do this anymore. Not this part. But the last time he'd brought up the subject, telling her that he was bothered by this, she'd told him to be quiet and do as he was told, or she'd find someone else to make love to. He knew she'd meant it, and would be easy for her. Many men wanted Lucinda, though not like he did. He needed her and she knew it.

As he climbed out of his truck, he saw Lucinda backing out of the front door, stepping on the hem of her long skirt making her stagger. She was tugging at something which looked heavy. John climbed the stairs two at a time as he watched her pull on a thick, dirty blanket that contained a thin body with long grey hair. It looked like a very old woman.

John pushed both Lucinda and his reservations about what he was about to do to aside and took the blanket from his lover. He pulled hard at first, thinking it would be heavy and took a few startling quick steps back. At a glance, he noticed Lucinda didn't look well. She looked pale and gaunt.

"Are you okay? You look tired," John said, regretting the words the moment he'd uttered them as Lucinda gave him a stern look that sent a chill down his spine.

He tucked the body in the blanket and scooped it up in his arms. The body felt light, as if it was hollow and dry. He noticed the smell of strawberries emanating from Lucinda was faint compare to its usual overpowering aroma. The body, like the previous ones, didn't smell at all. John didn't understand this. Dead bodies usually stank. From the house he caught a slight aroma of baked goods. Lucinda only baked when she wanted something. She would be out soon to charm someone into doing her bidding.

Without saying a word, Lucinda placed the shovel atop the body in John's arms. John carried the body to his truck and placed it in the box. He glanced back at the house and watched Lucinda walk through the front door, disappearing into the darkness. He glanced around the neighborhood to see if anyone was watching. Lucinda never seemed to care if someone saw them but John did. He cared a lot.

John looked at the body, wrapped in a blanket in the back of his truck, lying next to a shovel.

"How the hell did I get here?" he asked aloud as he climbed into his truck and drove off.

CHAPTER 16

VINCENT PERNELLI used to smoke. Something he had never done in front of his parents. Since he had been thirteen, he had acted tough around his friends, saying he didn't care who saw him smoking but the truth was he didn't want his mother knowing. It's not like she would beat him or anything, but the lectures about how smoking was bad for you would never end. Plus he didn't want to disappoint her. She would blame herself. Where did she go wrong, she would ask him? And because he loved his mother, Vincent eventually gave up cigarettes and replaced them with vaping. And since he assumed his mother wouldn't approve of that either, Vincent went for a lot of evening walks.

Under overcast night skies that blocked out the stars, Vincent stood under a streetlamp, vaping while he studied the images on the poster taped to the lamppost. He remembered Ezra MacDougal well. He was his best friend's grandfather. He remembered the times Ezra had let Thomas bring him along on fishing trips. Vincent had been a kid who couldn't sit still and so he didn't get to go fishing with them a third time. But he recalled how happy Ezra looked when he was with his grandson. So leaving and going to Florida without any warning had been out of character for an old man who loved his family as much as he did.

He remembered the girl in the picture next to Ezra's.

Sun-Yun and he went to the same school. She was hard to forget. At a very young age, while crushing hard on the older teenage girl, Vincent had been the one to give her the nickname of Some-Yum. Something he deeply regretted, even if she never had found out he was the one who did so. The rumor he had heard was that she had become pregnant and her parents had sent her to live with relatives to have the baby.

He inhaled a concoction of strawberry, cherry and mint while he scanned the other pictures that looked familiar, most of which he couldn't recall. A sudden aroma of menthol cigarette wafted through the air and caught his attention. He loved the smell of his favorite cigarettes. That was what he missed the most about having given up smoking. He didn't miss the times his throat burned or the head rushes after chain smoking too much. But he missed the smell of the menthol and tobacco. He sniffed at the air until a scuffing sound caught his attention.

He turned to see a woman in a long beige skirt and frilly blue blouse standing behind him. She had large hoop earrings that partially vanished in her long wavy blond hair, and faint crow's feet next to her piercing blue eyes. Her cheekbones were prominent, making her smile that much more mesmerizing. There was something about her that stunned him. Clutched in her hands was a light purple colored muffin with dark spots in it. She smiled as she held it out for him to take.

"What's your name, boy?" she asked.

The aroma of menthol cigarettes suddenly overpowering his senses, he found himself eager to answer her question.

"Vincent Pernelli," he replied.

"Would you eat this for me, Vincent?" she said as she placed the muffin in his left hand. "It's a very special recipe. I made it just for you."

"For me?" Vincent asked as he dropped his vape on the sidewalk. He clutched the muffin in both hands, and looked into the woman's eyes as he vigorously bit into it. It tasted bitter and yet he chewed slowly as if it was delicious. He had barely swallowed his first mouthful before biting off more.

"Where's home for you, my handsome child?"

Vincent answered by casting his gaze at a home up the street.

"That one?" the woman inquired while pointing and watching Vincent's reaction.

Vincent nodded slowly as he put the last of the bitter muffin in his mouth.

"Why are you so beautiful?" he asked, his voice muffled by the muffin as he chewed.

The woman smiled, then staggered, her knees buckling, clearly in pain. She reached out and clasped onto Vincent's arm to steady herself, breaking the eye contact she had maintained thus far.

"Are you okay?" Vincent inquired with real concern in his voice as he tried to help steady the woman before him.

"Help me home, my child. Help me get home."

Vincent helped her stand up straight as he placed his other arm around her waist as they began walking down the street. Vincent didn't think to ask where she lived. His mind was clouded and it was her doing, but he didn't know that.

***

Lucinda Mayweather's charms didn't work on everyone. Usually, she was able to sense when someone could resist her and she would need to increase her efforts. Sometimes an added charm in the right baked good helped. So tonight Lucinda had done it all. Increased her influential abilities to the point they were taking a drastic toll on her physically. And she had made the muffin, especially for someone like Vincent Pernelli. And while she didn't know for certain she wouldn't have needed all this with Vincent, she had done it just the same.

Weeks ago, she had seen him on his nightly walks and had decided he would be the next inhabitant of Leonard's bizarre basement cage.

***

John Fitzpatrick felt a drop of rain on his cheek as he stepped on the shovel and broke ground. It was past midnight and as he looked up he saw nothing but darkness. He had hoped to see stars in between patchy clouds. It was just a matter of time before the rain came so in the glow of his small battery powered lantern. He bent to the task of digging a shallow grave in this small clearing in a remote part of Maple Springs Park. The ground was soft so the digging was easy. Soon John was knee deep in a hole not much more than a few feet across by a little over three feet long. There wasn't much left of this one and John wanted to get this done quickly. He would make her fit, he thought. He reached out, grasped the old blanket which contained the frail remains and pulled it toward him. As he pulled, it unraveled and exposed a bony arm wearing a small leather bracelet with a tiny heart charm. He tugged the blanket and it opened more exposing the wrinkled face with its eyes and mouth open. John took a step back, clutched at his stomach which was suddenly not feeling so good.

Before he knew it, he was vomiting into the hole and all over his shoes.

"Why am I doing this?" he said aloud as he wiped his chin with a sweaty, dirt speckled forearm. Then he remembered how much he loved her.

John hadn't felt anything after his ex-girlfriend had ripped his heart out. She had said she never wanted to see him ever again, which, according to mutual friends, she had only said to hurt him and didn't actually mean it. But it left him numb and John hadn't felt a thing since. Not until he met Lucinda. It was as if she had cast a spell over him, he often thought, not knowing how true that was.

He stepped out of the hole, wrapped the body in the blanket, picked it up and dropped it into the cavity in the earth. He stood for a moment, marveling at how small the woman was.

A drop of rain on the back of his neck reminded him to hurry.

After filling the small grave, John planted a small shrub marking the spot where the body was buried. He had previously dug it up near the entrance of the park, a small bluish plant that looked sturdy enough. It would hide part of the freshly dug earth, if anyone happened upon it.

He stood back, examining his handiwork. If anything, it would look as if someone had simply cleared a space and planted a new bush. Over to his left were two other similar looking shrubs but much bigger than the one he had just planted. He recalled them being smaller when he first planted those. After planting the second one over the old man, he had told himself he would never do this again, and yet here he was.

John wiped sweat off his brow, leaving a trace of dirt in its stead. He picked up his lantern and shovel then turned to walk away but froze as a snapping sound came from the woods to his left. He clicked off the lantern and stood still, peering into the direction the sound had come from. He waited for his eyes to adjust to the sudden darkness. A scratching sound came from somewhere in the distance. John held the shovel like a club in his right hand.

Has someone seen me burying the old Asian woman, he wondered as he stepped forward into the copse of trees before him. He saw something move. Whatever it was, it was low to the ground. He flicked on the lantern to a bright setting and held it out before him.

A short distance away was a big dog that had an untamed look to it. Even in the shadowy darkness, he could tell it was mangy and matted. The dog barred its teeth and growled as it glared at John. Before it was a hole it had clearly dug and from it protruded a human skeletal leg.

"Fuck!" John uttered. He lifted the shovel up readying a strike as he took a step forward. The dog hunched down and growled louder, the hairs on its back bristled. A loud snapping sound came from behind the animal, making it twitch and leap sideways so that it could now look in both directions.

John felt a chill go up his spine and gooseflesh cover his forearms. He suddenly wished he was wearing his police issue gun belt. Another loud crack spooked the stray dog, making it bolt into the shadows and vanish from sight.

Holding the shovel at the ready and the lantern high, John stepped over the hole and peered into the dark woods. Light from the lantern's glow illuminated a monstrous, horned creature crouched in a thicket.

"What the f..."

Before he could finish uttering his disbelief, the horned creature rose before him to a towering height. It was like one of those creatures from the old stop motion movie matinees he watched with his father as a child. It was a weird, muscular horned ape with goat hooves and large monstrous fangs. Only it was real and standing tall in front of him. John shook in fear as he took a step backwards. The monster took a step toward him as John's bladder let go. He stepped back, tripping over the bones protruding from the hole. He fell backwards; the lantern hitting the ground hard and going out, casting them all into darkness.

In that moment, all of John's macho bravery slipped away as he dropped both the lantern and shovel, shot to his feet and ran as fast as he could in the direction he had come.

It would be a little more than an hour later when John, drunk on bourbon, came to the realization that there were more bodies buried in Maple Springs Park. More than the ones he had put there.

***

"Cool," Duncan whispered as he stepped past the giant horned monstrosity and out of the copse of trees. Duncan had loved how John, a grown man had wet himself and run in fear of his monster. That more than made up for Lucinda standing fearless before it.

"Whoa... is that?" Duncan said as he stepped toward the hole the stray dog had dug.

"Human remains," the shadow man said as he stepped out of the darkness facing the boy. "Yes. Yes, they are."

"Who was it?" Duncan asked, knowing full well the shadow man would know.

"That's not important," the shadow man replied.

"Wait until I tell..."

"You'll do no such thing," the shadow man replied.

"But..."

"Cover it up."

"Why?"

"Do you want me to take him away from you?" the

shadow man asked, gesturing toward the towering beast.

"No," a sullen Duncan replied. This wasn't the first time the shadow man threatened to take away his ability to give life to his giant horned friend. He had way too much fun with the thing to lose it now. And all he had to do to keep it was play pranks on the pretty lady in the long skirts and big earrings. The lady named Lucinda Mayweather, who always smelled like his grandmother's special oatmeal cookies.

"I don't understand how my playing tricks on her helps you get what you want," Duncan said as he half-heartedly pushed dirt into the hole with his foot. Stepping backwards, he glanced up at the giant horned beast and without saying a word, it knew what he wanted. The beast bent down, and with its large hands, it quickly filled the hole and scraped the dirt smooth.

"You don't need to understand the reasons for our little bargain," the shadow man replied. "You just need to fulfill your part of the bargain and you get to keep him."

Duncan cast a glance at the giant behemoth standing at his side.

"Kneel," he said to it and the giant monstrosity knelt as commanded.

Duncan scrambled onto its back and sat astride its hard shoulders, grasping the horns as makeshift handlebars.

"Home," Duncan said.

The creature rose to its feet and strode forward through the park with its boy master on its shoulders. Duncan ducked a few branches before glancing backwards at the smooth patch of dirt, wondering why he couldn't tell anyone about what he had seen. The shadow man was gone; probably back to the shadows like he always did. Gone but never far.

CHAPTER 17

LUCINDA SAT on a dusty old wooden stool; her back leaned against the bars of the cage in Leonard's basement. Vincent sat at her feet, on the old mattress. He sat, hugging her right leg as he looked up at her with a longing most dogs gave to their masters.

"You smell nice," Vincent said to Lucinda.

"Thank you," Lucinda replied meekly, forcing herself to smile as she suppressed a cough. Her lungs hurt now.

"Are... are you okay?" Vincent asked, his voice cracking with emotion.

"No," Lucinda replied. "But you can help me if you want to."

"Of course," Vincent replied. "Anything."

Lucinda glanced at the cage door which she had left open when she'd brought the stool in and sat down. Vincent had helped her walk to her house. He had helped her into the basement of the creepy house, and into the cage. In normal circumstances, Vincent would have thought the house was like something out of a horror movie. He would have told her so. But under the influence of multiple charms, his only concern was Lucinda's wellbeing.

"Will you stay here awhile?" she asked knowing full well what the answer would be. She wanted him to feel he had a choice. She wanted his staying to be of his choosing.

"For me?" she added.

"Sure," he replied without hesitation.

Lucinda coughed, clutched at her chest as she tried to regain her breath. Once she did, she wheezed with every inhale. She looked at Vincent who sat at her feet and saw tears running down his face.

"What can I do to help?" he asked.

"Stay here. Stay here with me. You can help me get better, but it's too soon for that."

"Why?"

"It just is," Lucinda replied. She knew from past experience that even though he was very susceptible to her charms, he would resist the shadow man at first. He would resist if she tried too soon to make him give the shadow man what it needed. Her charms were powerful but what she was asking was a lot and convincing them always took time, some more than others.

Vincent looked at her with concern in his eyes.

"Stay here for me," Lucinda said as she stood. She picked up the small stool, and exited the cage as Vincent watched her. She placed the stool near the large table in the center of the room. She returned to the cage carrying a full plastic water bottle and another light purple colored muffin with dark spots. She dropped the water bottle onto the mattress and handed Vincent the muffin.

"Eat this for me," she said softly, showing the boy a warm smile. She ran a hand through his brown hair and watched as he bit into the muffin hungrily.

The cage door clicked loudly as she shut the door behind her, leaving the boy where he sat, eating the muffin.

***

Hours later, as Lucinda slept upstairs, her charms began to wear off.

"Hello? Where am I?" Vincent shouted into the dimly lit basement. "How did I get here?" he asked, hoping someone would hear and perhaps enlighten him.

He was confused, his mind foggy. He felt as if he had not been forced to come here but had done so willingly. Yet he couldn't recall why or by whom. His head swam and his eyes grew heavy. He was tired again. *Perhaps it's best to lie down for a while*, he thought. Perhaps once he was rested, things would make sense. Vincent would never know the second muffin he had eaten was laced with something to make him sleep because Lucinda needed rest.

She didn't have the strength to fuss with the young man as he went through the process of being fully charmed.

***

It was 3 AM when an exhausted Robyn, finally home, climbed the dimly lit stairs with every intention of going straight to bed. She and Thomas had spent hours replacing posters that had been damaged, torn down or defaced. Now she felt emotionally drained. The torn posters she understood as they were most likely not damaged with ill intent. The ones with mustaches, glasses and missing teeth drawn in black ink annoyed her, probably the work of snotty kids having fun. The ones simply covered in spray-paint she assumed were casualties of overly energized youths, hopped up on too much caffeine and whatever else with nothing better to do. But finding many posters with all the pictures neatly cut out had been the most difficult of them all. The ones that had been defaced or torn were depressing but the ones that had been cut, removing only the images of the missing had really struck a nerve. The missing being missing from the posters was adding insult to injury. Who could have possibly taken the time to cut out each picture and yet leave the posters up for them to find? In front of Thomas, she had been angry but on her way home, Robyn wept. She felt exhausted and in dire need of sleep.

But strange blue flickering lights coming from under her brother's door made her freeze in her tracks. He had been acting strange. Ever since she saw him running from the giant monstrosity, she had watched him much more carefully than before. He had been behaving himself recently and that alone was cause for concern. Now this flicker of blue light from under his door had caused her to stop and stare. She felt her anxieties boiling to the surface. The blue light paused its flickering for a brief moment as if a shadow had been cast by someone passing by on the other side of the door. With a quivering hand, Robyn grasped the knob to her brother's bedroom door.

Taking a deep breath, she swiftly pushed open the door revealing the stillness of the dark room. Duncan's iPad sat on the floor, amidst some action figures, displaying some sort of dim, blue, psychedelic screen saver. The screen saver intensified casting the room in an eerie blue light. She stepped into the room and saw her brother sprawled in a mess of blankets, snoring away. Avoiding stepping on toys, she turned on the nightlight above the dresser. On her way to the door, she glanced at her brother but movement caught her attention. She turned and froze in place as there was something near the window. In the shadows she saw a patch of darkness. It was as if whatever was there was a deeper dark than the shadows themselves. She felt a sudden scream stuck in her throat as she swooned. A feeling of lightheadedness overcame her as she staggered and grasped the door to steady herself. When the room stopped spinning, she heard herself whimper.

The swirling blue light cast by the iPad intensified and then dimmed as if maybe the battery had died casting the room into more darkness than she could handle after seeing shadows move. In the soft glow of the now lit nightlight, the darkness concealed in the shadows, which she thought she had seen, was gone now.

Had she imagined it?

With a trembling hand, Robyn closed the door of her brother's bedroom and on shaky legs managed to make it into her room before real panic set in. She flicked on the lights and was almost to her bed when she heard a crackle and was engulfed in complete darkness. The bulb in her ceiling fixture had burnt. Her eyes began to adjust to the dim light from the window, a streetlamp casting faint light into her room. Anxiety and exhaustion combined had other plans for Robyn as the room went completely dark and she could no longer feel her legs.

Hours later Robyn woke stiff and sore, as the morning sun cast daylight into her room. She quickly realized that she had spent the night on the hard floor, next to her comfortable bed. Sleep addled; the reason why she had passed out eluded her at first. Then she remembered the light in her room going out before she made it to her bed.

She would be in the shower before she would recall the deep darkness in the shadows. Did it have a human shape? Chills went up her spine as she recalled the darkness moving. Robyn's tears blended with the shower water as she wondering if she was losing her mind.

***

Hours later, the short lady at the cash register gave Robyn a curious look as she rang in the seventh lamp. She glanced into Robyn's shopping basket and saw three more.

"You cleaning us out of lamps?" the cashier asked, almost as if they were hers and she didn't want to part with them.

Robyn had in fact, done just that. Taken every lamp, short or tall, modern or rustic, off the shelf of the small hardware store and placed it into her shopping basket. But now Robyn gave the cashier a reproachful look and took the last of the lamps from the shopping basket placing them onto the conveyer belt.

"Do you guys sell extension cords?" Robyn asked.

"Aisles seven," the cashier replied with a tone of annoyance.

"I'll be right back," replied Robyn as she hurried off in search of aisles seven. "Light bulbs," Robyn muttered aloud as a reminder to get some more light bulbs as well.

CHAPTER 18

LUCINDA MAYWEATHER sat at the table of her gloomy, dark kitchen in front of a battered, brown envelope. It sat amidst a pile of paper clippings which moments earlier had been the contents of the envelope. There were hundreds of pictures neatly carved out of the missing persons posters, exactly as she had instructed. The corners of Lucinda's mouth rose slightly in a gentle smile as she tried to ignore the arthritic pain in her hands as she held a picture of a young Sun-Yun.

The envelope had a note on one side.

Thank you for the gift, Dwight had written in black ink.

"No, thank you," Lucinda said aloud. Her arrangement with Dwight was a strange one. He would buy her shoes. She would wear them for a while until they held her scent and then she would give them back. It was a bizarre arrangement to say the least but it turned out that Dwight would do just about anything she asked for those shoes. She hardly had to use her charms at all on Dwight as he was more than willing to do her bidding as long as she kept her end of the bargain.

"You hungry?" Lucinda asked the darkness.

A voice from the darkness replied, "Always."

"It's time you met my new friend, Vincent."

"Yes, it is," the voice replied as the shadows in the corner bulged, moved and then stopped.

Lucinda stood from the table and staggered as the pain in her legs throbbed worse than ever. More pain shot through her abdomen, making her gasp. She had to feed the damned thing from the darkness or else she would soon begin to wish for death to take her and she couldn't allow that. She steadied herself on things while she walked to the basement door. Her lower body felt like she had eaten glass and it was tearing her up inside. The decent into the dimly lit basement would be slow and racked with pain as the young, tear-streaked Vincent clutched the bars of the cage.

"Okay," Vincent choked. "I'll do it."

Vincent tightened his grip on the bars and clenched his eyes, sobbing. Lucinda lovingly stroked his hair through the bars as the boy cried for the woman he had only met two and a half days ago.

"Thank you," Lucinda said softly.

"Is... is he here?"

"Yes," Lucinda replied as she watched the shadow man emerge from the darkness in the corner like he had done many times before.

The shadow man smiled, exposing his yellow pointy teeth as he positioned himself behind Vincent. Lucinda placed her fingers under the young boy's chin and gently lifted his face. He opened his teary eyes and looked helplessly into hers.

"I'm dying, Vincent, and only you can help me."

"Only me," replied Vincent as large tears streamed down his cheeks.

"Only you," Lucinda spoke softly as she held the boys gaze while the shadow man placed his cold, long fingers on each side of the boys head.

"I love you for this," she added.

Vincent's grip tightened momentarily as his eyes

rolled up as if he was trying to see inside of his own head. His body tensed at first and then loosened.

Lucinda immediately felt the pain in her abdomen and joints subside as the shadow man smiled.

After all this time, Lucinda still didn't want to know what he was exactly; only what he could do for her. She had made the deal with him, long ago in a small barn in a tiny hamlet. She had promised him bonding essence in exchange for youth and longevity; but not her own essence. Lucinda was smarter than that. The deal was struck long ago and an addiction created. She would use her special abilities and in exchange he would also make her more influential than she already was and that was impossible to give up.

She had known someday it would be her turn to die. But she had found a way to delay death with the help of this thing that looked like a man. She thought of this as cheating death, but the shadow man didn't seem to feel cheated at all. He smiled when he fed on the poor soul she had convinced to sacrifice itself for her.

With the pain in her abdomen and hands lessened, Lucinda touched at the crow's feet on her eyes. She smiled slightly as they felt less pronounced than they previously had moments ago, her vanity returning as soon as the pain of approaching death was removed.

"Thank you," she said to both the boy and the shadow man. She turned and walked up the stairs with a lot more ease now that her knees throbbed less and less.

***

"You feeling any better now, son?" Tim asked as he gathered a batch of printed wedding invitations and stacked them neatly into a box.

"A little," replied Duncan as he yawned and stretched.

He had fallen asleep in his father's desk chair.

"How's your stomach?"

"Better."

Tim closed the box and started filling a second box. He glanced at his son who sat at the computer. The boy looked groggy, as if he needed more sleep, even though he had just napped for a half hour.

He had dropped his son off at daycare like any other weekday but when Mrs. Litney called saying he had thrown up, he had sent Robyn to pick him up and bring him to the printing shop. He hadn't called his wife right away, not wanting to alarm her. She was worried enough as it is. He'd call her soon, now that he knew his son was fine. At least he looked fine. But he would call and make an appointment for Duncan to see the doctor, just to be sure.

***

Duncan felt groggy, sitting in his father's computer chair. He hadn't slept well the night before, after his sister almost caught him with the shadow man. He had dropped his iPad and leapt into bed, pretending to be asleep. But when he heard a noise, not long after, coming from his sister's bedroom, it had been his turn to check in on her. Finding her on the floor had scared him. He always teased and tormented his sister but he loved her like no other. She had been his world when he was little. But now his sister was too cool for her little brother but he loved her just the same. And finding her passed out on the floor of her bedroom had been frightening. She was too heavy for him to lift and she wouldn't wake when he shook her. He had wanted to get his giant friend with the horns to lift her into bed but didn't dare in case she did wake while in the process. But at last he only left her there because the shadows man said she would be fine. He would make sure of it. And even knowing this, for Duncan, sleep hadn't come for hours anyway.

Vomiting while Mrs. Litney wasn't looking had been easy. A few fingers down his throat had worked like a charm. That combined with his being constantly sleeping had sent Mrs. Litney into a panic. Now he sat at his father's computer, waiting for the perfect opportunity to set his plan in motion. The moment would only come later that afternoon when Tim had to leave him alone in the store for a bit.

"I'm just going to walk up the street to The Flower Shop to deliver these wedding invitations for Sandy's niece," Tim said. "I'll lock the door and put my *back in five* sign up."

"I'll be fine, Dad. Don't worry," Duncan replied.

"You sure you don't want to come with me?" Tim asked for the second time.

"I'm afraid of throwing up again," Duncan replied. "I mean, I feel better but I'd rather stay here and play games on the computer."

"Okay, but don't unlock this door for anyone."

"Even Robyn?" Duncan said with a smile.

"Except your sister," Tim replied dryly.

"Fine," Duncan said as he clicked away on the computer.

"I'll be right back," Tim said as he keyed the door locked from the outside and walked briskly in the direction of The Flower Shop carrying the boxes of wedding invitations.

A few clicks of the mouse later and Duncan had opened the file he had found previously and within seconds, the printer came alive and started spitting out page after page.

Duncan got up and ran to the door, pressing his face

into the glass leaving a greasy smear in the process. Looking down the street, he couldn't see his father anywhere. He ran back to the desk, grabbed his backpack and dumped out its contents on the floor. His favorite action figure bounced on the floor along with a rubber ball, a second action figure and a Hellboy comic book. He scooped a small battered box from the trash and set it by the printer. He gathered up the printed pages and shoved them quickly into the box as the printer spit out more. He ran to the door and looked down the street. A few doors down, his father stood, empty handed on the sidewalk talking to a man. Duncan recognized him as the local veterinarian, Robert Emerson, the one with the municipal election posters all over town. Robert was trying to pin one of the lame *vote for me* buttons he had made onto his father's shirt pocket. Duncan wouldn't forget him any time soon, not after what he had done with all those lawn posters. He had thought the idea a bit stupid at first but it had been fun after all. Duncan grinned at the memory as he watched the men chat while the printer drummed its rhythmic beat for a few more seconds before stopping as suddenly as it had begun. Duncan raced to the printer, scooped up the last of the pages, stuffed them into the box, and crammed the box into his backpack. He put his toys back into the bag, except his favorite one and put the backpack next to his father's desk where it had been previously.

When his father walked into the printing shop, a listless Duncan sat at the computer desk, his elbow on the desk, his face resting in the palm of one hand while clicking away on the computer mouse with his other hand. Tim noticed the greasy prints in the glass door as he removed his *back in five* sign.

"You feeling any better?" Tim asked.

"A bit, yeah." Duncan glanced at his father and saw him

pocket the button Robert had pinned on his shirt pocket.

"Pizza?" Tim asked.

"For supper?" Duncan asked sounding chipper.

"I'll finish this one last thing and shut down early. We can pick it up on the way home. I'll get Robyn to pick mom up with the delivery van and come home."

"Cool," Duncan muttered as he sat back and smiled at his action figure. *I should fake being sick more often*, he thought as he stood the figure on the desk and turned his attention to the computer to play a game.

CHAPTER 19

THE SUN HAD barely set when Lucinda showed up unannounced at John's home. She hadn't seen John since he'd removed the body of Sun-Yun from Leonard's house and disposed of it for her. Not wanting him to see her again in such a weakened and decrepit state, she had avoided John.

What she hadn't known yet was that John, after having disposed of the body, had had a brush with a giant demonic figure, and had since drank himself into a stupor then passed out. After half the bottle had been consumed, the balance of that night had been a blur, he would later tell her. John would also confess about fighting back a drunken urge to call Dwight and tell him to keep away from Lucinda. She was his, he had babbled aloud while in his drunken state. But while he didn't remember finishing the bottle, he did have a fuzzy memory of calling Officer Cortez while watching the sun rise and leaving her a garbled voicemail about how he wasn't feeling very well so would be taking the day off. He confessed to not having a clue why he had called her and not the captain. He remembered feeling disoriented and confused. As if some fog that had a hold of his mind had cleared a little, allowing him clarity but that was quickly dampened by more bourbon.

And when John told Lucinda about the giant horned

monster and the body in the park, she knew she couldn't let John keep those memories. She had already planned on blurring the last few days, helping John forget his feelings about the body and how she had recently been rapidly dying; but now that seemed less important seeing the situation.

John had seen that thing and so she knew now that it was real after all. Lucinda had wondered if perhaps her gifts were the reason why she had seen it. Maybe the monstrosity was from the deep darkness like the shadow man. Or perhaps because she was special, she was the only one who could see the behemoth. But now she knew it was real. John had seen it.

Having brought a special recipe, she would combine that with her charms and convince John that he had been home, alone, sick. Lucinda never needed to use much of her special baked goods with John. For such a strong man, he had a weak mind. And while John wanted to make love to her, she wasn't feeling strong enough for that just yet. Her joints still ached, although very little now, and the pain in her abdomen had subsided as well. She convinced John that he had already pleased her and that he needed to sleep now. And sleeping would have been difficult for him if she had not planned on that as well. They both consumed the sleep educing cookies she had brought. Lucinda needed more rest so she could be back to her full glory and she had plans for John when they woke the next morning; plans that would involve not leaving his silk covered bed for a while.

***

Fingers sat in the dark confines of his Lincoln Town Car having just returned from an errand in Stonevalley. He held his phone to his ear as he glanced at his watch, tilting it to catch the light from a nearby streetlamp. It was 2:12 AM and Leonard Legault's house had been deathly quiet for the past half-hour. He had parked across the street, watching, waiting for signs of life. He felt the butt of his snub nosed revolver through the fabric of the pocket of his suit coat as he spoke into the phone.

"Yes, boss. It's done, boss. The thing wid-da Chink lady."

Fingers pulled the phone away from his ear as sudden shouting emanated from it. He waited a few seconds then brought the phone closer to his ear, checking to see if it was safe to listen again.

"Sorry, boss."

More shouting, only not as loud this time.

"Yes, boss. The thing with the Chinese lady, not da Chink lady. Gotcha." Fingers nodded his agreement absentmindedly while stroking the revolver through the fabric of his suit coat. "Blend in better, gotcha." Fingers made a mental note to look up the word derogatory as he listened.

"I'm there now, boss. At Leonard's house, like you asked. All's quiet, boss."

Fingers listened some more.

"Yes, boss. Find out what happened to Leonard, gotcha."

Fingers looked at the phone as if making sure the call was really done before putting it into the inside pocket of the suit coat. He turned his attention back to Leonard's old house and watched for a few more minutes. Satisfied that all was quiet, he reached for the door and froze in the act when movement up the road caught his eye. Someone was coming.

He watched as a boy fearlessly strode up the street and stopped in front of Leonard's house. The boy, carrying a stiff looking doll plus a backpack, stood motionless in the street, as if he too wanted to know if anyone was home. Fingers watched as the boy glanced around, before walking to the picket fence that edged the property. The boy knelt, setting the backpack down, digging through it; he took out something shiny which reflected the dim lights from the streetlamps.

"What the hell?" Fingers muttered, thinking this small boy had just pulled a gun from his backpack. Fingers pulled his revolver from his pocket and rested it on his knee, waiting patiently to see what would happen next.

The boy dug in his backpack, pulled something else out and quickly stuck it to the picket fence with a dry, cracking noise. After the boy repeated this action a few times, Fingers realized the shiny thing was a gun after all. A staple-gun.

Clack-clack-clack, it went as the boy franticly dug out what looked to be pages from his backpack and stapled them helter-skelter to the fence.

"What the hell?" Fingers muttered again.

The boy feverishly worked away, stapling pages along most of the fence. He then hopped over the picket fence and stapled more pages to a maple tree, then moved on to the house. Fingers couldn't see him well but from the sounds coming from the house, he knew the boy was stapling page after page, the stapler making clacking noises that seemed to echo in the still of the night. Fingers tried to get a better view and saw the boy move around in the shadows, but with the house bathed in darkness, he couldn't see very well. But with the amount of noise he heard, the fence, and he assumed a good portion of the house, must be covered in pages.

The boy emerged from the shadows, scooped up his backpack and ran to the opening in the fence. He paused and glanced back at Leonard's house and watched as a few pages fluttered in the gentle breeze. Fingers watched as the boy turned and ran down the street, in the same direction he had come. It was difficult to be certain in the dark of night, but he was convinced the boy had been smiling as he disappeared up the street.

Revolver still in hand, Fingers stepped out of his car and slowly strolled across the street. He looked around the neighborhood, marveling at how no one else seemed to have heard the repetitive, loud clacking noise of the staple-gun. He stopped at the fence, tore off one of the stapled pages and looked it over. He recalled seeing this poster before. He had even called the number on the poster and spoke to a young girl. Or at least he had assumed she was young from the voice he heard. He had spoken to her about the missing people of Maple Springs, although he had really only been interested in one in particular and he wasn't on this poster. He looked around, examining the house, the fence, the tree. A few of the posters fluttered gently in the breeze. Some of the posters were about ten or twelve feet up in the air making Fingers wonder how the hell the boy had gotten those up so high.

What did Leonard get himself into, Fingers wondered? Did he have anything to do with the seven missing people on these posters? Is that what the cage in his basement was really for? Fingers always assumed the boss was right about Leonard being asexual; unless his love of playing with dead things was not just about animals. Leonard had held people in his cage a few times, but always for the boss. Always as sort of a hostage situation, until they or their loved ones made good on money owed, or some sort of information. But Leonard had never killed anyone. Not that he knew of, thought Fingers. He started to crumple the page but stopped himself. Instead he folded it and put it into the same pocket he had kept the gun in.

A sudden clatter came from a house on the other side of the street. Something that sounded like someone bashing metal trashcans, had broken the renewed stillness of the night. Fingers saw a light come on in a house up the street. He turned and walked back to his car.

It's one thing to be seen snooping during the day, but not at night. During the day, people minded their own business for the most part but not at night. At night, people were nosy, he thought as he got into his car.

While pocketing the revolver, a large black cat pounced loudly onto the hood of the car, startling Fingers in the process making his gun hand clench, firing the revolver accidentally. The bullet went thought his right foot and into the floor of the car.

Fingers winced and grunted from the pain as he struggled to pull the gun from his pocket. He raged at the cat as he yanked the gun free. He raised his hand to point the gun through the windshield but the black cat scurried up the glass and onto the roof of the car. Fingers shot twice through the roof as he heard the cat screech. In the rearview mirror, he saw the cat jump onto the trunk and off the back of the car, disappearing in the process.

Fingers dropped the revolver into the passenger seat, started his car and winced as he used his injured foot to quickly drive away.

***

Bewildered at first, Dwight had fallen asleep in his usual spot, the battered recliner in his dark living room. He awoke suddenly from what sounded like gunfire. Having been raised in family of hunters, he had been around it enough in his youth to know what it sounded like. That had to have been gunfire, something small caliber, he thought. He struggled out of his chair, stumbling in the dark. He muttered a curse as he stepped on an empty soda can, hurting his foot in the process. He kicked at the soda can, missed, connecting with the end table instead. Pain shot through his foot and up his leg as he held back a scream as if he didn't want to wake anyone, even though he lived alone. He clutched at his aching foot and fell on his side; landing on the empty soda can he had missed with his kick.

"Owwwww! Fuck!" he screamed, no longer holding back.

He rubbed at his toes and felt his side where the can would probably have left a bruise. He felt his foot and was relieved to find his toes didn't feel broken but the pain was still intense. He sat up and rubbed at his foot, while his eyes adjusted to the lack of light in his living room. Dwight struggled to his feet as he heard a car start. Before he could limp to the window, he heard the vehicle drive off and so it was gone when he peered through the blinds.

He grabbed a small pair of cheap binoculars that hung from an old curtain hook next to the window frame. He staggered on his sore foot as he peered at Leonard's old house, the place where the woman he was infatuated with lived. Confused, he cleaned the lenses of the binoculars on his shirt and peered again, this time adjusting them. Posters were everywhere he looked. The same posters he had cut up for her in exchange for a freshly worn pair of delicious pumps. The posters looked to be stuck to the house, the tree, and on the fence.

"Fuck me," Dwight muttered knowing full well Lucinda was going to be furious when she saw this.

He limped to his chair and found his phone. He searched quickly through the call history, found the number he wanted and hit dial. He let the phone ring six times before hanging up.

"Fuck," Dwight muttered. He had no way of knowing John and Lucinda were in a deep, drug induced sleep at that moment. He debated going over and tearing down all the posters but ever since he heard that voice, he hadn't dared step foot in that house. Not even in broad daylight. Dwight was convinced the place was haunted.

He'd pretend he didn't see the posters.

He limped back to his chair and flopped into it. *I never saw a thing*, he thought as he shuddered at the memory of the voice in the darkness. He would pretend like nothing had happened and he hadn't seen anything. Then it hit him. John would see the missed call on his phone and know it came from him.

Dwight bowed his head, closed his eyes and muttered quietly, "Sweet buttery Jesus... I'm fucked."

CHAPTER 20

IN THE DARK of night, Thomas walked down the sidewalk with a small battered box tucked under his arm as he looked back at Robyn as she finished taping a missing persons' poster to a signpost. He couldn't help but be amazed by her. She was fearless, even if she insisted otherwise, standing there in the shadows, determined to find out what really happened to her missing friend.

Robyn shoved the roll of tape onto her wrist like one of her bracelets and joined Thomas. "So you haven't seen or heard from Vincent in days and you don't find that suspicious. Not at all?"

"Vincent?" Thomas said while shrugging. "I told you. He moved away somewhere."

"He didn't tell you he was leaving?" Robyn asked incredulously. "He's been your best friend since kindergarten."

"Yeah, well... I don't know what else to say. I mean he moved."

"Who the fuck told you that?"

"My parents. I got home last night and found them sitting at the kitchen table eating muffins and having coffee with some old woman. Anyway, he quit school, moved in with a friend of the family, and got a job at a vape factory or something."

Robyn marched off, not looking to see if Thomas was

behind her as she did.

"My mom said he'd call me or something once he got settled in."

Robyn stopped, spun around and marched back to where Thomas stood. She grabbed the box of posters from under his arm and shook it in front of his face while she spoke angrily.

"Seriously! What the FUCK do you think we've been doing all this time?"

"What? I don't..."

"You don't what? Seven people that we know of... and now Vincent makes eight, all gone. With nothing but bullshit stories about why they're gone. A few, it's like they never even existed, for fuck sakes."

Thomas looked at her with bewildered sadness.

"Who was this woman with your parents?" Robyn asked.

"I don't know. She was old looking, but real pretty though. She had blonde hair with streaks of grey and amazing blue eyes. I don't think I've ever seen her before."

Robyn tucked the box of posters under her own arm and began walking again.

Thomas followed her. "I don't know who she is, but she makes really great muffins," Thomas muttered. "I must have had like three or four. Anyway, my mom said that Vincent would call me soon."

Robyn stopped suddenly and faced Thomas.

"Some strange old lady comes to your house, feeds you bullshit stories and muffins and you think this is normal? Now Vincent is missing and your parents tell you he just moved away? Just like that? And you believe them?"

"Well..."

"Doesn't that remind you of anyone?"

"But..."

"My best friend, who also suddenly moved away without any warning. Bullshit stories from everyone about her moving to Korea. A place she's never even been! Sound familiar?"

Robyn turned and marched on, leaving a bewildered Thomas where he stood. Robyn crossed the dimly lit street, as if momentarily forgetting about telling him she didn't want to be alone.

Robyn marched down the dark street until something caught her attention. She crossed the street and stopped in front of a white picket fence and stared as if in amazement. The fence was covered in the same posters she had in the box tucked under her arm.

Thomas caught up with her as they looked up and saw posters on a tree. A gentle breeze made a few flutter in the wind. They looked past the tree and at Leonard's house. Parts of the eccentric house, which was littered with the posed dead animals, was also covered in posters.

"When did you put these posters up and why so many all in the same place?" Thomas asked stupidly.

"I didn't put these up," Robyn replied.

She sounded baffled by the question as if she couldn't believe he had just asked it.

"If you didn't then... who did?" Thomas asked.

"Good question," Robyn replied.

They stood quietly marveling at the scene before them, both wondering why the dark, eccentric home of the legendary recluse, Leonard Legault would be covered in the very posters they spent many a night posting all over town.

"What do you think this means?" Thomas asked.

"I don't know but I can't believe how dark that house is," Robyn whispered. "Look at it."

"It gives me the creeps," Thomas replied softly.

"Maybe Leonard has something to do with all this," Robyn added. "Maybe he likes stuffing more than dead animals. Maybe he stuffs people too."

"Rumor is that Leonard is dead."

"What?" Robyn whispered.

"That's what Vincent said."

"Why?"

"Nobody's seen him in quite a while."

"That's normal for him though," Robyn replied.

"Someone said a woman lives here now," Thomas stated sounding sure of himself.

"We should go check it out," Robyn said with a quivering voice.

Thomas looked at Robyn who was physically quivering with fear.

"You sure?" Thomas asked just as they heard a door open and close.

Robyn and Thomas clutched at each other and looked around to see where the sound had come from.

"There," Thomas said as he pulled at Robyn, urging her to walk away, to get out of sight of whoever was now approaching.

From across the street, they watched a man, bathed in darkness, limping from a house and cross the street. They heard the man mutter as he stood before the poster-covered picket fence as he began removing the posters one by one, snatching them off the pickets, as he exclaimed, "Sweet buttery Jesus."

***

Tim woke at 3 AM, thinking he had heard something but convinced himself it was a dream. After which, he had lain awake for an hour before finally getting up to get a glass of milk.

He'd had a dream that his kids were in trouble. They were stuck in some dark room and couldn't get out. In his dream, he tried to open the door but found it locked. He had tried to break it down but it wouldn't budge. All the while he could hear his daughter, frantically screaming and crying, begging for someone to come and save them. And while he heard his daughter screaming, he also heard his son laughing and carrying on like he sometimes did when he was trying to annoy his big sister and get a reaction from her. And even if he couldn't see behind the door, somehow he knew his kids were in complete darkness. Something his daughter had struggled with her entire life.

Chills ran down his spine when he finally did get out of bed.

He needed to do something to get his mind off the nightmare.

Now, standing in his somber kitchen, Tim finished his milk and set the empty glass down on the counter next to the night light. He would check on the kids and then go back to bed and maybe read a little, he thought. That always helped him get his mind off things so he could eventually fall asleep again.

He crept quietly up the stairs in hopes that he wouldn't wake anyone. He would check on his son first. Duncan was always tired these days but otherwise looked fine, had gone to bed early. And his wife, having seen her son go to bed early, had done the same. She was worried for her youngest child, but she handled stress differently than he did. While it made sleep a difficult thing for Tim, it had the opposite effect on Gloria. Stress wore her out. She would run on adrenalin for a while and then, out of sheer exhaustion, fall into a deep sleep.

He opened the door of his son's bedroom and peered inside the dark room. *The nightlight above his dresser must be burned out*, thought Tim. He would check on that in the morning but for now, he stepped into the room and saw the boy was completely engulfed by the lump of blankets on the bed. He took a step closer but paused as the lump moved. He stood still and watched the mound of blankets, waiting to see if it would move again. When it didn't, he decided that was a good thing. The boy was asleep. And maybe, just maybe, he simply took after both his mother and father.

Duncan hated still having to go to daycare. He had whined about how the previous summer he got to stay home with his sister and it wasn't fair that he now had to go back to daycare because Robyn wanted a job instead of babysitting her little brother. So maybe, just maybe he wasn't sleeping well at night because of stress, like his father. But then would get worn out and have to sleep during the day, like his mother. After all, he was their child, a product of the two of them. Tim smiled at the thought and decided to let the boy sleep.

He quietly backed out of the room and gently shut the door behind him.

***

With Duncan's bedroom completely dark now that Tim had shut the door, the lump of blankets slowly flattened out like a balloon losing all of its air. The movement from the shadows in the corner was brief as the shadow man slipped back into the darkness.

***

"Is he gone?" Duncan asked the darkness.

"Yes," the shadow man replied.

"Good," Duncan replied. "I'm tired," he said as he set his favorite action figure down and watched it grow to giant sized on the lawn of his parents' home. The giant monstrosity picked up the boy and placed him onto the hip roof of the house. Duncan turned as the giant toy leapt into the air and shrunk back to normal toy size in mid-flight, small enough for Duncan to catch.

Duncan snuck through his bedroom window. He crawled into bed, fully dressed, and fell asleep within seconds.

***

Tim walked past his daughter's room and noticed the light emanating from under her bedroom door. He knew what this was. He had seen it enough times not to know. His daughter had always had a strong fear of the dark. She had slept with full lights on until she had been twelve, nearing thirteen. After that, she was able to manage with a few nightlights. But the light spilling from under her door was not from any nightlight. It was actually so bright that Tim had known it also couldn't be from the ceiling fixture either. And while he wanted to respect his daughter's privacy, he wasn't able to resist peering into her room.

What he found chilled him to the bone. There were thirteen lamps, all lit. Most were connected to extension cords or powers strips. The brightness in his daughter's bedroom was staggering.

His daughter lay fully clothed, atop the covers, sleeping what looked to be a fitful sleep as she twitched and kicked, moaning and groaning.

He had been so preoccupied, worrying about his son that he couldn't help but wonder if he had overlooked his daughter. Clearly her fear of the dark had not only returned but had intensified.

He scanned the room and noticed one of the lamps had a burnt bulb. Make that two. Two had burnt bulbs. Had they been burnt when he walked in? He was pretty sure they had been lit. All the lamps had been. Or had they, he wondered?

He watched as his daughter twitched and muttered something that sounded like the word no. She was repeating the word, over and over now. Tim stepped toward the bed with every intention of waking Robyn and ending whatever horror she was experiencing in her dreams. But as he got closer, his daughter seemed to settle down. That's when he noticed the roll of packing tape on her wrist, the memories quickly coming back. She had been out again, putting up those posters. He had forgotten all about the posters until this very moment when he recalled seeing them in town.

"Stupid conspiracy bullshit," he mumbled as he turned and walked to the door. He reached for one of the lamps, intending on turning it off then decided he better not. She would wonder who had shut it off and that would only feed her anxiety more. Best to let her do it but they would have a chat tomorrow. He would make sure of that, he thought as he got back into bed, flicked on his own lamp and reached for his copy of *Pines* by Blake Crouch. He would need to read for a while if he hoped to get any more sleep at all.

CHAPTER 21

DWIGHT SLEPT; face down, on the floor of Lucinda's kitchen. On the floor next to him, was a scattered pile of missing persons' posters. After having torn the bulk of them down, except the ones that were strangely high up, he had let himself into Lucinda's house with the key she had once gifted him. She had given it to him, telling him to keep an eye out for anything strange that he might notice. When he had asked what she was referring to, she had merely shushed him and told him that he would know it when he saw it. And the posters had certainly fit the bill as something strange. He had taken down almost all the posters but the staples with little bits of paper had remained. He would need light and something to remove those, if she wanted him to that was. But first he had wanted to leave the bulk of the posters on her kitchen table with a note explaining what he had found. But before he got a chance to write the note, Dwight had discovered a batch of cookies and without being able to resist, he scarfed one down in two bites. It was delicious. The second cookie, he bit into and chewed slowly, savoring the sweet yet bitter taste of both the dates and chocolate with a hint of something he simply couldn't recognize.

Dwight never knew what hit him when he collapsed onto the floor of Lucinda's kitchen, spreading a good chunk of the posters on the floor as he did so.

The laced cookies were strong, just like Lucinda had wanted them to be. Half of one would be enough to induce sleep for a full grown man. Dwight had eaten one and a half before succumbing to the effects.

***

It was almost 6 AM when Robert Emerson found the front door of his veterinary practice unlocked and ajar.

"Hello?" he said, as he walked in and closed the door behind him. The caller had said they had an emergency. Their dog had drunk poison and so this couldn't wait. He needed to be treated and fast. But he hadn't expected to find the door of his practice open, that part was peculiar.

"Hello?" he repeated as he walked past the reception desk and into the examination room. He froze at the door.

"Can I help you?" Robert asked.

Waiting in the room, in an office chair at a small computer desk, sat a rough looking man in a fancy suit and fedora. He had a large scar on the left side of his face and an unlit cigar in his mouth. His right foot wrapped in a blood stained towel was resting on a small stainless steel stool.

"You can't smoke that in here," Robert stated as he stepped into the room, looking behind the examination table, hoping to see a dog back there.

"Where's Roscoe?"

"Mr. Emerson," the man said. "I need you to fix my foot," he pointed to it as if it hadn't been obvious to Robert.

"But I'm a veterinarian, not a doctor."

"A wound is a wound," the man stated dryly. "Fix it," he added coldly.

Robert had the sudden feeling that he wasn't going to have a choice in the matter. Something told him that the bulge he now noticed in the jacket pocket would be a pistol of sorts and that the man sitting there didn't have a dog named Roscoe after all.

Robert had no idea who the man in the suit was but he didn't look like someone who was used to hearing no too often. Robert pulled an empty trash can out from under his counter and turned it upside down and sat on it. The stool he would have normally used was holding up the blood-stained, towel-covered foot of the man in the suit. He gingerly unraveled the bloody towel, exposing the wounded foot.

"What happened?" Robert inquired.

"Gun shot," the unknown man in the suit replied.

"Who shot you?" Robert asked before realizing that asking this question was probably not a good idea, considering the circumstances.

"Never mind that, just fix it."

Robert used the towel to dab at the wound to get a better look at what he was dealing with.

"You should really go to the hospital," Robert stated meekly as he looked at the scarred man with the cigar.

"Fix it," the scarred man said.

"Okay, but I should x-ray it to see..."

"Fix it," the scarred man said as he took a revolver from his bulging pocket and rested it on his injured leg.

Robert reached into a cabinet and took out cotton swabs and a bottle and set them on the examination table. He got up and went to a cabinet, unlocked it, and took out a vial and a syringe and started to fill it with a clear liquid.

"What's that?" the man in the suit asked.

"Something for the pain," Robert replied.

"Nuh-uh. I don't think so," the man in the suit said as he held up the gun and pointed it at Robert.

"It's a local anesthetic. I need to clean the wound and that's going to hurt a lot."

"I don't *wants* it."

"Well I don't want you to accidentally shoot me so," Robert said as he squeezed the syringe slightly to get the air bubbles out, causing it to squirt a little onto the examination table.

"This better not be some sort of poison," the man stated. "If it is." He pointed the gun at Robert to indicate that he would shoot him.

The thought had never occurred to Robert. He hadn't considered the option of injecting the man with Pentobarbital, putting him down like he would an animal; although the idea briefly crossed his mind now. He glanced at the gun and wondered just how dangerous this man really was. As Robert sat on the can again, he noticed on floor under the desk was a bloodied shoe and sock that had previously covered the wounded foot.

"This is going to hurt," Robert said while making eye contact to ensure the man was ready for it before giving him the first injection.

The man flinched, stiffened in the chair and braced against the desk, all while holding the gun at Robert.

"Don't shoot me," Robert stated as he proceeded with a series of injections around the wound. "You need more to numb the wound so I can clean it and see how much damage there is."

The man tensed but remained still as sweat began to trickle down his face. He pulled a handkerchief from a pocket with his free hand and dabbed at the perspiration.

Robert sat back. "We need to give it a few minutes to kick in so I can work without you shooting me," he said with a forced smirk as he noticed the computer was now out of sleep mode. On the screen he saw the results of a Google search.

Derogatory: Showing a critical or disrespectful attitude.

Robert dabbed at the wound, cleaning off the blood.

"How bad is it?" The man inquired.

"Well it looks like you probably have a chipped bone and if I was a betting man; you're going to lose a couple of toes if you don't see a real doctor."

"Which ones?" He inquired nonchalantly.

"The two smaller ones," Robert replied, leaving out the part where he assumed he was losing the toes no matter who looked at the wound.

The man shifted the cigar from side to side as he glanced back and forth between his injured foot and the man who normally treated animals.

"You got painkillers?"

"Of course but not for..."

"Never mind that. Remove the toes and sow it up. And get me some of those painkillers."

Robert hesitated.

"It's that or I shoot you in the foot and we both go to the hospital. You choose."

Robert fetched a few of the implements he felt he needed for the task at hand plus a few extra things. He turned and handed the man a rubber bone chew toy.

"What's that for?"

"You're gonna need something to bite on. And please put the gun away. I'd rather not be shot accidentally."

The man set the gun down on the desk, and set his cigar down next to it. He inserted the rubber bone sideways into his mouth, clamping it in place, ready to bit down hard on it when he needed to.

Robert hesitated; waiting to make sure the rough looking man in the suit was really going to let him cut off two of his toes.

He furrowed his brow and nodded as if to say, go ahead without actually verbalizing it.

CHAPTER 22

AT MID-MORNING under a patchy sky, a crowd consisting of retired members of the community and local shop owners had gathered around the large, ornate, white gazebo of the Maple Springs Park. Some sat on the wood benches while others brought lawn chairs. Most came for the free food, coffee, tea, hot chocolate and concert featuring beloved local talent, during which Robert Emerson would make a speech about how he was the best candidate for city council. Up until that morning, he had felt prepared to charm the town's folk with his wit, banter, and charm. But after the bizarre morning he had had, amputating toes off what he was sure was a mob enforcer, he felt rattled but was trying not to show it.

"I can't thank you enough," Robert said to Robyn as he signed for a delivery of flyers. "I had an emergency visit at the clinic this morning and I really didn't have time to pick these up."

Half-truths were easier to pull off than full outright lies for Robert.

Robyn stared at the giant bandage on Robert's right cheek.

"This?" Robert asked as he point to the bandage. "A dog bit me."

Robyn grimaced at the thought.

Robert opened one of the boxes and looked at the leaflet, hoping to change the subject. The last minute changes that Robyn had suggested, the spelling errors now fixed, Robert was thankful for her help but he had no intention of telling Robyn the truth about why he hadn't picked them up himself. He had no intention of telling anyone about the man with the scarred face. He didn't want anyone to know how he'd been forced to amputate two of the man's toes. He especially didn't want to tell anyone about how he had sat back during the removal of the toes, before sowing the man's foot back together. How he'd wiped his brow with the sleeve of the hand still holding a scalpel. He certainly didn't want to tell anyone how he accidentally grazed his own cheek with the scalpel, cutting his face open.

Robert turned away from Robyn as Mona, a silver-haired lady with too much makeup and perfume, carrying a tray of baked goods came over to where they stood. She grasped Robert by the arm, reminding him that the band was about to start. This was his event she said; insisting that he introduce them before they began playing.

***

As Robert walked away, Mona cornered Robyn, forced a Danish in her hand while smiling as she began explaining how Robert was going to help raise the funds to help renovate the bingo hall. They needed to bring it back up to code so the town's folk could resume their regular bingo games she loved so much and Robert had promised he would get this done. The more Mona prattled, the tighter her grip became, clutching onto Robyn's arm, preventing her from walking away like she wanted to.

Robyn listened to Mona go on and on about how great the Danishes were, insisting that she take another one to go. Robyn watched the people mill about, looking for a way out of the chat she had been cornered into.

From a distance, Robyn noticed the blond woman who had torn her poster off of a lamppost. She recalled the woman's name was Lucinda. She was talking to Sandy, The Flower Shop owner who was eating a muffin of some sort while Lucinda clutched what looked like containers full of baked goods.

Could Lucinda be the woman Thomas had described, the one who visited his parents when Vincent had disappeared, who had fed them muffins and lies? Did she have something to do with all this, wondered Robyn? She fit Thomas' description only she wasn't old or had grey hair like he had said.

Robyn bit into the Danish and marveled at how good it was after all. *Now all I need is a coffee and this morning would suck a lot less*, she thought as Mona waved at someone else and finally walked away.

***

Under the patchy morning sky, Duncan kicked at the dirt by a hole in the ground, marveling at the decayed human remains inside it. His curiosity had finally gotten the better of him and he had returned to see if it was still there. He desperately wanted to see it again but without the shadow man to stop him this time. This meant he had to do it in broad daylight, when there were no dark shadows for him to emerge from. But this had also meant sneaking out of daycare again, and this time he hadn't intended on getting caught. He intended to return before Mrs. Litney figured out that he wasn't sleeping in the closet. He had made sure she saw him carrying a large duvet and pillow into the closet. He had made sure she was watching when he had tugged the door closed from beneath the blanket. But once he heard little Mandy Taylor getting upset over what he assumed was some mundane thing, he knew Mrs. Litney would be sufficiently distracted and wouldn't notice him boldly sneaking out the front door.

And now, having found the remains dug up again, a few bones protruding from the ground, Duncan's curiosity took a turn he hadn't expected. He had previously thought it would be cool to see this again. Maybe even hold a real human skull in his hands. But now that he saw that parts of the body looked like they had been clawed and gnawed on, he felt icky and uncomfortable in a way that he hadn't thought possible. He couldn't help but think of his mother and sister as he looked at the body before him. He glanced behind him at the giant horned demon toy as he spoke.

"Who do you think that was?" Duncan asked the giant toy, knowing full well it couldn't answer his question. The thing was nothing but a giant puppet. It could obey commands and perform tasks but didn't actually have a mind of its own.

"I wonder how she died?"

From under the bones protruded a small piece of purple fabric. It looked like it had an intricate, fancy hem which gave the garment a feminine look and this humanized the remains. He no longer saw them as a thing but as someone.

"I wonder who put her here?" he said as he stared at the remains. The head was partially exposed but all he could see was what looked like the back of her head and wisps of blonde hair partially covered in dirt.

A sudden low growl coming from the woods made gooseflesh crawl up his bare arms. Up until that moment, he hadn't heard the mangy dog coming. The big dog stepped from the woods into the small clearing, barred its teeth and growled louder.

Frightened, Duncan stepped backwards and tripped

over the giant foot of his horned ape goat hybrid. Landing on his rear, he panicked and scrambled backwards as the dog stepped toward him, still growling. He tore his gaze away from the dog and looked at the overgrown toy, standing there motionless, as if he expected it to bravely defend him. In his moment of fear, it had slipped his mind that he controlled it. It could follow simple commands but without him willing it to life, it wouldn't do anything without his wanting it. He willed the giant toy foreword, stomping its hollow plastic legs as it did.

The stray dog took a few steps backwards as the fur on its back bristled while it growled still.

Duncan emboldened by the sight of the dog stepping back from his giant monstrosity, made the toy take a few more steps toward the dog and raise its arms as if to make it even more imposing. The dog lowered its head and scurried to the edge of the trees where it stopped, turned and sniffed at the air. Duncan got to his feet as the dog stepped toward the horned monstrosity, still sniffing at the air. Duncan willed the creature forward a few quick sudden steps, spooking the dog which turned and ran back into the woods.

"Ha!" Duncan exclaimed triumphantly only to watch the dog turn around and come toward him again, still smelling at the air, as if it was assessing the threat of the giant beast that stood between it and the rotting bones in the hole. Duncan smiled as he made the plastic horned creature stand as tall as it could, raise its arms high and begin to run toward the dog as it crashed through branches in the process.

The dog turned tail and ran through the woods while being chased. Having forgotten his fear, Duncan laughed as the dog vanished into the woods, being chased by his giant toy.

***

Robert Emerson, the would-be city councilor, walked up to the microphone and encouraged the audience to again applaud the marvelous talents of the Clancy sisters and their rather bizarre bluegrass renditions of old hard rock songs. He glanced at the crowd sitting on benches and lawn chairs around the Maple Springs Park gazebo, marveling at how much grey hair he saw; his target audience, a great number of which were clients of his veterinarian practice.

"Thank you for coming out to entertain the good people of Maple Springs," Robert announced. "And now I'd like to take a moment and talk about some of the things, I as councilor, will be focusing on like.... HOLY CRAP!!"

Shocked looks appeared on many of the faces in the crowd until they saw what he had seen.

From the trees burst a ten-foot-tall, horned demonic figure that looked like it was part ape and part goat. The monstrosity ran into the crowd, arms raised, and stopped in the middle of the scattering throng of people.

***

Duncan suddenly wondered what he had done as the shrieks reached him and he realized it was early morning and not late at night. He stood there, next to a hole, where a long-dead woman decayed in the ground. The screams seemed to grow louder.

***

Robyn dropped her coffee and screamed as the giant, horrific creature she had convinced herself wasn't real had just emerged from the woods and now stood in the middle of the crowd, its arms raised up as if it was being held at gunpoint.

The crowd scattered in all directions, some of the older people struggling with canes, arthritis and bad hips. Mona, the silver haired bingo fanatic went pale and dropped to the ground, fainting at the terrifying sight before her.

Robyn witnessed the incredible boldness of Lucinda Mayweather. Mona, who was now sprawled on the grass, had confirmed Lucinda as the muffin maker for Robyn.

Unlike the others, Lucinda stepped toward the monstrosity. She showed no fear while everyone else had backed away from the giant demonic figure. An old, white-haired man picked up a nearby walker and positioned himself between Lucinda and the monstrosity, clutching the walker as a weapon as he quivered in fear, yet stood his ground.

Robyn saw Robert Emerson hiding behind the Clancy sisters who had backed themselves into a corner of the gazebo, one of whom clutched her mandolin by the neck as a club.

Robyn watched Lucinda step up to the monstrosity, reach out and lay a hand on its leg as if she was checking to see if it was real.

Robyn's head spun as she fought off a bout of anxiety. This was confusing enough as it was, but what happened next made absolutely no sense to her.

***

Lucinda touched the giant creature as it stood motionless, towering above her. It felt cold, hard and artificial. The legs looked as if they were covered in fur, but they only looked that way. The creature felt like plastic and yet moments ago, it had burst from the forest, running like a living thing. She heard someone shout from behind her, something about this monster eating people. That's when the realization dawned on her that no matter how much she tried to convince people that the disappearances were perfectly normal, there would always be those who wouldn't believe it. They would believe in monsters in the park. And even though she knew this wasn't true, one now stood before her.

Lucinda took the walker from the old man and struck the giant monstrosity as hard as she could. A loud cracking noise echoed as a result. She stepped back, expecting the monster to strike her in return. But the monster stood stock still. She pulled the walker back and struck the creature again, this time, cracking the thing's leg open.

Plastic! The damned thing was made of plastic.

Turning to the remaining people around her, she yelled, "Help me! Help me kill it!"

A few of the remaining people grasped at wood handled election signs, walking canes and chairs. Most stood their ground, frozen in fear but a few stepped forward, attacking the giant monstrosity with their makeshift weapons, striking it over and over, an attempt to protect the woman named Lucinda Mayweather, whom they were smitten with.

***

Robyn looked around for something to use a weapon, thinking she might just be brave enough to help fight whatever this creature was. She grasped at a plastic folding stool, but judging it too weak to be any good against a giant monster, she tossed it aside. She proceeded to pull a wood staked election sign from the ground and after a brief struggle, tore off the plastic sign her father's printing shop had supplied.

Before she could join the fray, she saw her little brother burst from the trees where the creature had previously emerged. He was panting, out of breath as he stopped at the edge of the woods, a look of panic on his face.

***

"NO!" Duncan shouted. "NO! Don't!"

Duncan reached out his hand as if trying to will the people to stop attacking his giant toy in the same way he willed it to do things. Only his ability to control the creature didn't work on people. He watched helplessly as they beat at it with pieces of wood and various other things. He saw it crack and break into large shards of plastic as they struck it repeatedly.

"No!" he said as he made the creature take a step backwards on what were now broken and cracked legs. A well timed blow felled the creature onto its back as it now placed arms in front of itself to shield from the blows, as a boy might do if he was in its place.

Duncan felt defeated as he released the bond with the giant broken toy, making it instantly shrink back to its normal size.

He turned and walked back the way he had come, back into the woods.

***

During the chaos, Lucinda drew back the battered walker to strike the broken monster when it simply vanished. Now with the creature suddenly gone, some of the others that had helped her beat at it turned and ran away. Those few brave souls that had helped her weren't ready for what looked like demons and magic. Her rallying cries had helped instill bravery but that was short lived in regular people, especially when the creature suddenly vanished before their very eyes. The few that remained were baffled as to what had just happened.

A grey haired older man who had beat at the monster

with his now battered cane made it halfway to the gazebo and collapsed from the exertion.

Lucinda wiped the sweat of her brow and glanced around as if ready for something else to come at her. That's when she noticed the small remnants of the broken plastic doll on the ground. The torso and head, while battered, seemed intact. Stomping her foot, she crushed it into the grass, shattering the plastic to bits.

The giant monster had simply vanished and left everyone struggling to understand what had just happened but Lucinda now new this was conjured by someone. No one else seemed to notice the small pieces of broken plastic in the grass. What turned out to be a giant toy now reduced to small shards of plastic, part of which had been stomped into the ground.

Lucinda looked around, trying to find the one responsible for this chaos, assuming he had to be close by and most likely relishing in the mischief. She noticed small footprints in a patch of wet soil by the tree line and had a good idea who they might belong to.

***

An hour after the chaos at the gazebo, a dirty, sweaty Duncan marched into the Thrifty Dollar Store and disappeared down an aisle as the cashier with the shiny nose ring and the heavy eye shadow watched. Moments later, the son of her boss emerged from the toy aisle carrying one of the cheap import action figures; the creepy ape one with goat legs and giant horns. He walked to the cash register, plopped a fistful of change onto the counter and immediately walked out of the store carrying his newly purchased action figure.

"Do you want your receipt?" the cashier asked while counting the change, as the door closed behind the boy.

CHAPTER 23

ROBYN'S PHONE rang as soon as she pulled the company van into a parking spot by the curb in front of Mrs. Litney's daycare. She glanced at her phone. It was Thomas. It must be important since Thomas never called. He texted, messaged via Facebook, but never called. With a shaky hand, she put the phone to her ear.

"Hey."

"Did you hear?" Thomas blurted. "Someone spiked the food at Robert's concert in the park. They think someone put acid in the hot chocolate or something."

"Who told you that?"

"People said they saw monsters on unicorns with swords and shit, others saw trees come to life or something."

"Bullshit, Thomas. I was there. I know what I saw."

"What was it like? Doing acid I mean?" Thomas inquired eagerly.

"There was no acid, Thomas. None!"

"It was in the drinks," Thomas replied. "You probably had a coffee or hot chocolate and then..."

"No! There was no acid, Thomas. A monster came out of the woods," Robyn stated firmly, leaving out the part about having coffee and a Danish. "I saw it. The same monster that I saw chasing my brother. It's real. At least it was. I think they killed it."

"What are you talking about?" Thomas asked as if she was the one not making sense. As if what he had suggested was perfectly normal and she was the one who was crazy. That's what his tone of voice conveyed to Robyn and this angered her.

"It's her, Thomas. The woman who fed you muffins and lies. She's behind this somehow."

"It was an acid trip, Robyn. Mona, the old bingo fanatic, said so. She used to do a lot of acid in the 70's and she said that was just like the good old days. That's what she told my mom, anyway."

"Fuck you, Thomas. I know what I saw," Robyn blurted before ending the call.

She looked at her phone, wishing she could throw it as far as she could, but knew then she would have to fork out the money for a new one. But a part of her did doubt what she saw, only because she didn't want it to be real. She didn't want monsters like that to exist. That was crazy. But she couldn't think about that now.

Exiting the van, she marched across the street and up the steps to Mrs. Litney's daycare. The first thing she needed to do was make sure her brother was okay. Every time she saw that monstrosity, he was there. It's as if the thing was after him. Was he going to vanish like all the others, she wondered as she made her way into the daycare.

"Hi," Mrs. Litney said as she saw Robyn walk in.

Robyn assumed Mrs. Litney knew why she was there as she gestured toward the closet where Duncan frequently napped.

Robyn went to the closet and opened the door expecting to find it empty.

Instead, what she saw was a dirty, sweaty Duncan, curled atop the duvet, sleeping soundly. What she didn't see was his new favorite action figure's leg, protruding from under the duvet, where he had hidden it from Mandy and Mrs. Litney.

Robyn was startled when Mrs. Litney spoke.

Standing behind her, Mrs. Litney was looking over her shoulder at the boy sleeping in the closet.

"I think he plays video games all night," Mrs. Litney stated confidently. "That's why he's always tired when he comes here."

To Robyn, Mrs. Litney spoke as if she had cracked the mystery. The boy was tired because he stayed up all night, playing games. But maybe Mrs. Litney wasn't as crazy as she seemed, thought Robyn. Maybe there was something to this theory. Although it might not be video games, but just maybe he was staying up all night. Doing what though? That was the mystery, thought Robyn.

***

A little past midnight, a plain-clothed John Fitzpatrick sat in his truck concealed by darkness. He had parked a short distance from the Skidmoore house where he now waited, pondering his next move.

Having gone a few days without a visit from Lucinda had left him perplexed. Had she found a new lover? If so, John had decided he would kill him. After all, he was getting good at disposing bodies. Lucinda had made sure of that. And after everything he had done for her, how could she simply cast him aside? He felt rage building up inside.

A Glock rested on the passenger seat, just in case. He glanced at his cell phone, scrolling through the missed calls, seeing Dwight's number and wondering if he had anything to do with Lucinda not coming to see him the last few days. He set the phone down next to the Glock and watched the house.

He glanced at the house he was parked directly in

front of and saw an election sign on the front lawn.

Vote for
Robert Emerson
Councilor at Large

Was it Robert she was seeing?

He had heard rumors about all the excitement at the park that afternoon, by the gazebo. Someone had spiked the drinks with acid and all hell had broken loose. The event had been organized by Robert Emerson himself and from what he'd heard, Lucinda had been there. Sure, she often went to social events and always brought baked goods, but maybe she was there to see Robert this time. Maybe he would pay the vet a visit in the morning and have a chat with him. But that would have to wait until morning. Right now there were more pressing questions, like what was Lucinda doing at the Skidmoore house at midnight?

***

In the glow of a nightlight, at a little past midnight, Lucinda stood over the Skidmoores' kitchen stove. She stirred the contents of a large pot, simmering a strange smelling concoction, the fumes of which wafted through the house like a living thing, twisting and turning, as if seeking something. Lucinda picked from a small mound of pungent greenery she had on the kitchen counter as she stirred the pot. She put some of the leafy greens in her mouth and chewed slowly. She swallowed her mouthful and replaced it with the rest of the leaves and suckled on those as she turned off the stove.

"I know you're here," she said to the darkness. "I know you come see the boy."

Lucinda walked past the kitchen table where she had set a small surprise for the Skidmoore's to find in the morning.

She went up the stairs, holding on to the handrail, walking carefully in the dimly lit house. She chose the first door of the upstairs hallway, entering a bedroom to find Gloria sleeping soundly as some of the fumes from her concoction seemed to hover over the mother.

Tim lay on the floor, a few feet from the bed, also sleeping soundly, fumes hovering over him.

Lucinda didn't know that Tim had heard her in the kitchen and doing what any worried father would do, had tried to go check on what he assume would be one of his children. She wouldn't care about that even if she did. All she cared about was that the fumes hovered over him as well as he slept where he had collapsed.

"Show yourself," Lucinda said aloud as she watched the fumes writhe like a living thing before they dissipated into misty air, their job done.

After waiting a few moments, she took a small satchel from the folds of her skirt, pulled open the drawstring and took a pinch of a fine grey dust inside it. Lucinda smiled and sprinkled dust over Gloria's face.

Gloria swatted at the air, as if she was swatting away a bug, but never woke.

Lucinda stepped over to Tim and sprinkled more dust over him as well. She took a step back toward the door and watched as the couple began twitching in what was now a fitful sleep. Tim's legs twitched as if he was dreaming of running while muttering incomprehensible gibberish. Gloria gripped her blankets with blanched knuckles as she pulled them up to her neck and twitched; expressing discontent through moans and groans.

"Sweat dreams," Lucinda said with a smile as she

closed the door behind her, leaving the couple trapped in vivid nightmares.

Lucinda opened the next bedroom door and walked in, making no effort to be quiet in the process. Upon seeing the boy, fully dressed sleeping on top of his covers with his plastic doll. A very familiar hybrid of a muscular horned ape with goat hooves and large monstrous fangs, she spoke loudly.

"SHOW YOURSELF!"

No shadows moved.

"I know you use the boy to make me weak so that I'll have to feed you more frequently."

Lucinda walked to the dresser and picked up one of the many action figures on its top.

"Toys! You gift the boy with magic and he wastes it on toys. But now what can he give you in exchange for those magical gifts? He's far too young to understand what you want."

Lucinda set the toy down and walked to the bed, took a pinch of the grey dust and sprinkled it over the boy's face. She watched as he scrunched his nose and grimaced as if he was about to cry.

"He probably won't give you his essence to take, not on his own, but I can convince him to give it willingly. If that's what you're after," Lucinda said to the darkness, knowing full well he was listening. She touched the boy's face, ran her fingers down his cheek as she smiled. "Or maybe I'll just take something very precious to him and blame you for it. He'll hate you and won't want anything to do with you then. Even if it means giving up his precious toys."

Lucinda smiled, looked into the darkest corner, knowing full well this would be where the shadow man always emerge.

"Maybe I'll take her now," Lucinda said as she exited

the room, not bothering to close the boy's door and walked in through the next door down the hall. She squinted at the brightness from the room as she pushed the door open. As her eyes slowly adjusting, she stepped on the towel at her feet. The one Robyn had put on the bottom of the door, so that the light from her bedroom wouldn't show in the hallway. She marveled at the sight as there were thirteen lamps, all lit. Most were connected to extension cords or powers bars. The brightness in the bedroom was overbearing. Lucinda squinted and saw Robyn, sleeping atop her blankets, fully clothed. On the floor next to the bed was a small stack of missing person posters with Sun-Yun's picture on them.

From under the bed, emerged a large black cat.

Lucinda took a step back, a look of shock on her face as she watched the cat hop onto the bed. The cat sat next to the sleeping Robyn and looked fixedly at Lucinda who stood in the doorway.

"Odessa!" Lucinda said in shock, as her gaze went back and forth between the girl in the bed and the cat. "That would explain why she didn't seem to be affected by my Danish. She's been touched by darkness, hasn't she?" Lucinda asked aloud to the shadows as the realization that the girl before her was special, dawned on her.

Odessa licked her paw and rubbed at her ear, watching Lucinda while she did this.

"Is she?" Lucinda asked the shadows that had yet to answer any of her questions.

The shadow man had to be listening, she thought. But he wouldn't show himself. Not with Odessa here. He would fear her, and rightly so. He had gone against the natural order of things, broken rules and Odessa was here because of that.

Lucinda's head suddenly spun as she staggered. The

herbs she suckled were wearing off and the fumes from the simmering concoction emanating from the kitchen were beginning to take effect on her as well. She had to leave, and quick before she too would end up in a deep sleep.

Clutching the wooden railing, she struggled down the stairs, her vision blurring as she hurried to make it outside before her own black magic concoction worked against her. She staggered outside, down the steps and on the lawn until her legs gave out from under her, plopping down on the grass, her large black skirt pooling around her.

John, who had still been watching the house, hurriedly got out of his truck and rushed to her side.

"Are you okay?" he asked.

"The herbs only slow down the effects," she said groggily. "Help me, John."

In her groggy state, she knew John didn't understand what she was referring to but it didn't matter. All that would matter to John was that she wanted his help and she knew this.

He scooped her up into his strong arms as if she was a small child, his eagerness to please her back with a vengeance, spurring him on.

"Take me home with you," Lucinda said meekly as she struggled to remain alert. "Take me home."

His face contorted with emotions; John carried Lucinda to his truck. He had no way of knowing that her grip on him was still strong and that pheromone charms were making him forget all about his jealousy.

She needed him and that's all that mattered.

CHAPTER 24

IT WAS NEARING 2:00 AM; and in the dim light of the antique imitation torch sconces, Vincent sat on a thin mattress, wrapped in a dusty green sleeping bag, leaning against the back wall of the basement cage. He quivered with fear. He didn't understand why he was so frightened but only that he felt fear like he had never experienced. He had awakened to find a large black cat, sitting quietly before the cage door. Somehow he had known right away this was no ordinary cat. There was something about it that felt off.

"Hello," he said aloud, hoping she was home.

"Lucinda?"

The cat sat so still that Vincent wondered if it was alive. Could it be another one of Leonard's stuffed creatures he had adorned his home with? And if it was, then the question would become, who had put it there?

Chills washed over him when the cat cocked its head to the side.

It was alive after all. This should have been a relief as it could have merely found a way to sneak into the house. It could simply be hunting mice or maybe rats.

Vincent glanced at the empty paper plate that sat inside the bars and saw crumbs from the cold pizza pockets Lucinda had left for him. He thought hard, as during his time in the cage, he often had food lay about but had never seen a single rodent. Come to think of it, he had never seen a single insect either. He shifted his gaze back to the creepy cat and watched as it inched closer to the cage door. It cocked its head again and this time, Vincent heard a series of loud clicks as the cage door opened slightly.

While still seated against the back wall, Vincent glanced at the shadows in the dark corner; the place where the shadow man emerged from even though there was nothing there but solid concrete. He wiped away a tear as he struggled with the decision of what to do next. He felt he had to leave the cage as the man from the shadows frightened him almost as much as this cat. But he loved her. If he left, would she be mad at him? Would she still want to sit with him, let him lay his head down on her lap and stroke his hair like she had done those first few nights?

Vincent knew she would be upset if he left. But the man from the shadows, who seemed to come through the walls in the darkness, frightened him enough to make him want to leave the confines of the cage, now that he could.

As if sensing Vincent's apprehension, the cat turned tail and sauntered up the staircase. Vincent got to his feet and stood before the unlatched cage door as he heard the door at the top of the stairs creak open as the cat disappeared from view.

He pushed the cage door open and with an emotion filled voice, called out again.

"Lucinda?"

Glancing back into the dark corner, he decided he would at least go upstairs. He would go upstairs and then decide what to do from there.

The stairs creaked as he climbed them slowly, pausing every few steps, as if unsure and doubting his decision. He pushed the basement door wider and held his breath as he fully expected to see someone or something standing there, waiting for him. As he stepped past the doorway into the dimly lit room, he felt as if all of Leonard's creations were watching him. At any moment, he expected them to come alive and attack him. Chills washed over him as he saw the open front door, the streetlights and starlit sky illuminating the outside more than faint lights did the interior of the dark creepy house.

The large black cat emerged from shadows near him and walked through the door, only pausing at the walkway before the steps. It turned and looked back at Vincent, as if waiting for him.

Vincent made his way out the door and stood on the veranda, watching the cat that had spooked him not long ago. The cat turned tail and sauntered past a stuffed raccoon that was perched on the lawn near a bush. The cat walked behind the bush but never came out on the other side.

Vincent stepped off the veranda and walked past the picket fence and into the street where he stopped and turned to look at the creepy house he had just come from. He wiped away a tear and thought of her.

Would she be upset with him? He knew she needed him and he loved her so.

Looking up at the starry sky, he wondered what time it was. He wondered what day it was as well. How long had he been in that cage? He tried to remember their conversations, hoping that might give him some sort of clue as to where she could be.

He had to find her, he thought as he began walking down the middle of the street, toward his home, where he has first met Lucinda.

***

In the dark of night, Thomas stood at the corner of a driveway, under a streetlight near the old Legault house. He had a folder with a new version of the posters tucked under his arm, one hand in his pocket with his phone in the other.

"Where is she?" he muttered quietly as he checked his phone, hoping he simply hadn't heard the chime indicating he had received a text message.

Earlier that day, Robyn had told him she would meet him at this very spot near the house where she supposedly lived. He had read the text multiple times to be sure, but now he worried. It wasn't like Robyn to not show up. She would at least let him know. She was considerate. Something he hadn't thought she would be, back when they were still strangers. She said to meet here at 1:30 AM and now it was 2:00 and she hadn't shown.

"You coming?" Thomas texted Robyn. He waited a moment and then sent another text. "Did you fall asleep or did you disappear on me too?"

Thomas opened the folder, tilted it to catch light and looked at the new posters, a few new faces added to it.

Maybe Robyn was right. The thing about Vincent leaving, moving away to work in a Vape shop did sound bogus, now that he thought about it. He had known Vincent since kindergarten and even though he liked to pretend he was some cool, tough guy, Vincent was a momma's boy. He wouldn't ever leave Maple Springs or his momma, thought Thomas.

Thomas closed the folder, tucked it back under his arm and looked at his phone. Three painful minutes had passed since the last time he checked it. Now, feeling that he had waited long enough, he decided he would walk to Robyn's house and see if she had indeed forgotten. Perhaps something had come up, he wondered. Or maybe she was gone. Disappeared like the rest, a thought which sent a chill down his spine.

He walked from under the streetlight's glow only to pause in his tracks at the sight before him.

Farther up the street, someone bathed in darkness, walked with a familiar stagger. The shape of the silhouette, the clumsy stride, could only be one person, thought Thomas.

Gooseflesh covered his arms as he raised his hands, waving; about to cry out to the shadow, convinced it was his best friend Vincent. But before he could make a sound, a strong hand grasped him by the nape of his neck, fingers digging in. He felt a sharp stabbing pain in the side of his neck.

Weakness washed over him as he felt his knees buckle. Everything around him felt like it spun. He didn't know how it had happened but he was prone now and yet it felt like he was still falling. His mind clouding over, his last thoughts about whether or not he was about to suffer the same fate as the missing people on the posters. Then all went black.

CHAPTER 25

LUCINDA HAD awoken in John's bed while morning light peeked through the bedroom window as the sun crested the horizon. Her mind had been groggy as John snored softly, still deep in slumber. She had sat on the edge of the bed, a feeling of weakness washing over her.

She should have fed the shadow man the night before. The previous day had taken its toll and she felt it. She would need to feed the shadow man to keep age at bay and regain her vigor on most days. But today she felt emptied, as if she had used up all the magic she had in keeping the people of Maple Springs under her spells, recently feeling her influences waning.

She had recalled waking earlier and making love to John. But her own concoction had worked against her in that she had been completely exhausted and had slept much longer than she had anticipated.

But an hour after waking, she found herself now standing on weak legs, on the walkway before the creepy house she lived in, wondering why the front door was wide open. She glanced at the neighborhood, looking for clues as to what might have happened in her absence and found none. She wondered if she would find Dwight passed out in her house again, like the time he ate her baked goods laced with her own sleep additives.

Lucinda walked in, pausing at the front door as she

saw the door to the basement was also ajar. Under ordinary circumstances she would find comfort in the stillness of the house she called home. But this day, hearing not a sound worried her. The basement door had been locked from the outside. She felt the strength drain out her legs as she descended into the basement. It was no surprise when she found the cage door open and the boy gone.

"She was here," a familiar voice said from the darkness.

"Odessa," Lucinda murmured.

"Yes," the shadow man said as he emerged from the darkness in the corner of the cage. "She's found us."

"Because of you!" Lucinda barked. "Your greed is the reason she found us."

"It is you who cheat death," the shadow man replied. "It's your soul she wants released as it should have been, long ago."

"Maybe you forget; she's not the one who takes the essence. YOU ARE!!"

"I don't take anything not given to me willingly," the shadow man said with a devilish smile as he stroked his chin with long, bony fingers.

"She's here because you've been playing with that child, him and his toys."

"I know not what you speak of," the shadow man muttered.

"Because of that boy's mischief, I've had to use too much magic and that's the reason she found us."

"I CANNOT HELP MYSELF!" the shadow man barked before calming himself. "I need to feed!"

"And you do," Lucinda replied. "Each time someone dies, you and those like you get to feed on what's left of their essence."

"But that is not enough!"

"That's why our little arrangement worked so well but like before we came to this little town, your greed will ruin everything."

"I SHOULD TAKE YOUR ESSENCE AND BE DONE WITH YOU!"

Lucinda spoke softly. "Then who would charm these pesky weak souls into giving up their essence for you to feed on? How else would they give it willingly before their time? How else would you get to feed more than you should? You need me as much as I need you."

"Tis-not true, I could stop taking others instead of yours and let you die."

"But again, who would make them give you their essence willingly?"

"Perhaps you've lived long enough," the shadow man stated, showing his impatience.

"Never!"

"Odessa is here to right what we've done and you know it."

"She only found me because of you," Lucinda said, her voice filled with bitterness. "That's why you're going to help find the boy Vincent for me, before the day is over!"

Lucinda's stomach began to ache fiercely as she grasped the wood handrail, making her way up the basements steps. She needed to feed the shadow man and soon. She made her way across the hall and out the front door. She had to find Vincent and quickly before her charms begin to wear off and she had to start over, making her use even more of her magic, making her weaker still.

***

Robyn opened her eyes, squinting against the bright light in her bedroom. The thirteen lamps keeping her room as bright as day, she happily thought was a small comfort against her renewed anxiety toward the darkness. She rubbed the sleep from her eyes and glanced at the window and saw full daylight. She had assumed the brightness was from the lamps but now saw that almost all of them were off and the illumination came from the new day. She didn't recall opening the curtain of her window, which was normally always closed.

Reaching for her phone, she saw that it was nearly 8 AM. She had overslept. The smell of coffee had pulled her from what had to be the deepest sleep she'd had in months. She stretched as she sat up, realizing that she was still fully clothed and atop the blankets which was not all that unusual for her. But seeing her curtain open was bizarre and her bedroom door was ajar as well. The towel she had used to block light under it, still on the floor. She knew her parents hadn't opened the door as they would have picked up the towel and thrown it in the hamper. She assumed her brother opened the door to her room.

Climbing out of bed, she turned off the only two lamps still lit. While doing this, she noticed that the other lamps hadn't been turned off, instead their bulbs were burnt. The LED as well as the regular bulbs, all blackened. Had there been a power surge during the night, she wondered?

A glance at her phone made fresh anxiety well up. Thomas had texted her, his last message just after 2 AM.

"Did you fall asleep or did you disappear on me too?" he had asked.

The text jogging her memory, she recalled telling Thomas she would meet him near the old Legault house to do some of their own investigating.

Robyn typed a reply.

"Sorry!! I fell asleep."

A text she followed with a sad emoji.

The smell of coffee was strong and the chatter coming

from the kitchen loud. She glanced at the time, confused. From the sounds coming from the kitchen, they would all be late this morning. This was abnormal for her family. She couldn't help but think something strange had occurred the night before.

Entering the kitchen, she found her family sitting at the well-worn table with mugs of coffee, her little brother with what had to be hot coco in his. Each of them had a crumb-covered plate before them. In the center of the table sat a wicker basket which contained a couple of familiar looking muffins and Danishes.

"We saved you some," Gloria said as she sipped coffee.

Robyn glanced at the half full coffee pot and then back at the pastries. In her head, she could hear Thomas's voice.

"I got home last night and found them sitting at the kitchen table eating muffins and having coffee with some woman."

She stifled a scream as she debated throwing the baked goods into the trash, or better yet, throwing them outside for the crows to peck at. But the looks of bliss on her parents' face told her they wouldn't understand this. They would most likely be angry with her. They might even try and punish her for wasting food and for being so rude.

She watched Duncan as he glanced at her and then back at the muffins. He clearly hoped she wouldn't want them so he could have another.

"No thanks," Robyn replied as she got a mug and poured coffee. "I'm not hungry," she lied. She was famished but there was no way she would eat those pastries. They looked like the ones Lucinda was handing out in the park that day all hell broke loose.

"I'm gonna grab a shower," she muttered, making her way back upstairs while clutching her coffee like it was something precious.

***

Thomas opened his eyes, squinting against the brightness of the room. He struggled to straighten himself but found he could hardly move. His throat was painfully dry and his head ached. From hands to elbows, he was taped to the arms of a chair that rolled a little when he struggled. It was an office chair with wheels, he thought as his sight adjusted. His feet were bound together with more tape he assumed as from his vantage point, he couldn't see them.

"You can't do this here," he heard someone say. "You have to leave."

"Yeah-yeah. I'll leave when I'm done."

Before him, looking down at him was a mustached balding man with a large bandage on his right cheek.

"Dammit. He's awake."

"Good," the other voice said.

Thomas glanced at the room and realized he was at the vet, in one of the exam rooms. The balding man with the bandage was Doctor Emerson, the local vet. Behind him was a rough looking big man in a suit. Half his face looked like melted cheese that had congealed. He had a large unlit cigar in his mouth. In his right hand, he held a crowbar. Thomas watched as the man limped, placing his weight on the crowbar which he used as a cane, the bottom end of which had a rubber tip, just like a normal cane but the upper end had prying prongs.

The suited man stood before him and tapped him on the chest with the heavy metal crowbar as he spoke. Thomas groaned from the pain of what had looked like a light tap, but hurt like hell.

"What were you doing hanging around Leonard's house last night?" the suited man asked.

Thomas glanced back at Doctor Emerson and saw a look that wasn't good. The doctor looked like he wasn't about to piss off the man with the crowbar. The light tap had hurt and the crowbar felt heavy and yet the man held it as if it weighed nothing.

"Look, Mr. Fingers. Not here, please," Doctor Emerson said meekly.

The rough looking man in the suit the vet had referred to as Fingers reached back, grasped one of the posters from the exam table and showed it to Thomas, then using the crowbar cane he pointed to one of the new pictures on the posters as he spoke.

"This guy... Leonard. What do you know about his disappearance? Where is he?"

"I don't know," Thomas replied suddenly realizing this had to be the infamous mobster named Fingers people spoke of.

"Nobody's seen him in months, maybe more. That's why we added him to the poster," Thomas added.

"Who's we?" Fingers asked as he pulled the unlit cigar from his mouth and breathed out as if it was lit and he was exhaling smoke.

In that moment, Thomas knew he had messed up. He should have said, I and not we. This Fingers character didn't look like someone you wanted to mess with.

"Please don't kill me." Thomas muttered.

"I can't promise notin," Fingers replied. "But help me find Leonard and we'll see."

Thomas opened his mouth to speak but stopped when he heard his phone ring. From behind Fingers, on the exam table under the posters, his phone rang a second time.

Fingers picked up the phone and looked at the call display.

"Who's Robyn?"

"Robyn Skidmoore," Robert murmured.

Thomas' eyes grew wide with fear at the idea of endangering his friend. He glanced at the vet and wondered what was under that bandage.

Fingers answered the call.

"I got your friend here," Fingers said abruptly. "You want notin to happen to him, you come to the vet's. You know where that is?"

"Who's this?" Robyn replied.

Fingers held the phone in front of Thomas.

"Robyn, don't..." Thomas muttered before a feeling the curved end of the crowbar jab him in the gut.

"You're going to have to leave," Robert said meekly. "I have appointments."

Ignoring everyone, Fingers spoke into the phone.

"Listen kid, we both *wants* the same thing; to find Leonard. Come to the vet's if you *wants* your friend back in one piece."

Fingers ended the call and pocketed Thomas's phone.

"Don't try and run, kid." Fingers said as he pulled a snub nosed revolver from his pocket.

Thomas saw the gun. Fingers didn't point it at him but instead held it in a way to be sure he saw it.

"You can outrun me but not a bullet. Cut him loose, Doc."

CHAPTER 26

OFFICER JOHN Fitzpatrick hadn't been on the road in his cruiser long before the urge overpowered him. He'd awakened yet again to find her gone. On his phone were two missed calls from Dwight, Lucinda's personal neighborhood watch. The thought of her going to him infuriated John.

She was his, he thought as he headed toward her house.

With every fiber of his being, he resisted the urge to turn on the sirens and speed.

"Where is she?" he muttered.

She hadn't answered the calls. Lucinda loathed telephones of all kinds. But she had a strange way of knowing when something was off. It was like she had some sort of sixth sense, thought John as he sped up. She had to be home, dealing with whatever trivial matter Dwight had seen fit to call about in the middle of the night.

***

At about 9 AM Vincent Pernelli stood under a streetlamp, not far from Leonard Legault's old house, befuddled at the sight before him. Stapled to the wooden power pole was a poster of the missing people of Maple Springs. The part that baffled him was that he was one of them.

Being tired and hungry was affecting his ability to think, but he recalled his best friend Thomas saying something to him about posters of Sun-Yun, the missing girl he had long ago nicknamed Some-Yum. But until this very moment, Vincent hadn't thought of himself as missing. He knew where he had been, in the basement of The Grill Reaper's house. Knowing this, he hadn't felt lost at all. He felt as if he had been sent by some unseen force to help the beautiful Lucinda. She needed him and only he could help her. She had told him so and she wouldn't lie to him, he thought.

A sudden feeling of desperation overwhelmed him, a gasp escaping his lips while large tears flowed down his face. A sickening feeling washed over him and he felt he would throw up, even though he really had nothing in him to vomit out.

Where was she, he wondered? Why had she left him? All he wanted was to help her. She had to know this, he thought. Wiping away the tears from his eyes, Vincent returned his gaze to the poster. He saw a picture of an old man he recognized. It was Ezra, Thomas's Grandfather, on the poster with him. But Ezra had moved. Gone to Florida. His parents had said so.

Vincent found himself craving a menthol cigarette, something he hadn't done in months. In the past, he had used smoking to help curb hunger pangs, something he found himself feeling now. Lucinda had left him food but it had been so long ago, he struggled to remember what it had been.

But now all he could think about was finding her. Making sure she was okay. Concerned with her wellbeing, he had wandered back to Leonard's old creepy house.

Lost in thought, he hadn't noticed the large black cat approaching. Somehow he knew this was the same cat that had come to him as he sat in a cage, mere hours ago. Vincent stepped toward the cat, suddenly finding himself wanting to pet it. Without warning, the cat arched its back and hissed. Vincent took a surprised step backwards away from the cat, watching it as it hissed, before turning tail and disappearing into a nearby hedge.

***

Lost in thought, Officer John Fitzpatrick never saw the large black cat in the middle of his lane until the last second.

The cat sat perfectly still, as if watching the cruiser coming at him without flinching.

Out of instinct, John stepped on the brakes and swerved to miss the cat but felt a thump under his cruiser as he drove past. He glanced in his rear view mirror and saw the large black cat, sprawled on the asphalt. Still watching it in his rearview mirror, he looked for movement, wondering if he had killed it.

With his attention on the cat in his rearview mirror, John never saw Vincent standing in the road until he heard the noise of the impact and saw the boy sprawled on the hood of his cruiser.

Slamming the brakes, John brought his cruiser to sharp stop, leaving skid marks on the asphalt in the process. As the vehicle stopped, Vincent slid off the hood and tumbled on the hard surface.

Shocked into the moment and into action, John radioed for an ambulance, giving the necessary information before running to the boy's side and checking his vitals.

"What's your name, kid?" John said in as calm a voice as he could muster under the circumstances. "Look at me. What's your name?"

John assessed the injuries as the battered boy seemed

disoriented. John was pretty sure the boy would survive this but he had no way of knowing how injured he really was. In that moment, the Officer John Fitzpatrick who had buried bodies to please the woman he was infatuated with had vanished, replace by the old officer he had been.

Guilt washed over John as he was the reason the boy was in this state.

"Help is coming, kid. Stay with me… talk to me." John cast a glance down the road and noticed the cat was gone.

"Stay with me, kid. Help's on the way."

***

Something felt wrong, thought Lucinda as the pain in her lower abdomen intensified. She needed to feed the shadow man and soon. She needed to find Vincent quickly, but Lucinda knew things were unraveling and finding the basement cage empty had been unexpected. Odessa had to be the reason behind it. That damned black cat was a guardian of the darkness. She didn't know much about them, only what the shadow man had told her. She knew he wasn't supposed to take the bonding essence from them before it was time. It would ebb normally, flowing as the person aged until their time had come. Only then were his kind allowed to feed off what was left, releasing the soul to the other place. This was how it should work. Odessa was one of the guardians who made sure this wasn't tampered with. Feeding the shadow man slowly was the key to not being noticed by the guardians. But the shadow man's greed had ruined everything, thought Lucinda as she paused in her tracks, near the edge of Maple Springs Park.

A moment ago, she had felt something rock her body from the inside out. Something bad had happened to Vincent. She could feel it. Her link to the boy's essence was still strong. The boy was hurt and bad, but yet she knew his life wasn't in any danger. The bond to the boy's soul was still strong and in no danger of fading. He wouldn't die this day. But the boy was hurt and so her bond with him would slip away unless she could get to him. Use her charms to convince him to help her still. Feed the shadow man. She would have to convince him to help her still, even though he himself was hurt.

Now she felt pain in her hips and knees. Walking was going to more difficult now. She needed to find Vincent and fast. Otherwise, she would have to start over and that might take more energy that she had.

She closed her eyes, tried to ignore the pain as best as possible and concentrated on Vincent. She could feel he wasn't far and needed to go find him, even if it would drain her to do so.

CHAPTER 27

A **T A LITTLE** past 10 AM the newer model Lincoln Town Car with two bullet holes in its roof pulled up in front of Leonard Legault's house. Its driver parked and stopped the engine.

"Listen, I'm not gonna hurt youse. Not unless you piss me off. You're not gonna piss me off, are you?" Fingers said as he felt the snub-nosed revolver through the fabric of his pocket.

"We told you," Robyn said with bitterness in her voice while she looked at the bullet holes in the roof, fascinated by how the hell they had gotten there. "We don't know where Leonard is. That's why we added him to the poster. Nobody's seen him in months."

"Okay. I get it. But what I don't get is why you know he's missing, but nobody else thinks he's missing."

Thomas and Robyn exchanged puzzled glances.

Fingers pulled a folded paper from underneath the sun visor of the Town Car and proceeded to unfold it.

"When I asked around town about your missing people on this poster, almost everyone had something to say about it. That they weren't missing and whoever made those posters was confused."

Fingers looked in the rearview mirror and saw Robyn roll her eyes at his last statement.

"The old guy moved to Florida, the blonde chick here,

she moved away to be with some guy she met on the web," Fingers said pointing at the poster. "The kid here, nobody knew who she was and this gook girl here..."

"Hey," Robyn blurted.

The girl obviously knew that term, thought Fingers. Although she probably hadn't actually heard anyone say it out loud too often as it clearly angered her to hear it now. Remembering all the lectures about blending in better from the boss, Fingers watched Robyn via the rearview mirror as he corrected himself.

"The Korean girl they said went back to Korea."

"That's bullshit," Robyn muttered.

"And while they all had something to say about all of them, nobody had anything to say about Leonard."

"I don't get it?" Thomas replied in obvious confusion.

"It's like everyone didn't even know he was missing." Fingers watched Robyn's reaction as he spoke. She clearly was the brains of this operation. "Nobody seemed to know except youse two." Fingers said this as he held up the pleated poster so they could see it. He refolded the poster and tucked it into his pocket as he exited the car.

"Hand me that, will ya," Fingers said to Thomas, pointing to his cane.

Thomas had to use both hands to extend the crowbar cane to Fingers who handled it as if it were light as a feather.

"Come," Fingers said as he limped through the opening of the picket fence, leaning heavily on his cane. He paused near the blackened deer, waiting for the kids to catch up.

"This place gives me the creeps," Thomas stated.

He was looking at a large stuffed grey squirrel perched on the veranda railing.

Seeing where Thomas's gaze was cast, Fingers replied. "Wait-til you see the inside." Fingers pulled a key from his pocket and opened the front door and stepped into a somber room.

Thomas squinted as he stepped inside the darkness, away from the bright outdoors. He could see nothing but the faint glow of what looked like wall mounted lights.

Robyn hesitated at the doorway, the darkness causing her anxiety to resurface.

"Come inside," Fingers said.

Robyn swallowed hard and stepped briskly past the doorway and stood next to Thomas as Fingers closed the door behind them.

Fingers watched as Thomas didn't move from where he stood looking about, examining the inside of the house. He and Robyn had obviously wondered about what they would find inside. Wondering if it would be as strange inside as it was outside. Fingers watched Thomas as his gaze went from the stuffed coyote in the hallway and then to the large moose with a black lacy bra hanging from its antler.

Fingers reached into his pocket and pulled out a short piece of a cigar and clamped it between his teeth.

In the dim light they could see a large hawk perched on the handrail going upstairs.

"This place is creepy as fuck," Thomas blurted as Robyn grasp his arm in a grip that would leave a mark.

With a quick glance at the kids, Fingers confirmed that they both thought the inside of the house was even creepier than the outside. This amused him.

"I think there's a broad living here now," Fingers said as he limped to the large wood door that was slightly ajar.

"Lucinda," Thomas replied. "My dad said her name is Lucinda."

"That's what the old lady called her," Fingers replied.

"But Leonard didn't like broads."

"What old lady?" Robyn asked.

Fingers opened the door revealing a musty yet sweet smelling basement staircase, gesturing for the kids to follow him.

"The old lady I found in the basement."

Robyn let out an audible gasp and took Thomas's hand in hers. Thomas glanced at her as he followed Fingers down the dark stairs, looking around the dimly lit basement.

There were dried flowers, cloves of garlic hanging and jars on wood shelves. As they walked past the jars with the eyeballs and teeth, Thomas spoke.

"They're not real," he said to Robyn.

"Some are," Fingers said, correcting him as he walked past a series of jars with a dark liquid in them. A large wood table dominated the center of the room. Fingers pointed to a metal cage in the corner.

Robyn gasped.

"What the fuck is that?" Thomas asked.

"Long story," Fingers replied. "But there was an old lady in there, the last time I was here."

"Did you leave her there?" Robyn asked.

"I didn't have the key," Fingers replied, when in reality he simply hadn't cared. Without knowing why the old lady was put there, it was best to leave her be, he had thought.

Robyn squeezed Thomas's hand.

"You don't have her on your poster," Fingers continued. "She looked like a gook... I mean Korean. She looked Korean but had long grey hair and was old."

"How old?" Robyn asked.

"Old," Fingers stated firmly as if that would explain just how old the lady had been.

"What the fuck is this place?" Thomas asked.

"It's probably where Leonard used to do his taxidermy. But what I want to know is why did he have a cage in his basement?"

Robyn let go of Thomas's hand and walked to the bars.

"Now's not the time for that," Fingers stated.

"Fuck that," Robyn replied. "Is Leonard the reason people have been disappearing?"

"No. At least not people from Maple Springs," Fingers replied as he took the cigar from his mouth and exhaled as if it had been lit. "Look, why he had a cage in here is not important right now. What is important is what the hell happened to him. Where's Leonard? I know the cops don't *got* him, I can tell you that much."

Clearly angered, Robyn faced Fingers as she spoke in a tone that made Thomas cringe.

"Listen, I know you want to find Leonard but we want to find our people too. My best friend is missing and I need to find her."

"I... I saw Vincent this morning," Thomas said in a voice that was barely audible.

"What?" Robyn said loudly.

"Who's Vincent?" Fingers asked.

"My friend, he's on the poster," Thomas said meekly.

"The vape kid?" Fingers asked.

"When were you going to tell me that?" Robyn asked while looking at Thomas.

Fingers notice a change in her stance, as if her nervousness slipped away, replaced by a boldness as she spoke.

"Sorry, but I was busy getting abducted," Thomas answered.

"Look, whoever this broad Lucinda is, she's probably involved in something. I made some calls and asked around, my people don't have a clue about no Lucinda."

"My parents love her," Thomas added.

"My parents fight about how pretty she is," Robyn said with a sigh.

"I can't go back to the boss without answers," Fingers stated. "I need to find out what happened to Leonard."

"Listen, Fingers or whatever the hell people call you." Robyn said as she'd clearly begun letting her frustration out.

Fingers could see this tone of voice was making Thomas nervous.

"I need you to trust us," Robyn continued. "We both want the same thing. To find someone that mysteriously disappeared. And you obviously think they're linked as much as we do so we need you to trust us."

"What's your point?" Fingers asked as he pocketed his unlit piece of cigar.

"I have something I need to check out," Robyn replied.

"What is it?" Fingers asked as he pulled the snub-nosed revolver from his pocket. He didn't bother pointing it at the kids. Just showing it to them usually had the effect he was looking for.

"I can't tell you," Robyn replied. "You'll have to shoot me or trust me."

Fingers pointed the gun at Thomas.

"Okay-okay!" Robyn blurted. "I think my idiot brother knows something and doesn't at the same time. It's hard to explain."

"Duncan?" Thomas said aloud, garnering a dirty look from Robyn.

"He a little guy, about yea high?" Fingers gestured holding his gun hand at about his waist.

"Why?" Robyn asked.

"He's the one I saw putting up the posters all over this house," Fingers stated confidently.

"That would explain where the posters came from," Thomas muttered.

Fingers saw Thomas looking nervously at the gun that was still pointed at him.

"He could have printed them himself," Thomas added.

"Look, I don't know what he knows, if he knows anything at all. He's a kid," Robyn said in obvious frustration. "But I do know that for some reason, he's involved in this. I doubt he really knows what's going on. He's not that bright."

Fingers could tell that was a lie. Clearly she thought her brother was too smart for his own good and this was proof of just that. Fingers was good at reading people's intentions. This is what made him good at what he did. But this didn't make him a patient man.

"Then let's go see him now. Where is he?" Fingers asked.

"NO! We are not going to see him," Robyn said firmly. "Thomas and I are going to see him. I don't want nobody pointing a gun at my kid brother."

"Fine," Fingers replied, pocketing the gun. "But call me if you find out anything."

"You too," Robyn replied boldly, surprising Fingers.

"If you find out what's going on here, call me. My number's on the poster in your pocket. Come on, Thomas. Let's go."

As they hurried up the stairs and out the front door, they never looked back to see if Fingers was following them.

Fingers knew they came to Leonard's house in his car so the kids would need to walk back to the vets to get the company van Robyn had arrived in. He hesitated, thinking he should go drive them. This would be quicker, he thought. But then again, they clearly had wanted away from him. Instead Fingers decided he would take some time to snoop through the house and see if he could find clues as to what had befallen the eccentric mob accountant.

CHAPTER 28

HIS HEAVY-DUTY cane leaning against his leg, Fingers sat on the edge of the bed in what used to be Leonard's bedroom, only now there were too many feminine garments and accoutrements making the room barely recognizable. In his left hand was the poster of the missing people of Maple Springs, in his right hand was his phone, on the bed sat his fedora.

Fingers wasn't adjusting well to lying to the boss for the first time ever, saying he was following up on some leads as if he was some sort of detective. Although he did have leads, they weren't much to go on.

Some broad is living in Leonard's house, he had told the boss. Something strange is going on here, he had said. That part wasn't a lie. But the fact that he felt he could handle it, was. Fingers was good at reading people and getting information out of someone. He excelled at making people change their minds and sometimes making them disappear altogether. The basic mob enforcer type stuff he was good at, but now he felt like he was in over his head.

He couldn't help but wonder if Leonard was involved in this. Did he lose it and start doing taxidermy on people too? He assumed that wasn't the case because Leonard would have had one perched somewhere in the house, if he had. A human in its natural state, posed at the fridge perhaps, drinking milk from the carton. Fingers smiled briefly at the thought.

But was he really missing or did the cops get him? And yet if they had gotten him, nobody would be living in his house, so that idea didn't make sense either. Perhaps it was that rival gang of mob bikers that as far as he knew, had a working understanding with the boss. The understanding was that they didn't fight over territory. You don't try and take my slice of the pie and we won't come after yours; unless they had gotten greedy and come after Leonard, the man with access to all the secrets. But these bikers were not the espionage types and so there would have been a trail of bodies displayed in public places, not missing people.

The puzzling part was all the random people on this poster the kids had made. It also didn't explain why most everyone he spoke to claimed said people were not missing at all, and yet the kids seemed to think otherwise.

Fingers pocketed the phone and the poster, pulled a pill bottle from his inside breast pocket. He shook two of the painkillers into his palm and examined them as he recalled the vet telling him that he shouldn't take more than two at a time. Not if he wanted to remain upright and functional. Even if he didn't show it, the pain in his foot was getting worse. But taking the vet's advice and staying off his feet wasn't an option.

He popped the pills into his mouth and dry swallowed.

He lay back on the bed and closed his eyes. He would rest for a few minutes and wait for the pills to kick in.

***

Lucinda Mayweather needed to find someone to fall under her charms and quick. She needed someone that wouldn't take days to cave to her wishes. She didn't have the time for that. She often could sense those with weaker wills, unable to resist her charms and magic. Although in her youth, many times she had ignored those senses and chosen people that took time to break. A part of her had enjoyed that part. But that was then and this was now, many decades later, and she no longer had the luxury of time, even if that was what she was working on acquiring. The time between needing to feed the shadow man had gotten shorter and shorter and so she felt she had no time to waste.

The ache in her joints had returned but it paled in comparison to the pain in her lower abdomen. That had returned with a vengeance and it was worse than ever. It felt as though something was alive in there, slowly clawing its way out.

She had painstakingly made her way to her destination, now standing under the ornate sign that simply read The Flower Shop with "The" underlined twice.

Sandy, she recalled, was especially susceptible her to her charms. She had met her at the park on the day when the giant plastic demon toy was so easily defeated. She had noted her susceptibility, keeping her in mind for just such a time when she might need someone like her. Someone that wouldn't resist, that would give freely what Lucinda desperately needed. And while convincing people a shop owner, up and left town would be more difficult than she preferred, under the circumstances she felt she had little choice.

Lucinda opened the glass door which tugged on a spring and jingled a set of small bells, announcing her arrival.

The afternoon sunlight shone through the glass storefront, illuminating the store in natural light. There were plants everywhere. A large display of hydrangea in the front of the store with a sign noting they were 50% off.

On the right side of the store hung English ivy, beginning somewhere in the back of the store behind the counter, reaching all the way to the front windows. Under it was an overpowering display of African violet.

On the counter sat an Aloe Vera plant which looked to have been recently cut a few times. A cooler with a glass door sat behind the counter holding clusters of roses and carnations.

"Why do I smell Orchids?" Sandy asked aloud as she emerged from an archway at the back of the store. "I don't have any."

Lucinda leaned against the counter and clutched her side, trying to mask the pain.

"I remember you," Sandy stated. "You're that nice lady with the baked goods at the park. My heavens, those muffins were delicious." Sandy set her hand on top of Lucinda's as she spoke. "Tell me your secret? Please?" Sandy asked, smiling all the while. "I promise I won't tell anyone if you don't want me to. I just want to know why your muffins are sooo good."

Lucinda smiled her best smile, masking the pain she was in as she spoke.

"I'm happy you remember me," Lucinda began. "I'll tell you about my muffins later but right now I need you to help me with something."

"Oh," Sandy gasped while blushing. "Me? You, want *my* help?"

Before Lucinda could continue, as if out of nowhere, a large black cat leapt onto the counter and placed itself between them, startling both women in the process.

"My heavens!" Sandy blurted in surprise as she staggered back, bumping into the refrigerator behind her, making it contents rattle and shake. "Where the heck did you come from?"

Lucinda stepped back, nearly tripping over a small potted shrub.

The large black cat hissed at Lucinda, fur bristling on its back. This was no ordinary cat. Odessa had found her again.

Sandy took a bold step toward the cat.

"What's the matter with you?" Sandy asked, as if she could speak cat. "Don't hiss at the nice lady," she added in a pouty tone.

Odessa turned her attention to the approaching Sandy for a brief moment. She purred as the hairs on her back went down when Sandy reached out for her. Sandy took this as a sign that the cat wouldn't harm her and scooped it up in her arms.

Odessa, now in the clutches of the flower shop owner, turned to face Lucinda again and flattened her ears and moaned.

Lucinda knew in that moment, that Odessa wouldn't let her find a new volunteer to feed the shadow man. Odessa would dog her every move. The only way to survive this was to leave town. To start anew, like she had done before, but this time, Lucinda didn't know if she had the strength to do it.

She needed help and fast, Lucinda realized, as she turned and exited the store.

"Come back," Sandy said weakly, speaking to a closing door as the bells chimed their goodbye.

***

"What's wrong with you?" Sandy said to Odessa as she held up the cat who lazily returned her gaze.

Odessa squirmed and so Sandy set her down on the counter.

"Where did you come from?" Sandy asked. "And what

am I going to do with you? I can't take you home. My Mittens doesn't like other cats. It's nothing personal, you know."

Odessa turned, hopped off the counter and scooted across the floor, slipping into the gap between the refrigerator and the wall.

"Get out of there," Sandy said.

She opened a junk drawer in a cabinet near the front counter and dug out a small flashlight. With her head against the wall, she flicked on the light and peeked in the space between the refrigerator and the wall only to find it empty.

"How the heck?" Sandy muttered in confusion.

There was nothing back there and no other way out, but the black cat was gone.

***

A sullen Duncan sat next to his sister in the back seat of the family car, his arms crossed, and his face pressed against the glass.

"What's wrong, son?" Tim asked.

Duncan had been abnormally quiet that morning. Now at half-past-five, on the way home, the boy was even more sullen and distant.

From the front seat, Gloria turned and looked at her son.

"You wanna taco-bout it?"

Robyn rolled her eyes and looked out her own window. Her usual reaction to the cheesy jokes her parents used when trying to cheer her brother up.

"It's best to taco-bout your troubles, son," Tim added.

"Tacos for supper," Robyn blurted. "Great! The spices give the little twerp gas."

Robyn and Duncan made eye contact.

Supper would be awkward this night.

Much to the chagrin of Mrs. Litney, Robyn and her friend Thomas had paid Duncan a visit earlier that afternoon. They'd brought Duncan outside and had tried to pry information out of him.

"What do you know about the lady who lives in Leonard's creepy old house?" they had asked. "Why did you put posters all over that house and that house only?"

Duncan was probably wondering how they knew about the posters, thought Robyn as she watched his reaction.

"Do you know how she's involved in the mysterious disappearances?" Robyn had asked, doing the bulk of the talking as Thomas had looked puzzled.

"Why are monsters trying to get you? Yes, monsters?" Robyn had repeated, clearly confusing Thomas even more.

To which her brother had asked what a lot of people already thought about his big sister.

"Are you on drugs? You losing your mind?"

She had wondered if her irrational fear of the dark was getting the best of her. Not many people were aware of this fact but her brother knew. He sometimes teased her about it.

"Fingers saw you put up the posters on Leonard's house. Where Lucinda lives," Robyn had stated.

"Who the hell is Fingers?" Duncan had asked with a childish grin. "Is his first name Chicken?" Duncan asked with a smile.

The more they spoke, the more Robyn realized that Duncan didn't know anything about missing people. The more they spoke, the more she realized that she was telling him more than he was telling her. And the more they talked, the more Duncan seemed to grow immature and unlikely to answer her questions.

Something was for sure, her brother knew something but she now thought that he didn't realize he did. And when he began to ask why she was making posters of her friend who had gone back to Korea, saying she was missing, that was when Robyn's patience with her little brother wore out. And when he asked if dad knew about the posters yet, Robyn had known she had to let this go, for now at least. She figured dad knew but strangely he had yet to confront her about them and she didn't want to open that can of worms.

Now, sitting in the back seat of their parents' car, they either spent time glaring at each other or looking out their perspective windows, wondering what the other knew and would they say anything to mom and dad?

CHAPTER 29

ON HER WAY home, Lucinda limped when she walked. Her joints stiffened and the pain in her lower abdomen had gotten worse. She was in trouble, and she knew it.

Not having fed the shadow man in a while, she could feel herself getting weaker. Her enhanced abilities diminishing back to what they were before she had met the shadow man long ago.

Now that Odessa had found her, she wouldn't leave her be. Twice that afternoon, she had been in process of using her witchcraft, applying her pheromone charms to a new volunteer and twice Odessa had appeared out of the shadows to meddle in her affairs.

The first occasion, at The Flower Shop, had taken Lucinda by surprise. Sandy was especially susceptible to her charms and wouldn't have been able to resist her otherwise.

Her second attempt had failed when Odessa appeared and leapt at the man Lucinda had been seducing using her pheromone charms. Odessa had struck the man in the chest, scrambling over him and scratching his chest and neck in the process. All of Lucinda's enchantments had been broken instantly, sending the man off in a panic.

Lucinda knew she was in trouble. She hadn't wanted to, but she would have no choice but to feed John's essence to the shadow man. He was already under her spell, and she had no other options. But John hadn't been home.

Where was he, she wondered as she turned up the walkway of the house she had claimed as her own. She needed to get John alone and quickly. She could make him do anything and so he would feed the shadow man for her. She would sacrifice her lover. This wouldn't be the first time. She had been feeding the shadow man, and cheating death, for a very long time.

She longed for the old days, back in the beginning, when she wouldn't need to feed him as often. Now he needed to be fed frequently. Lucinda's time was long overdue, and it was taking its toll on her volunteers. Although without volunteers, time would take its toll on her.

Lucinda grasped the veranda's railing as she climbed the stairs of the old Victorian home, her knees aching with each step. She paused at the front door, grasped the doorknob as pain coursed through her wrist into her forearm. She felt weak. She needed to feed the shadow man soon, but she lacked the strength to fend off Odessa to do it. Feeling defeated, weakened, she lacked the will to go find help. She staggered into the kitchen and took the antique rotary dial phone from the counter and placed it on the table and sat.

Phones were something Lucinda despised but she had to call John. She let the phone ring over and over, until she tired of hearing it. John would have answered if he knew it was Lucinda calling. He wasn't capable of ignoring her calls. Something must be wrong; she thought while getting up, staggering to the kitchen cupboards to fetch her special tea.

***

His eyes closed, it took Fingers a moment to realize

where he was. He didn't recall climbing onto the bed, but he did remember taking the painkillers to ease the ache in his throbbing foot. The pills, which he had taken a smidge too soon since the last ones, had made him feel very tired and so he had decided he needed a short nap.

That had been over eight hours ago.

"You'll need to stay off your feet for quite a while," Robert Emerson had told him after amputating two of his toes.

Sadly, this was advice Fingers felt he wasn't in a position to take.

Now, he lay splayed out on his back in what used to be Leonard's old bed, wiggling his socked feet, marveling at how the pain in his foot had subsided.

Any normal person would have been laid low by such an injury but there was nothing normal about Fingers.

Minus a few toes, he would soon be back on what was left of his feet, he figured.

A faint aroma caught his attention. Where was it coming from?

In the dimly lit bedroom, Fingers open his eyes and shot up into a sitting position. Suddenly he knew he wasn't alone in the house anymore. He heard a creak in the floor downstairs. He scrambled to the edge of the bed and swung his legs out over the side and sat up. Using his heavy-duty cane, he got to his felt and got a sudden reminder of why he was on painkillers.

Snub nosed revolver in one hand, cane in the other, he limped around the bed and down the stairs to the first floor. Walking softly, he tried to be as quiet as possible, but he was too heavy and clumsy, making the old staircase creak and groan under his considerable bulk. A glint of flickering light came from the kitchen. As quietly as he could manage, he stepped past the giant moose in the hallway and into the archway that opened into the kitchen.

In the dim light, standing there holding a cup and saucer before her, was a mature blonde beauty of a woman, her large hoop earrings almost touching her shoulders. The earrings were partially hidden by long, blond-grey hair. Her clingy blouse showed her figure as his gaze wandered over her, sizing her up to be sure the garments strewn about were hers.

Fingers followed her stare to his right hand which hung at his side, his snub-nosed revolver in its grip.

"Who are you?" Fingers asked. "And why are you in Leonard's house?"

Lucinda clutched her side, obviously trying to mask the pain she was dealing with as she spoke.

"I'm an old friend of Leonard's. I live here now." Lucinda smiled as she set the cup and saucer down on the kitchen table. In the center of the table sat a few containers of baked goods.

"Didn't Leonard ever tell you about me? My name's Lucinda."

"Leonard didn't have any friends," Fingers replied gruffly.

"Tea?" Lucinda asked.

"Where's Leonard?" Fingers asked in response, shifting his weight to the cane as he spoke.

"I can help you with your foot," Lucinda replied, ignoring the rough looking man's question. "I can help with the pain."

Fingers saw Lucinda clutch her side and try to hide her own pain as she pulled back the kitchen chair and sat.

"I think you need some of that help yourself," Fingers replied as he limped in her direction.

"What do you think the tea's for?" Lucinda replied with an air of sarcasm.

"That old Asian lady in the cage, was that you? Are you the one who put her there?"

"Does it matter?" Lucinda inquired.

In that moment, Fingers smelled a strong aroma of cigar smoke mingling with the smell of Lucinda's tea. He reached into his pocket and pulled out a short piece of a cigar and clamped it between his teeth. The temptation to light it was fierce, but he resisted the urge as he watched Lucinda sip tea. Revolver still in one hand, cane in the other, he nudged the chair facing Lucinda and sat down.

Lucinda struggled to her feet and staggered slightly as she made her way to the kitchen counter. She took out another cup and saucer, scooping a generous amount of her special tea leaves into the cup and carried it over to the table, setting it in front of the rough looking man in the wrinkled suit.

"You're the one they call Fingers, aren't you?" Lucinda said while pouring hot water into his cup.

Lucinda sat again and plucked a muffin from one of the containers and set it down in front of her. She smiled, plucked another muffin from the second container and held it out to Fingers.

"You didn't answer my question," Fingers stated as he set the revolver down and took the muffin from Lucinda. "You know where Leonard is, don't you?"

"Maybe," Lucinda replied as she broke off a piece of muffin and ate it.

"I don't want to have to hurt you, but you know I will if I have to."

"I'm already in more pain that you could possibly do to me," Lucinda replied nonchalantly.

For the first time, Fingers didn't know quite how to respond to this. Somehow, he knew this wasn't a bluff. He recognized agony when he saw it. Instead, he pocketed the piece of cigar and took a bite of muffin to quiet the churning his stomach had begun to make.

"Maybe... after we have our tea, you'd be willing to help me with that," Lucinda said as she raised her tea to her lips and sipped. She tried to push out her mystical aura of pheromone charm but felt too week to give it anything extra.

"I'm not exactly sure how I could do that," Fingers replied.

"We'll show you how," a voice from the shadows said. "Won't we, Lucinda?"

Lucinda frowned as she set her tea down.

"Not yet, he's not ready," Lucinda stated.

Fingers glanced at the shadows in the corner of the kitchen, where the sound of the voice seemed to come from and then back at Lucinda. He placed his hand on his revolver as he spoke.

"Who else is here?"

"Just little ol' me," the voice from the shadows said.

"No!" Lucinda said sharply.

From the shadow in the corner emerged a smiling, gray haired, pale-skinned thin man. The shadows seemed to cling to him at first but then ran off him like an elasticized liquid and returned to the corner. His smile revealed yellow pointed teeth. He wore a top hat and clothes that were quite old from the look of them.

The hairs rose on the back of Fingers' neck as he watched in disbelief.

"Feed me, damn you," the man from the shadows said firmly. "Feed me or I can't help you," he said while looking at Lucinda.

"What the hell?" Fingers muttered.

"Something like that," the shadow man replied with a creepy grin.

"Go!" Lucinda barked. "I'll call on you when..."

"Fuck that," Fingers muttered as he pointed his revolver at the scrawny man from the shadows and fired three consecutive times, hitting him twice in the chest and once in the abdomen.

Lucinda squinted and winced against the loud cracking noise of the snub-nosed revolver.

The shadow man stopped in his tracks stunned, marveling at the three black holes in his body. With long bony fingers, he touched at the holes, inserting his fingers in them with a look of curiosity.

"GO!" Lucinda barked as she looked at the shadow man.

Fingers pointed his gun at the shadow man's head but hesitated, waiting. No man alive could stay upright from a bullet to the heart, let alone two bullets plus one to the kidney for good measure.

Frowning, the shadow man stepped backwards as he melded into the shadows hence he came, vanishing from view.

"He's gone now," Lucinda said as she sipped her tea, as if a walking corpse appearing from the shadows and being shot three times with no affect was perfectly normal and certainly nothing bizarre.

"Who was that?" Fingers asked.

"The more appropriate question should be what... what was that?"

Fingers, a man who had felt real fear only a few times in his life, was feeling something close to it now. He looked at the muffin in his hand and wondered what was in it but saw that Lucinda was eating hers with gusto.

"That wasn't human, was it?"

He set his revolver down and using both hands, took a large gulp of tea.

Lucinda sipped her tea and set her cup down.

Fingers saw her glance at how much of the muffin he had eaten as she spoke.

"I'm dying."

"So?" Fingers replied dryly, wondering why she thought he should care.

"Unless I can keep my end of the bargain with that thing you just saw, the one from the shadows."

"You made a deal with that thing?"

"You could say that."

"Is he... is he the devil?"

"It's quite difficult to explain," Lucinda said.

"What did he mean when he said, feed me?"

"Like I said, it's difficult to explain."

"Did he... did that *thing* eat Leonard?"

***

Lucinda glanced at the muffin, the strongest batch she had made ever and yet it seemed to be having no effect on the gruff looking man who called himself Fingers.

"Leonard was merely helping me," Lucinda said. "He did it for me. He fed the shadow man for me." Lucinda tried to use her charms but felt they had no effect. Not many had the ability to resist her charms. Those who did were special, touched by darkness, or where stone-hearted and felt nothing. Emotionless, those people were rare and so to have one sitting before her now, in a time of desperate need made her feel more doomed than ever.

"More tea?" Lucinda reached for the kettle and poured more water in each cup.

"So, Leonard is dead. The boss isn't going to like that," Fingers stated.

"I wonder if you would consider helping me? Helping me feed the man from the shadows so he can make me feel well again?"

"How? How would I do that?" Fingers replied.

Lucinda could see a sudden curiosity in Fingers. He had to wonder about what this woman before him, who had charmed a man full of hate like Leonard into helping her, had to offer him in return. He would have to know it couldn't have been sexual as Leonard wouldn't have been interested in that, thought Lucinda. Leonard had been a bizarre man who was interested in dead things more than live ones.

"Help me find someone to feed him."

"You mean someone for him to feed on, don't you?"

"Not in the literal sense," Lucinda said with a smirk.

"What's in it for me?" Fingers asked as he took a bite of muffin.

"I'm 98 years old," Lucinda said matter-of-factly. This was a lie. Nobody would believe the real number if she said it.

Fingers swallowed his half chewed muffin.

After having seen that thing come and go via the shadows, Lucinda knew Fingers would want to believe her. Although in her current weakened state, she wanted to think she didn't look older than late fifties at best. She knew with her piercing blue eyes and high cheekbones, she was very attractive to most people.

"I know I don't look like much now, but you should have seen me last week," Lucinda said with a pain wracked smile.

She knew Fingers would wonder how much difference a week could make in her case.

"I'll help you under one condition," Fingers stated as he finished the muffin he was eating and reached for another.

Lucinda glanced at the muffin Fingers had just picked

up, reached over and took it from him.

"Not that one. Not unless you want to sleep another day away." She took another muffin and handed it to Fingers. "This one. You'll like it. Trust me. Now about that condition?"

"I need proof that Leonard is really dead."

"There's not much left of him," Lucinda replied with a slight frown.

"Show me his remains and I'll get what I need."

"I can't say I didn't warn you," Lucinda replied. "But first I need your help, or I won't live long enough to help you get what you need."

***

Fingers pondered this. If he helped her first, would she keep her end of the bargain and still help him? But if she wasn't lying about how long she had left, how weak she was, it might not be a risk he could take.

"Deal," Fingers replied, feeling he didn't have much choice at this point.

Fingers assumed that wherever Leonard was, that his remains would be partially intact enough for him to get what he needed. Most bodies can be identified via dental records or DNA. But what fingers wanted was one femur and one humerus; the ones that had the steel plates and pins in them from when Fingers had recruited Leonard to be the accountant for the boss.

Leonard had worked for someone else; until Fingers had convinced them they couldn't control him. He didn't have vices like most people and so they decided on having him taken care of. Which was perfect timing as Fingers, having been tasked with finding a new number cruncher for his boss, had rescued Leonard from what would have been his execution. From that moment on, Leonard had declared his loyalty to Fingers and no one else. But now Fingers had to prove that Leonard hadn't double crossed the boss or else Fingers might be the one that needs replacing.

Fingers and Lucinda sipped tea and ate muffins, as he wondered what was in them as the pain in his foot subsided.

CHAPTER 30

WITH THE SUN setting over the neighboring houses, the blinds shut tight, all the lights off, Duncan's bedroom was as dark as he could make it. He sat on his bed surrounded by a dozen action figures with his favorite in his hands as he spoke.

"Why won't it work anymore?" Duncan whined. "I don't understand."

Concentrating on the figure, he tried to get its eyes to glow red but nothing happened. Having spent a half-hour trying to get the toy to grow into the giant he loved to play with and failing, he felt cheated.

"Why? Why won't it work anymore? Why won't you talk to me?" he said firmly to the shadows. He wanted to scream but was afraid his family might hear him. He wiped a tear off his cheek as the frustration got the better of him.

Duncan reached over to his nightstand and got his iPad. Turning it on, he quickly made his way to the videos. He clicked on the video of the night Lucinda faced off with his giant plastic demon in the alley next to the pharmacy.

He watched as she turned and saw the monstrosity. He marveled at how instead of backing away in fear she had stepped forward, the look in her eyes fierce and unflinching.

"What are you?" she barked at it.

Duncan rewound the video repeatedly, playing that

bit over and over making her repeat this multiple times.

"I don't understand," Duncan whined. "We had a deal. I played the pranks on her like you asked."

He turned off the iPad and stared into the dark corner near the closet, between the dresser and the wall, the darkest of shadows where the shadow man emerged when he came.

"You there?" Duncan asked meekly.

***

In her brightly lit bedroom, Robyn lay on her bed atop the covers still wearing her black jeans and Black Sabbath T-shirt, exhausted yet fighting the temptation to go check on her little brother. He's probably just playing with his dolls, she thought as she heard murmuring through the adjoining bedroom walls.

He had barely eaten anything at supper. Their parents assumed it was because he had gotten his hopes of for tacos, but the plan had fallen through as they were out of shells. And while Duncan also loved his mom's spaghetti and meatballs, they assumed that was the reason he had been sullen and zestless.

Robyn on the other hand assumed her little brother's lack of appetite was due to something else. Something he wouldn't tell her and the stress of it all was getting to her. She took after her mother. Exhaustion setting in and comforted by the bright lights, she felt herself falling asleep until a chime from her phone roused her from the edge of the desperately needed slumber.

Robyn didn't have the ability to ignore messages.

Moving as little as possible, she reached for her phone on the nightstand, grasped it and held it up to read the text message.

"Vincent is in the hospital," Thomas had texted her.

Robyn sat bolt upright in her bed. She replied to the text with a simple question mark.

"He's in a coma," Thomas texted back.

"Can you call me?" Robyn texted in reply.

"My mom is taking me to the hospital to see him," Thomas blurted when Robyn answered his call.

"I don't understand," Robyn muttered as she tried to wipe the sleep from her eyes.

"Vincent, he was hit by a car, this morning, I think. I just heard about it and so I called his mom. She was confused but said that Vincent is in the hospital in Stonevalley. He's in an induced coma."

"Induced?"

"Yeah, my mom said the doctors induced a coma as he had swelling on the brain and so they've basically sedated him while they work on bringing the swelling down."

"Where? How?" Robyn muttered. "Who ran him over? Where was he?"

"My mom said a cop ran him over or something. The cop said he never saw him."

"Where?"

"In town, not far from Leonard's old house."

"Where was he all this time?"

"I don't know," Thomas replied. "I asked his mom, but she was confused and couldn't answer the question."

"What does this mean?"

"I don't know but I had to tell you."

"When did you find this out?"

"About twenty minutes ago. I called his mom because I didn't believe it at first. My mom called the hospital, and they wouldn't tell her much, but they confirmed he was there."

"Could they all be still alive?"

"I don't know. I mean we assumed the worst but...

anyway, I had to let you know."

"I'm glad you did but I don't know what to think about this," Robyn replied as she tried to rub the exhaustion from her eyes.

"Me either. I just had to tell you. But I gotta go, my mom and I are going to the hospital to see him."

"They won't let you," Robyn said coldly. "Sorry. I didn't mean for it to sound insensitive but unless you're immediate family, they won't let you see him. Not if he's in a coma because that means he'll be in intensive care."

"True, but I gotta go anyway."

"I understand. I'd do the same thing if it was Sun-Yun."

"I miss my grandpa," Thomas said in a voice filled with emotion.

"Call me if you find out anything about where he was or how he got back."

"I will."

"I don't want to sound mean but if he wakes up, ask him where he was," Robyn stated.

"I know," Thomas replied. "He may be able to help us find out what's going on."

"He probably knows something that can help us figure all this out," Robyn replied. "Help us find the others."

"I'll let you know what I find out," Thomas replied.

"Thank you," Robyn said before ending the call.

Flopping down again, she stared at her ceiling, her mind reeling with thoughts.

Are they alive after all? Or did Vincent just get away before the monster could eat him? And what does Lucinda or this Fingers character have to do with all this? And why was a monster trying to get Duncan? What's going on, wondered Robyn?

Exhaustion returned with a vengeance as she felt herself slipping away, her last thought before sleep came was about dreams.

Sweet dreams, she wished upon herself.

No more nightmares, please.

***

Still sitting on his bed, Duncan shoved all his action figures off the duvet and onto the floor. He cocked his arm back readying to throw his favorite action figure into his bedroom door as hard as he could until he realized that it would do him no good. Feeling defeated, he set the action figure down on the bed before him and stared at it.

He knew, thought Duncan. The shadow man knew he went to see the body in the park. The one he had told him to bury. The shadow man had told him not to tell anyone about it or he would take away his toy. But he hadn't told anyone. Sure, he had gone back to see it, but he hadn't told anyone.

"That's it, isn't it?" Duncan asked aloud. "That's why it won't work anymore."

Favorite action figure still in hand, Duncan hurriedly climbed out of bed and slipped on his running shoes. He peeked out his bedroom door down the dimly lit hallway at his sister's door and saw the light emanating from underneath it. With the bedroom lit that much, she had to be in bed. On the other end of the hall, his parents' bedroom door was shut which meant mom was in bed already and dad was either reading or downstairs watching television. He shut his bedroom door and went to the window and opened the blind.

"Shit!" Duncan exclaimed as he staggered backwards in shock.

On the roof in the dark of night, sitting at the window staring at him was a large black cat. He started to go to the window and remembered that he wouldn't be able to climb down without help from his enlarged demonic looking toy. He would have to sneak out the back door.

Maybe I should wait, he thought. But he felt a sense of urgency and so waiting wasn't going to be an option. Duncan crept downstairs and through the kitchen only to pause there.

In the junk drawer he found what he was looking for, his father's favorite flashlight which he had bought at a flea market for ten dollars. Duncan snatched it up and snuck out the back door. On the back stoop he paused and tried his toy once again, concentrating on making it grow to giant sized like he had done many times before. Disappointment in the lack of results increased the sense of urgency as he ran in the direction of Maple Springs Park. This would have gone a lot faster if he could have gotten a shoulder ride on his giant demonic action figure, he thought as he scrambled over a neighbor's fence, marveling at how the giant toy had merely stepped over it even with Duncan on its shoulders.

CHAPTER 31

STANDING OUTSIDE under a starry night sky, Fingers spoke on the phone.

"Yes, boss. I just need a little more time, boss."

Leaning heavily on his cane, Fingers held the phone away from his ear for a moment, until the shouting subsided.

"Yes, boss. If everything goes smoothly, I'll have this wrapped up by morning, boss."

Fingers turned his attention to the house behind him as he dug out a half smoked, fat cigar out of his breast pocket and placed it in his mouth, moving it around as if trying to get comfortable. The house was quiet, but the lights were on suggesting that someone might be home.

"Yes, boss. Wrap this up. Gotcha."

Fingers pocketed the phone and climbed onto the veranda and rang the doorbell. He peered through the door sidelight, seeing the brightly lit home and rang the doorbell a second time.

"Excuse me," he heard someone say.

Fingers looked around, wondering where the voice had come from.

"Can I help you?" he heard someone say.

Fingers turned and saw a short lady, wrapped in an oversized sweater that hung to her knees, curlers in her hair and a Yorkshire terrier on a leash, standing on the sidewalk before the house. He removed the cigar from his mouth and breathed out imaginary smoke as if it was lit.

The lady clutched at her sweater as she spoke, while her little dog sniffed about.

"The Pernelli's aren't home," the lady said. "Is there something I can help you with?"

"Do you know when they'll be back?" Fingers asked.

The lady's dog looked toward Fingers and began to growl.

"Their son's in the hospital. I don't think they'll be home anytime soon."

"Hospital? There's no hospital in Maple Springs, is there?" Fingers inquired.

"No, there isn't," the lady replied as her dog let out a subtle bark. "The closest hospital is in Stonevalley."

"Thanks, lady," Fingers muttered as he limped off the veranda and in her direction, leaning on his cane.

His foot throbbed now and the last time he checked, it was turning red. Infection was setting in. He walked slowly as he watched the lady hurriedly walk away, tugging her dog's leash dragging him along.

Once at the sidewalk, he glanced up the street where he had parked and then back at the house, contemplating his next move.

The boy was no longer an option, thought Fingers. He needed a back-up plan and quick. Lucinda promised that she would take him to Leonard, but only once he had gotten her a sacrifice for the shadow man and the boy Vincent had been the best option. The only option, according to Lucinda, but Fingers had a back-up plan.

A half-hour later, Fingers was at a different door, ringing yet another doorbell. This time, the plan was a little different. This time, he wouldn't leave empty handed. He hooked his crowbar cane onto the crook of his left arm as he waited. In his left hand he had his plan, in his right hand was the snub-nosed revolver.

"What can I do for..." Robert Emerson began asking until he realized who was at his door at almost eleven at night.

Standing in his doorway was Fingers, the man who was responsible for the stitches on his right cheek. Robert wore a grey bathrobe which he had on over a pair of dark grey pajamas and matching slippers. In his left hand he held a mug of what smelled like hot chocolate.

Fingers stuck his left hand out to Robert as he spoke.

"Eat this," Fingers ordered.

In Finger's hand was the very muffin Lucinda had told him not to eat. Not unless he wanted to sleep for hours that was. Fingers pointed the revolver at Robert as he waited for him to take the muffin.

"Why?"

"Don't ask questions," Fingers replied gruffly. "Just eat the damned muffin."

"Does it have flax seeds in it? I'm allergic to flax seeds."

"What do I look like, a baker?" Fingers asked. "Just eat the damned muffin."

"But it's too late for me to have a snack," Robert replied, glancing away to what Fingers assumed was a clock somewhere in the distance.

"I don't think you appreciate the gravity of the situation, doc. You either eat the muffin or I shoot ya, so which is it gonna be?"

"I thought you broke fingers and that's why people called you Fingers?"

"We can do that instead if you prefer," Fingers answered. "But either way, you're going to eat that muffin and so I suggest you cooperate and eat with your fingers not broken."

"Or shot," Robert replied. "Can I eat it without being shot too?"

"Sure," Fingers replied.

"So are there flax seeds?" Robert asked as he took the muffin and examined it.

Fingers stepped into the house and closed the door behind him.

"Let's sit, shall we," Fingers gestured with his gun that Robert should lead the way.

Robert proceeded to the dining room, sat at the table and watched as a limping Fingers sat across from him.

"Would you like some hot coco? It's no sugar added and I make it with milk so it's richer. No?"

"Just eat the damned muffin," Fingers replied firmly.

Robert delicately bit into the muffin, as if half expecting it to contain something bad, chewing slowly at first.

"This tastes like one of Lucinda Mayweather's muffins," Robert said as he took a second bite of muffin with much more zest than his previous bite. "I love her muffins," he mumbled through his mouthful. "How's your foot?" Robert asked between bites as he continued to eat the muffin.

"Hurts," Fingers replied.

"It should," Robert said, giving off an I told you so vibe.

"I think it's infected," Fingers added.

"You need to see a real doctor."

Robert sipped hot coco and took the last mouthful of muffin. He got up from his chair as he spoke.

"Let me make you a hot coco," Robert said as he took two steps toward the kitchen and stumbled foreword until he lay face down on the tile floor.

The muffin had taken affect before Robert knew what had happened.

Fingers set his revolver down, reached over and took

hold of Robert's mug. He smelled at its contents and then took a sip, tasting the hot coco.

"Not bad," Fingers muttered sipping more of the coco as he looked at Robert, sprawled on the kitchen floor.

***

Officer John Fitzpatrick sipped coffee from a paper cup as he sat in the waiting room of the Saint Grace Memorial Hospital. He couldn't wrap his head around the idea of getting back behind the wheel of his police cruiser. Every time he closed his eyes, all he could see was the look of disbelief on Vincent's face as he bounced off the front of the police cruiser and sprawled on the asphalt as John slammed his brakes.

He simply couldn't get the image out of his mind.

By early evening, he had known that Vincent wasn't bleeding internally but had a badly broken leg, broken arm, bruised ribs and a serious concussion. And no matter how much she tried, Officer Cortez had not been able to convince John to go home and let the doctors do their job. Vincent was in a coma to get the swelling in his brain down so they could fully assess the damage.

For hours, John sat in the waiting room, practically laying in a chair, staring at the ceiling in a daze. He walked the hospital grounds when he got restless, waiting for more news. After getting an update that the treatments were working and the swelling was going down, John sat in the waiting room, sipping horrible coffee.

Vincent wasn't out of the woods yet but the prognosis was good.

John ignored the sound of a phone ringing at first but after the third ring he realized it was his. Pulling his phone out of his breast pocket, he glanced at it and was tempted to ignore the call. Chances were good that Cortez was calling to ask him if he had gone home yet. He'd lie, he thought, but there were ways she could track him down if she really wanted to and he didn't feel like arguing.

"Hey," he said as he took the call.

"John, I know you're off duty and with everything that happened today you should be home resting."

"I'll go home once I know the kid isn't going to be a fucking turnip because of me," John replied in anger.

"That's not why I'm calling," Cortez replied. "I actually need your help and I think it'll help take your mind off the boy for a while."

"What is it?" John asked as his frustration subsided.

"We have a situation in Maple Springs Park and I need everyone I can muster to get here fast. Can you come?"

John hesitated, wondering if he should say no.

"I could really use you," Cortez said, filling the silence

"I'll be there as soon as I can," John replied, thinking it would take a lot less time if he turned on his cruiser lights and hurried.

"Just make it here when you can and be careful, John."

John ended the call and sipped the coffee; grimacing at the taste while wondering what Cortez needed him for. She never mentioned what the situation was and he hadn't thought to ask. Before he could pocket his phone, he noticed he had a missed call.

He clicked on *view missed call.*

"Fuck," he muttered when he saw he had missed a call from Lucinda Mayweather.

She never called unless it was critically important. He was suddenly reminded of how much he desired her. It came rushing back, just how much he obsessed over her.

Suddenly conflicted, he wondered if he should go to Lucinda instead of the park for Cortez.

Hitting redial, he returned the missed call and let

it ring four times before giving up. Lucinda would have picked up if she was there, he thought. Chances were good that by now she had enlisted someone else's help. Probably that Dwight or maybe Robert, they all wanted to take her from him, he fumed at the thought.

She lived at Leonard Legault's house and that was very close to the park. He'd drive by her house on his way to the park. He walked to his cruiser and frowned at the dent on the hood, the only damage the car had actually sustained in that day's horrific incident.

CHAPTER 32

DUNCAN DIDN'T have a plan when he set off in the dark of night to go find the body in the shallow grave in Maple Springs Park. He just assumed that if he went back and found it dug up again by that mangy stray dog, he could bury it and maybe that would make the shadow man happy. Maybe then he would come and give him back the ability to play with his action figure. That was the idea, when he left the house equipped with his father's flashlight and his dull lifeless toy. He never considered what he might do if he came across the mangy mutt, this time without a giant demon to protect him from it. But to Duncan, what he found was worse than the mangy mutt.

He'd seen the lights from far away, through the trees.

Turning off his flashlight, he crept closer until he saw a sight that made his heart sink.

Strung from tree to tree, a bright yellow plastic tape with words printed on it.

POLICE LINE – DO NOT CROSS

With his action figure still clutched in one hand, Duncan ducked under the tape and scrambled through the brush, scrapping his hands and knees in the process until he was close enough to see four cops, standing around talking as if everything was normal. Near them, they had set up lights on stands pointing toward the hole Duncan recalled seeing, where the body of a woman had been. But what confused Duncan is that not far from that hole, were two more holes, much like the first one.

"Holy crow," Duncan whispered in amazement.

From the opposite side of the lit area, Duncan saw something emerge from a copse of trees. The mangy mutt walked to one of the holes and sniffed at the area. One of the cops pulled his gun from his holster as he nudged another officer to get her attention. The cop with the drawn gun took a step toward the dog as he said something Duncan didn't understand.

The dog growled and barked as the hairs on its back bristled.

The cop stepped toward it and the dog took a step backwards.

As if out of nowhere, a large black cat strolled in between the officer and the mutt. The dog whined, tucked its tail between its legs and sprinted off, dodging the clutching hands of a police officer. While the officers watched, the cat sniffed the corpses the dog had exposed and before anyone could react, the cat hopped into the hole with the body.

"What the hell?" the gun-toting officer said as he stepped forward, peering into the dark hole. "Where'd it go?" he questioned as the black cat was gone.

With everyone distracted by the cat and the body, Duncan crawled back a bit until he felt he could get up without being seen and ran toward home.

He was almost there when he realized he had the flashlight in one hand and nothing in the other.

***

Officer John Fitzpatrick was almost at the park, but he

had a detour to make on the way. He slowed his cruiser as he approached Leonard's old house, hoping to see lights on for a change or something that would indicate what was going on with Lucinda.

Instead he saw the house pitch black as usual with only faint light coming from the closest streetlamp.

The porch light was on at Dwight's house, but that was normal for him.

John slowed his cruiser to a crawl in front of Lucinda's house. He switched on his spotlight and played it over the creepy taxidermied animals.

He would go to the park, see what was going on, and if he wasn't truly needed, he would fake being ill and come back to check on Lucinda. The plan seemed sound enough, thought John as he sped up and headed toward the park.

Moments after parking, he called Officer Cortez. "I just got here," he said. "What's going on?"

"It'll be easier to show you," Officer Cortez said to John. "I'll meet you at the gazebo," she added before ending the call.

***

As he walked through the gravel footpath near the park's gazebo, Officer John Fitzpatrick's heart sank as he realized what Officer Cortez was about to show him.

It had to be the bodies.

John paused on the path, wondering what Cortez knew.

He suddenly felt ill as he realized he had allowed himself to be distracted by Vincent and his obsession with Lucinda Mayweather. Did Cortez know he was the one who had buried some of the bodies?

"There's no way," he murmured aloud.

If she knew, she wouldn't ask him to come to the scene.

Cortez was much smarter than that. Unless she wanted to see his reaction when he saw what they had uncovered. But again, she wouldn't tell him to come here. Tipping him off would give him a chance to run. That would be stupid and Cortez wasn't stupid. Wondering what could have led to them finding the bodies, John walked on.

"You don't look so hot," Cortez said. "You feeling okay?"

"Not really," replied John as he approached the gazebo. "But that's to be expected, after the day I had."

"You gotta see this," Cortez said as she led the way toward where John recalled seeing one of the bodies, he hadn't been responsible for burying.

Sure enough, there it was. The very body he had stumbled on when he'd buried that old lady for Lucinda. Not far from there, were two more holes that looked to also contain bodies. Two more that John hadn't been responsible for putting in the ground. And near one of them were what looked like paw prints in the loose dirt, probably from the same mangy dog he'd come across.

"Damn," John muttered, wishing he'd shot the dog when he caught it digging up the body.

"Something tells me there are more," Cortez said to John.

She's right, thought John, who looked around, seeing a few more members of the small Maple Springs Police force there at the scene.

He knew of at least three more bodies and could show her where they were buried.

"Does the chief know about this yet?" John inquired.

"Yup. The big city crime scene guys have been called in. Although they don't know how messed up this situation is just yet."

Neither do you, thought John.

"How'd you find all this?" John asked.

"A stray dog," Cortez said while gesturing toward the dog prints near a hole. "It dropped a leg, including the foot onto Mona Hopkins's stoop."

"Mona? Bingo nut, Mona?" John asked.

"Yup," Cortez replied. "We tracked the dog back to the park and found this."

***

Fingers pulled his Lincoln Town Car over to the side of the road making sure to stop directly under a street lamp so that the inside of the vehicle would be bathed in dark shadows, concealing the vehicle's occupants to anyone that might be watching. While looking at the slew of police cars in the Maple Springs Park parking lot, he said, "What now?" to the woman sitting next to him.

"I wish you'd have told me you were going to give him one of my muffins," Lucinda said as she leaned against the passenger side door and closed her eyes. "A little would have been enough. With an entire thing, he's going to sleep for too long."

"Either way, it doesn't look like I'm going to get what I need so maybe I just shoot the doc and let you fend for yourself."

"What you want is over that way," Lucinda said pointing behind them. "We should be fine, if we're quiet that is."

"As a church mouse," Fingers said as he put the car in reverse and began backing up slowly. "Tell me when to stop."

"They're by the gazebo," Lucinda said referring to the cops without saying it. "What we want is over there," she said pointing toward a patch of deep dark shadows in the park.

"Under that Forsythia over there," Lucinda said pointing toward the edge of the park.

"The what?" Fingers inquired.

"The big bush with the small yellow buttercup flowers."

"Why didn't you just say that?" Fingers muttered as he glanced up and down the street, making sure no one was watching.

"Wait here," he said as he exited the car, opened the back door and took a shovel from the back seat. Quietly closing the car door, to not attract attention, he limped across the street and tucked himself into the shadows until he was at the bush Lucinda had referred to.

"Foreskinthia," he muttered as he grabbed hold of a handful of branches and tugged at them. "What am I, a bushologist?"

Bracing himself on the shovel for support, he tugged at a lower branch and marveled at how easily the thing plucked out of the dirt, roots and all. He grabbed more and tugged it out just as easy as the first bunch. He repeated this a few more times, plucking out more of the bush until he heard a voice, startling him.

"He's not deep," Lucinda said.

Fingers paused for a moment, looking around to see if anyone else was sneaking up on him. He didn't notice anyone, but he did see a few more Foreskinthia's along the edge of the park. He wondered if those contained more of Lucinda's friends as he returned to the task at hand. Once the bush was removed, he took the shovel and stuck it in the ground, scooping away some of the loosened dirt. Pulling out the bush roots and all had done wonders for the soil underneath it. After a few shovels of dirt, he began uncovering the body buried beneath it.

"Not very deep, indeed," he commented.

"I buried these myself," Lucinda replied, confirming Fingers' suspicion that there were more in this part of the park as well.

He knelt on the damp ground, taking the pressure off his sore foot and scooped away the dirt with his large rough hands until he revealed the raggedy, bony mummified remains of something that looked like it could have been Leonard Legault.

He looked at Lucinda and at the body he had just unearthed and wondered how a little woman like her could have done this to a bitter fuck like Leonard. Leonard wasn't a pleasant man, which is why Fingers always assumed he preferred to spend time with dead things rather than living ones. And Fingers wasn't wrong.

Fingers took hold of the late Leonard's right arm and pulled it out. He scrambled to his feet, took the spade and using it as a makeshift axe, he chopped off Leonard's right arm at the shoulder with little effort. He picked it up and held it out to Lucinda.

"Here, hold this," handing it off to her as he turned his attention to the body in the dirt for the second part. Without ceremony, he drove the shovel into the soil, severing the leg at the hip with a crunching sound. He scooped up the leg, tossed the shovel aside into the pile of freshly torn out bush and took the severed arm from Lucinda.

"Let's go," he muttered as he glanced around.

***

Fingers limped as he walked back to his Lincoln Town Car because of what was left of his sore infected foot.

Lucinda limped because in this moment, her guts felt like they were passing glass and her joints felt like they had been taken apart like Fingers had done to what remained of Leonard.

All her aches and pains were intensifying and it was becoming unbearable. But she had someone to feed the shadow man and so far, Odessa hadn't come around yet. All she needed was to get away so she could convince her new friend to do this for her.

Feed the shadow man.

But first she needed him to wake up and that would take a while.

CHAPTER 33

ROBYN KNEW this night wouldn't be any kind of normal when she found her father's flashlight on the kitchen counter. It looked like it had been rubbed in dirt. Plus, it was out on the kitchen counter instead of being in the junk drawer where it belonged.

Only one person would leave the flashlight out. Her little brother.

Knowing this, she went upstairs to check on him and had found him in bed, sound asleep with toys strewn about on top of the covers. She had made sure he was asleep this time, poking him until he stirred. But he had been outside and with dad's flashlight, this she knew, as he too looked like he had been rubbed in dirt. Robyn had wondered what he had been up to, as she herself set out in the dark of night to meet Thomas by the park.

His text at nearly 2 AM had surprised her as she hadn't expected him to be home that night. And after a brief exchange of text messages about not being able to see Vincent as she had predicted, they both knew that sleep would be hours away. Best to take advantage of the time awake and replace some posters that had been vandalized or torn down.

"They still don't know where Vincent was and now his mother is all confused," Thomas said as they walked down the street past Leonard Legault's creepy house.

"But he's going to be okay, right?" Robyn asked.

"It's too early to tell. I mean bones will heal and all but it's the swelling of the brain I'm worried about."

"I thought you said that was already showing progress?"

"That's what the doctor said but I'm still worried," Thomas replied.

"I get it. But you're lucky. I hope you know that. I'd give anything to know what happened to Sun-Yun."

Robyn regretted saying this as it was obvious Thomas didn't know what to think. He said nothing at first. She knew he understood as he would give anything to know what happened to his grandfather as well.

They stopped at a streetlamp and put up a new poster over the remnants of a torn one.

"I wonder where that Fingers character disappeared to?" Thomas asked as they turned and walked along a street parallel to the park.

"I thought about calling the number he gave me but I'm not so sure I want to," Robyn replied. "I mean maybe he was lying to us all along. Maybe he has something to do with the missing."

"I doubt it," Thomas replied. "If he did, I'm pretty sure I'd be missing too after the way he grabbed me."

"That's true."

"I'm pretty sure all he cares about is creepy Leonard."

"I think my brother was out tonight, but doing what, is the part I'd like to know?"

"Do you think your parents know? That he sneaked out tonight?"

"Hell no," Robyn replied. "My parents are brainwashed, like half this town is. I think maybe my dad knows that I—"

"What's that over there?" Thomas said, interrupting

Robyn as he grasped her arm to get her attention.

He was pointing to what looked like a fire truck parked across the street. There were men in uniform laying out sawhorse barriers in the street.

"What are you kids doing out at this hour?" a voice asked.

Robyn turned and saw a police officer walking up behind them.

"Doing your job, that's what we're doing," Robyn replied out of frustration, this side always came out whenever she saw cops.

"What's going on? Why are they blocking off the street?" Thomas wondered aloud.

"You the kids putting up the posters?" the officer asked as he pointed his tiny flashlight at the black folder under Robyn's arm. "You'd better come with me."

Thomas gestured with a nod for Robyn to look behind them.

By the light of the streetlamps, they could see someone putting up more sawhorse barricades at the corner they had just walked past. Near there was a rescue truck with its lights flashing. Up the street on the side of the park, what Thomas assumed were cops were stringing police tape from streetlamp to streetlamp. It looked as if they were closing off the entire park.

"What's going on?" Robyn asked; her anxiety building as she spoke. "What's going on in the park?"

The officer spoke into the radio clipped to his shoulder as he watched the men putting up the police tape. "Cortez?"

"Go ahead, Martin," they heard a voice on the radio reply.

"I got those kids who been putting up those posters all over town, over," Officer Martin replied.

"Bring them to the station, over," the radio crackled in response.

"You kids come with... HEY!" Officer Martin exclaimed. He turned to the officers stringing up the police tape. "You guys see where those kids went?"

***

Robyn had the flashlight off as she stumbled through the woods with Thomas in tow. She needed to know what was going on. It was obvious that the cops had found something and she needed to know what that was. Sectioning off one part of the park was one thing, but it looked like they were about to close off the entire thing.

"This is not good," she whispered to Thomas.

"I know," he muttered in reply.

They trekked through the woods until they saw lights ahead. Aiming for those, they marched on until they got close enough to see.

"Oh my God!" Robyn said aloud.

Thomas stood beside her as they examined the sight before them.

It was like something out of a movie, Thomas would later tell his parents. There were giant lights all around, little red flags dotting the ground in some areas near a hole. A hole they saw had a bony arm protruding out of it. The part that scared them was the other holes nearby, all of them looking freshly dug.

There were people in baggy white, full body suits with masks on their faces, walking around taking pictures and placing more of those little flags marking things. The reality of what they were seeing was sinking in. Robyn choked back a sob as she wiped a tear with the back of her hand holding the flashlight.

"Check this out," Thomas said in a crackly voice.

He was pointing at something at their feet, something that looked out of place in the shadows.

Robyn bent picking it up as Thomas spoke.

"No, don't. It could be evidence."

Robyn picked up the action figure, a hybrid of a muscular horned ape with goat hooves and large monstrous fangs. This is where he had been, thought Robyn as she noticed the doll was covered in dirt.

"Whose there?" they heard someone say.

One of the people in the white jumpsuits turned one of the powerful lights in their direction, Robyn and Thomas shielding their eyes from the sudden glaring light.

"Martin?" Officer Cortez said into her shoulder radio. "We found your kids, over."

CHAPTER 34

WITH HIS PANTS around his ankles, Fingers sat on a toilet in the men's room of the Greens gas station, his crowbar cane leaning against the toilet paper dispenser. Having the washroom to himself, he had the privacy he needed and so this had seemed like the perfect time to make the call he had been dreading. After a quick dial, there was no going back as he heard the greeting on the other end of the call.

"Boss. I hate to break it to ya but Leonard is dead."

Fingers listened a moment before continuing.

"Yes, boss. Proof I got, it's in the car."

Fingers listen some more.

"No, boss. It wasn't no rival gang or anyone looking to hurt us. Looks like Leonard got mixed up with some broad."

Fingers pulled the phone from his ear but the shouting subsided quickly this time.

"Yes, boss. Leonard got involved with a woman, not a broad. Gotcha."

Fingers listened.

"I know it's hard to believe, but it's true, boss. I got her with me now, although she don't look so hot."

Fingers listened more.

"No, boss. I don't mean she's ugly. As matter of fact, she's hot for an old broad... I mean, for an old woman. But she looks sick, like she might die or something."

Fingers listened, wriggling his leg as he grimaced in pain. His foot was throbbing badly now.

"Yes, boss. Come home. Gotcha. I told her I'd help her so she would get me proof that Leonard was really dead and she wasn't messing with me. I'm gonna ditch her outside of town and then I'm coming straight home, boss."

Fingers listened still.

"Drive careful, sure boss. So cops don't bust me for speeding. Gotcha."

Fingers ended the call and pocketed the phone. He pulled a bottle of pills from his inside suit coat pocket; dry swallowed a couple of pain killers before putting the bottle away again. He pulled a half smoked, fat cigar out of his breast pocket and placed it in his mouth and finished using the toilet, washed up and limped out of the bathroom.

***

Fingers ravaged a foot-long roast beef sandwich as he watched the Greens convenience store clerk ring up and bag the rest of his purchase. He figured the sandwich should hold him until he ditched the old broad. For after, he had two more sandwiches, a pound of beef jerky and six Twinkies. Road trip munchies, he thought as he handed cash to the clerk. He was famished.

For a moment, he wondered if Lucinda might want something to eat as well. He couldn't help it. It was as if he was warming up to her. He was almost starting to like her, even though she had barely said a word since they dug up Leonard's remains. She had leaned against the door of the car and closed her eyes as if struggling to bear the pain.

He didn't know what it was about her, but maybe Leonard had felt the same way, once he got to know her. Perhaps that's how Leonard ended up in a shallow grave in the park near his house, after beginning to grow fond of the woman who would be his demise. The idea of Leonard liking a woman enough to be duped by her was mind-boggling.

Fingers took the bag from the clerk, pocketed his change and limped out of the store. He paused outside the door under the lights, shoved a hand through the plastic bag handles so it hung from his arm. With his free hand, he reached in and took out one of the Twinkies. While leaning heavily on his cane, he limped toward the side of the building where he had parked. He bit and tugged at the wrapper, engrossed in the act of opening the sweet tasting, cream-filled sponge cake as he limped around the corner. With a mouthful of the sweet cake, half a Twinkie in one hand and his cane in the other, he paused looking at the scene before him.

Askew to his Lincoln Town Car was an ambulance with its back doors open, its lights flashing brightly, illuminating the night sky. The passenger side door of his Lincoln was open and Lucinda lay on the asphalt while a heavy set paramedic applied an oxygen mask to her face. Near them stood an older couple, gawking at what was happening.

"Is she dead?" the old man in the socks and sandals asked.

"Give us some space," the heavy set paramedic replied as he fiddled with the oxygen tank.

"She's dead, isn't she?" the old woman in the flower print blouse with the huge purse questioned.

The second paramedic with red hair pulled a stretcher from the ambulance and propped it up.

"You're going to be okay, lady," the first paramedic stated with certainty, an obvious attempt to sooth his patient. "We're going to take you to the hospital," he added.

In that moment, a police car pulled up, the pair of police sprung into action.

"Give-em some room, folks!" the lanky officer stated with authority while gesturing for the couple to step back.

The shorter police officer stepped up to the Lincoln as she peered inside it.

"Whose car is this?" the officer asked.

"His," Fingers heard a voice say.

The store clerk was standing behind him, watching with a look of excitement on his face.

The officer placed her hand on her gun belt, unsnapping the holster as she spoke.

"Are those bullet holes in the roof?" the officer inquired.

Fingers watched as the officer rested her hand on her still holstered gun. The officer glanced into the car and back at Fingers as she spoke.

"Are those what I think they are?"

Fingers knew the officer was referring to the dirt speckled, mummified severed limbs in the back seat of his car. The door was ajar and the dome light was lit, making them visible.

With his cane in one hand, half a Twinkie in the other and a full plastic bag dangling off his arm, Fingers knew he couldn't possibly outdraw the cop if he decided to go for his gun. He also knew he couldn't outrun the officers either. Even on a good day, he wouldn't stand a chance in a footrace. His infected foot throbbed, reminding him that he needed to have it looked at and soon. Shooting it out with cops, if he managed to survive it, would put him on the run and then the infection wouldn't get looked at and he'd risk losing his foot.

This is what he was contemplating when the Lincoln Town Car suddenly rocked as a few rustling thumps emanating from the trunk.

"What the fuck was that?" the spooked officer blurted in surprise as she pulled her gun from the holster. She glanced back at her partner who was now watching Fingers as well.

The decision was made for him. He would let them arrest him, take him in and so that way his foot would get looked at much faster.

"Keys," the officer demanded as she pointed her gun downwards, readying for action as she stepped toward Fingers.

"Left coat pocket," Fingers said as he slowly took a small bite from the Twinkie and let the officer pat the pocket.

"Don't even flinch," the officer said as she reached in and pulled out the keys to the Lincoln.

"Guys," the paramedic kneeling next to Lucinda said. "We need to take her now."

The lanky officer pointed his gun at Fingers. His partner turned her attention to the Lincoln Town Car and pushed the trunk button on the fob.

From the opened trunk sprung a large black cat as it leapt striking the officer in the chest, startling her. She discharged her weapon accidentally as the cat scrambled over her and sprung off her shoulder and bolted.

The cat now gone, the officer heard a moan coming from the trunk.

Inside the trunk, lay a balding man with a mustache and stitches on his right cheek. He was dressed in a grey bathrobe. The officer noticed blood oozing through the grey fabric around a fresh bullet hole in his chest, and even though he had just been shot, the man in the grey robe looked to be unconscious.

Fingers popped the last bite of his Twinkie into his

mouth and chewed slowly. He savored what he believed might be his last bite of the delicious yellow cream filled cake, at least for a while.

The lanky officer pointed his gun at Fingers and stepped toward him.

His partner used her shoulder radio and called for backup.

The lanky officer holstered his gun, pulled out his handcuffs and wondered if they would fit around Fingers' thick wrists.

The paramedics lifted Lucinda onto the stretcher.

"I'm going to need one of you over here," the officer said to the paramedics as she gestured toward the trunk of the Lincoln.

The plastic bag of road munchies still dangling from one arm, Fingers didn't resist as the lanky officer pulled his arms behind him, letting his cane fall to the ground with a loud clatter.

The officer marveled at how the cuffs barely fit over Fingers' thick wrists, not thinking that the cane might have been more than just a fashion accessory.

Fingers mumbled something about his foot as he staggered and pitched forward, falling face first onto the asphalt, scrapping his forehead in the process.

"Geeze," the lanky officer muttered.

The store clerk remembered his cell phone, took it out and began taking video.

"Graveyard shift hasn't been this exciting in a long time," he muttered.

***

Dwight was worried. He hadn't heard from Lucinda in almost a week. That wasn't like Lucinda to go a week without calling on him for some sort of favor, task or grocery list. The last time she had given him a grocery list, it had consisted of only ingredients. No instant meals or frozen dinners, just ingredients for baking. That in itself was odd.

Dwight always wondered how she stayed in such amazing shape, eating all those meat pies, pizza pockets, frozen TV dinners and other unhealthy foods she made him buy. Especially with the amount of baking she did. She was always making a batch of muffins, cookies, Danishes or some other type of baked goods. Although he often saw her giving some of it away. He knew she frequented the gym and walked everywhere. But the amount of food he supplied her with was a lot. It's like she was feeding someone she had locked in the basement or something, he had once jokingly told the cashier at the grocery store after she had commented about all the frozen foods.

But now Dwight was worried and so had decided that since sleep wouldn't come this night, he would cross the street and check up on her. See if she was okay.

He worried that he might find her dead. Lucinda had her ups and downs when it came to her health. Some days, she looked like she was on top of the world, healthy and happy. Other days she looked like she wished death would come calling, and quickly. On those days, if death did come, he got the impression it would be as a friend, like she might welcome it, he thought. On those days, she looked tired and in great pain. But those days never lasted and she always bounced back. Or at least she normally did, he thought as he looked up at the starry sky.

He heard a lot of commotion and knew something was going on near the park and wanted to go check that out as well. But first, he would look in on Lucinda.

He paused next to the blackened deer on the front lawn, looking at it like he did ever since the fire, with utter curiosity wondering if he had ever actually seen it move.

He walked slowly, noticing how dark the house was. It was always dark, but tonight it seemed darker than usual. Like the darkness had depth to it, as if it hid something. Since he had heard voices when no one was there, he had convinced himself the house was haunted even though he had never believed in ghosts. He'd always wondered if they were real but there was always a seed of doubt in him.

He walked up the steps to the veranda and paused at the front door, his hand on the doorknob. He realized in that moment he hadn't brought the key. But as he thought about going to fetch it, he tried the handle and realized that the door wasn't locked.

Walking on the balls of his feet in an attempt to be as quiet as possible, Dwight entered the dark house. He pushed the door closed but made sure it didn't latch shut.

He paused and listened. The house was quiet as usual and he hadn't decided if he liked that. Lucinda often spent nights away from home. Recently she had been spending them with that cop, John Fitzpatrick. But on nights when Lucinda didn't feel well, she didn't typically go out. Dwight had seen Lucinda limping and stumbling, clutching at her sides recently and so he knew she wasn't well. *She should be home*, he thought, but all was quiet and he hadn't figured out if this was good or bad yet.

"Hello?" Dwight spoke at little more than a whisper at first.

"Lucinda?" he said with a slightly louder tone. "Are you home?" He looked about, as if expecting one of Leonard's creations to move. When they didn't, he stepped toward the staircase placing his hand on the banister.

"Hello?" he said with increased volume.

The house remained as quiet as it had when he'd entered it.

He checked the kitchen, walking as far away as he could from the giant moose in the hallway as he did. The kitchen was empty so he returned to the staircase. He climbed it slowly while listening. He paused near the top of the stairs, peeking about in the darkness, the antique imitation torch sconces barely illuminating the hallway.

"Hello," he said louder this time.

"She's not here," he heard a voice say in reply.

"Who said that?" Dwight asked as gooseflesh coursed over his forearms.

"Does it matter?" the voice replied.

Dwight thought he saw movement in the shadows at the top of the stairs. His knees buckled at the thought that he wasn't alone.

"Lucinda!" Dwight said loudly, trying to hide the fear in his voice.

"She's not home, Dwight," the voice replied.

The voice came from downstairs that time, making the gooseflesh on his arms intensify.

"Who are you?" Dwight asked, wondering how this person knew his name. He could only assume Lucinda might have told this person about him.

"Me? Who am I?" the voice answered as if it came from the kitchen.

"Why, I'm a friend of Lucinda's," the voice replied, but this time from upstairs.

Dwight turned and ran to the door, yanked it open and stood in the doorway.

"A-r-r-are you a ghost?" he stuttered.

"Not exactly," the voice replied.

Dwight saw movement in the kitchen, as if someone had walked through the room, but the voice then came from upstairs as it spoke again.

"What I am, is not important, Dwight."

A creepy smiling pale face emerged from the shadows in the kitchen archway, illuminated by the antique imitation torch sconces.

Dwight turned and ran home as fast as he could, stumbling over the curb, up his steps and didn't stop until he was inside, locked in his bathroom. Once there, he scrambled into the tub and sat down. Terrified, he grabbed the first thing he saw, his plunger, and held it as a weapon waiting for someone to burst through his bathroom door.

"No! I'm not living next door to that," he muttered as an idea formed, the only logical thing he could think of doing. "No house, no ghosts," he muttered.

CHAPTER 35

OFFICER CORTEZ couldn't remember his name. Jackson, Jefferson, Johnson?

It started with a J, she thought as she watched him talk on the phone. He had taken over the crime scene and had been barking orders ever since. One of those big city detectives who always came in to take over on the bigger cases and this definitely qualified as a big case. They had found about a dozen bodies so far and everyone assumed there might be more. They were bringing in special equipment, scent dogs and the whole park was already being divided into search grids. The whole thing was being taken over by this Detective Jefferson or whatever his name was, thought Cortez.

"You look terrible," Cortez said to John as they waited for the big city detective to finish his call.

"I feel like shit," John replied. "I haven't slept in like two days and I need a drink some fierce."

"I get the feeling you'll be able to get both soon," Cortez replied. "I'm thinking they're about to dismiss us, now that the big city boys are here."

"I don't know about you but I won't argue if they do tell us to go home," John replied.

Detective Jamison ended his call and approached the officers.

"We got it from here, so you two can go home and get

some rest," Detective Jamison said. "But before you do I have a couple of questions."

"Shoot," Cortez replied.

"Have either of you heard of a guy known as Fingers?"

***

John glanced at Cortez, gauging her reaction to mean she hadn't heard of Fingers.

"I've heard rumors," John replied, knowing full well his expression had given him away so there was no use trying to deny it. "I've heard people talk about a guy they called Fingers but I assumed that was just urban legends."

"Fingers is real enough, although we don't know his real name yet," Detective Jamison replied.

"Why do you ask?" Cortez inquired.

"We picked him up at a Greens gas bar on the edge of town," the Detective stated.

"For?" John inquired.

"We think he's our guy," Detective Jamison replied.

"For this?" John inquired.

"I'm told he had an old dying woman in his car and a man in his trunk at the time."

"I see but, how does that tie him to this?" Cortez replied.

"He had a couple of severed limbs in his back seat that we're sure came from the freshly dug up body on the edge of the park."

"A guy they call Fingers had severed limbs in his car?" Cortez said with an air of disbelief.

"I know," Detective Jamison replied. "I see the irony. Anyway, until we confirm anything we need the local P.D. to keep all this as quiet as possible. Go home; get some rest. But come back bright and early as we're going to need your help in managing this with the locals."

"No problem," Cortez replied.

***

Officer John Fitzpatrick hadn't meant to drive by Leonard Legault's old house. Not on this starry night. It was late and he was beyond exhausted. He had every intention of going straight home to bed, but sometimes habits are so deeply ingrained that we do them without thinking. Like driving by the eccentric house to catch a glimpse of the woman he had become infatuated with. So out of habit, John had turned the cruiser with the dented hood toward her house without realizing it.

At first glance, John was confused as the house seemed lit for a change, as if someone had turned on every single light in the house. The confusion quickly turned to panic as he realized the light he saw was fire.

Flames were climbing up the side of the old house, engulfing all of Leonard's creepy creations in its path.

He pulled his cruiser over onto the sidewalk and ran toward the house, leaping over the picket fence and stopping next to the already burnt deer.

"Lucinda!" John screamed, his heart racing.

"She's not home," John heard someone say.

"What?" John asked, looking about to find who had said this.

Illuminated by the glow of the flames, John saw an old man wearing checkered flannel pajamas standing on the other side of the picket fence. The old man had a cordless phone in one hand.

"I saw her leave earlier. She got in a fancy car with a man in a suit. She's not home," the old man said.

John briefly thought about going inside to see for himself but something told him he should believe Lucinda's neighbor.

"I called 911 when I saw the fire," the old man added.

"What happened?" John inquired, still reeling from shock, his exhaustion temporarily abated as adrenaline kicked in.

"Dwight," the old man replied. "Dwight lost his mind, I think."

"He what?"

Using the cordless phone, the old man pointed across the street where Dwight stood, gaping at the burning house.

On the sidewalk next to Dwight sat a red gas canister.

"I'm up all night peeing on account of my prostate, you see," the old man stated. "So I heard some ruckus and when I looked outside, Dwight was pouring gas on the porch and before I knew it, he was setting the house on fire."

"You saw Dwight do this?" John heard someone say. He spun around and saw Officer Cortez walking up behind him.

Up the road, fire trucks roared, sirens blaring and lights flashing as they approached the burning house.

"Yes, ma'am," the old man said while nodding. "When I came outside, he said something about the house being haunted. Dwight was rambling but I'm sure that's what he said."

"You know what I think," Cortez said loudly, glancing at John as she spoke, trying to be heard over the approaching sirens. "I think we might have found our dumpster fire arsonist."

She pulled the cuffs off her belt, readying them for Dwight.

They watched the flames engulfed the house as the fire trucks arrived.

***

At the Skidmoore house, breakfast wasn't just considered the most important meal of the day; it was also the most chaotic. Gloria had a load in the dryer while Tim made his son breakfast.

"You want pancakes too," Tim asked Robyn who sat across from her little brother, clutching her hot coffee in both hands waiting for it too cool a little.

"I'm not hungry," Robyn replied while in a daze watching her brother.

In the kitchen chair across from his sister, Duncan slouched with elbows planted wide on the table, his head in his hands making his cheeks puff as he stared at his favorite action figure which stood on the table before him.

Robyn knew he had been out the previous night. She knew he had been to the crime scene, but lucky for everyone, the cops hadn't seen him. It had taken an hour to convince the cops that she and Thomas had merely stumbled upon everything and new nothing about any of it.

The posters had helped. Why would they be putting up posters if they knew about any of this?

The cops asked a series of questions still, rewording a lot of them so that if they did know something they might trip up and reveal it. But Robyn and Thomas had been able to evade arousing suspicion and were eventually taken home by one of the officers.

But now Robyn couldn't help but wonder what her little brother had been doing there as she sipped her coffee.

***

Duncan starred at his action figure, wondering how in the heck it ended up on his nightstand.

Was it him?

Was it the man from the shadows?

He hadn't realized he had dropped it until it was too

late and he had evaded being seen as he ran out of the park and headed home. By then he knew he couldn't turn back and go get it. It was too risky. He would simply have to get a new one. Best to replace it and quick so no one would ask questions, he had thought at the time.

But when he woke, there it was standing on his nightstand and he knew it was the same one because it still had dirt all over it. Now it stood on the kitchen table, freshly cleaned and still damp in some places.

Tim placed a plate with one large round fruit riddled pancake in front of his son who gave him a puzzled look.

"Moon shaped," Tim said with a smile as he pointed to a raised lump on the edge of the pancake.

"Rocket ship," Tim added.

"Ketchup?" Duncan asked.

Robyn grimaced.

Tim frowned but handed his son ketchup.

"Whatever works," Tim muttered. "At least he eats breakfast," he said glancing at his daughter.

"You sure you don't want a pancake?" he asked Robyn.

"Sure," Robyn replied with a sly grin. "But shape mine like Uranus."

Duncan guffawed as Tim shot his daughter a look but couldn't suppress a smile.

"What's so funny?" Gloria asked as she walked through the kitchen with a basket full of folded laundry.

"Pancake?" Tim asked his wife.

"Sure," she replied.

"Mars," Duncan replied as he cut a piece of pancake and dipped it in ketchup. "Make mom's the shape of Mars."

***

After dropping off Duncan at daycare and Gloria at the Thrifty Dollar Store, Tim had stopped the car in front of a sawhorse with a large orange sign that had the word DETOUR on it.

"I wonder what's going on here?" he said to Robyn who sat in the passenger seat, sipping her much needed second coffee from a travel mug.

Robyn hadn't said a word since they had left the house that morning. During breakfast she blamed being groggy on being tired and that part was true. She hadn't slept much and so she felt exhausted but the part she left out was why.

All she could think of was the holes she had seen at the park. It was obvious they had found bodies and Robyn was now convinced Sun-Yun would be one of them. Closure would be better than not knowing, she now thought as she looked at the detour sign. But this was not the kind of closure she had hoped for.

"I don't know," Robyn lied, regretting it right away. Her dad might eventually find out she had been caught snooping around the crime scene the night before and so then he would know she'd lied.

"I saw something on Facebook this morning about this but I thought it was a joke," she said, covering her tracks with more lies. She said this hoping that if she slipped up and said the wrong thing, it would cover her tracks but it wouldn't help if her lie was exposed. She sipped coffee and turned on the radio.

"Maybe there'll be something on the radio about it," she added.

The radio played the song; *You're So Vain.*

"Isn't this Fleetwood Mac?" Robyn asked.

"Carly Simon," Tim replied as he turned into the direction of the detour. "Local radio's no help. Call your mother. See if she's heard anything."

***

"Do I look okay?" the reporter asked the cameraman as she fidgeted, adjusting her jacket and patting down stray hairs that stuck out, doing their own thing.

"Perfect," the cameraman stated as he adjusted his camera to catch the crime scene tape behind the reporter.

"Let's do a take," the reporter said as she cleared her throat, patted her hair once more and readied herself.

"And go," the cameraman said pointing at her as he hit record.

"This is Wendy Woodcock reporting live in Maple Springs. We're here at the park in the center of town where police have the entire park closed off as one giant crime scene, and while police have yet to issue any kind of statement, sources say they've uncovered bodies buried in the park. It's believed there are at least 13 so far and that number could go up as police are searching the entire park. Sources also say that police already have a suspect in custody but this has yet to be confirmed. We'll bring you an update as soon as we have more information so stick with us. This is Wendy Woodcock for Channel Seven News."

The cameraman stopped recording, giving Wendy a thumbs up.

"How was that?" Wendy inquired.

"Perfect," the cameraman replied, readying to send the footage back to the station.

***

Phone in hand, Robyn sat on boxes of paper next to the wall near her father's desk in the back of the printing shop while Tim sat at his desk, computer mouse in hand.

"Leonard Legault's house burned down," Robyn stated with disbelief as she surfed the internet on her phone while her father did the same on his computer.

"What?" Tim asked.

"Leonard Legault's house, it burned last night. The article on the radio station's Facebook page has a picture. See," Robyn said as she showed her father the picture on her phone of the house going up in flames.

The phone on the desk rang almost a full ring as Tim quickly answered the call.

"Hello," he blurted, caught up in the moment and forgetting his customary greeting. "Bodies?" he blurted as he listened. "It's mom," he said to Robyn. "She says she heard they found bodies buried in the park."

The reality of it all finally hitting Robyn as tears flowed down her cheeks. She wiped them only to have more take their place. She had felt numb all morning, knowing but trying not to show it. Now, feeling like she was finally able to let her guard down, the tears flowed freely.

"Channel Seven. Thanks, hunny. I'll check it out," Tim replied. "I'll have to call you back," he said to his wife as he noticed his daughter beginning to cry.

***

Under a clear blue sky, Officer Cortez stood near the blackened hole in the ground that used to be Leonard Legault's basement. A ladder leaned against the side of the opening and at the bottom; the fire chief was poking around in one of the less cluttered areas.

"I almost didn't call you," the fire chief said as he poked at something that seemed to still smolder slightly. With his search for hotspots almost over, and nobody else there except Officer Cortez, he said, "But I figured you might want to see this."

"I'm not going down into that hole," Cortez replied.

The fire chief picked something up from the charred debris.

"Catch," the fire chief said as he tossed his find at Cortez who caught what looked to be a rusty tin can.

"What is this?" Cortez asked as she watched the fire chief climb the ladder.

The fire chief took the can from Cortez; pulled a multi-tool knife from his pocket and proceeded to pry open the rusted can.

"I think they were stored inside jars filled with liquid of some sort which explains the rust."

Cortez watched as the fire chief opened the can and handed it back to her.

"Careful," he said. "The edges are rusty but very sharp."

Cortez gently reached into the can and pulled a plastic bag which contained a wad of rolled up bills. She peered into the can and saw a second identical wad in the bottom.

"Money?" she asked.

"I almost didn't call you," the fire chief said with a smirk. "I found six cans."

"How much?"

"I don't know. I only opened three, counting that one," he said gesturing at the can Cortez held in her hand.

"Six?" she asked to be sure.

"Yes," the fire chief stated.

"Did you tell anyone else?"

"Only you."

"Six is a perfectly divisible number, if you ask me," Cortez replied as she watched the fire chief, gauging his reaction.

"It is, isn't it," he replied with a smirk.

Cortez couldn't help but wonder if the fire chief was really looking for hot spots after all as this was the house of a man reputed to be a mob accountant who may or may not have had money stashed in his home.

CHAPTER 36

VISITING HOURS finally over, all was quiet and the lights dimmed ever so slightly in the intensive care unit of the Stonevalley Saint Grace Memorial Hospital. Vincent, who had been in an induced coma, had finally opened his eyes for the first time that afternoon. His mother had stayed by his side for hours, even though all he wanted to do was sleep. Sleep came but was fitful for most of the afternoon and early evening. He awoke often while reliving the accident that left him in this condition. The intensive care unit was typically kept very calm and serene but not that day as new patients were being brought in.

Lying in the bed nearest to him was an unconscious Robert Emerson, the veterinarian from Maple Springs, who was running for city council. He had overheard something about Robert being shot and from what he understood, the surgery had gone well and he was expected to recover.

On the other side of Robert in the next bed, was a man in a weakened state that Vincent couldn't see from his vantage point. He had overheard the nurses discussing the patient, about how serious his infection was and that he may lose his foot. This made Vincent wonder about the state of his own broken and battered body as his eyes grew heavy once again.

A faint aroma of menthol cigarettes roused Vincent

from a sleepy stupor. The scent was coming from behind the curtain to his left. Instead of bringing cravings, the scent brought memories instead. He had overheard his mother conversing with a nurse.

Cancer, he recalled the nurse whispering about the old lady in the bed next to his. He remembered how the nurse had said it was the worst case she had ever seen and that she couldn't understand how she had survived until now. But that smell. The last time he had been around that aroma is when she was there. Vincent felt a familiar yearning in his heart, as if it suddenly began to ache with desire. A tear rolled down his face and onto the pillow as he wept softly.

Suddenly, the room went dark as the lights in the intensive care ward went out. A sudden clattering made him jump as someone dropped a tray. Vincent's eyes adjusted to the soft glow of all the medical monitors and equipment when the emergency lights kicked in and the room was lit enough to function.

"I'll call maintenance," he heard a nurse say as she exited the room.

The curtain separating Vincent from the cancer lady began slowly pulling back. Vincent noticed long bony fingers clutching the curtain, pulling at it slowly.

"She needs you, Vincent," he heard a voice say as the curtain pulled back all the way revealing the shadow man in his strange garb.

Vincent looked and saw a nurse in the process of picking up the dropped tray full of supplies. The second nurse had left to get someone to look into the lights. The third nurse was tending to Robert and had her back to him.

The curtain between Robert and Vincent began to slowly pull forward rounding the end of the bed, concealing him from the rest of the room. Vincent looked at the shadow man who stroked Lucinda's hair.

"She needs your help, Vincent. Only you can help her and you know it."

Lucinda had a breathing tube in her mouth, a pair of IV drips going into both arms. Fresh tears flowed down Vincent's cheeks as he noticed her eyes fluttering.

Was she awake, he wondered?

"Will you help me stop her pain?" the shadow man asked.

Lucinda's eyes flickered, as if she was trying to look around.

Vincent nodded gently, not even realizing what he was doing while tears streamed down his face as he choked back sobs. His desire to help her made his heart ache as he watched the man from the shadows come around to stand behind him. Vincent felt the shadow man's hands slip around his head, long fingers splayed over his face as he watched Lucinda struggle to breath.

Vincent's eyes rolled back into his head and his mouth opened, letting the drool drip onto his already dampened pillow as the shadow man took the essence he needed to do what was required.

***

Vincent had no idea how long he had slept but when he woke, the lights in the intensive care were on again, his curtain pulled back and a nurse from the graveyard shift was checking his bandages.

In the bed nearest to him, Robert was also being tended to by a second nurse who was in process of changing an IV bag.

On his left, Vincent saw that bed was empty. Bewilderment washed over him as he vaguely remembered her being there. Had he imagined it, he wondered as he touched his face recalling the cold fingers of the man from the shadows.

"The lady," he said to the nurse. "The lady in the bed over there?"

"Oh dear lord," the nurse replied. "She was at death's door, that one," the nurse said as she paused and crossed herself before pulling Vincent's blankets back up. "I don't understand it, she could barely breath. Becky said she saw her being pushed down the hall in a wheelchair by some creepy guy in a Halloween costume. She said she was fully lucid and looked good considering, better than good actually. It's nothing short of a miracle, if that's true. But she won't get far without treatment. She's very sick."

Vincent felt sad as a tear ran down his cheek but his sadness quickly changed to confusion as he recalled being kept in a cage in a dark basement somewhere, the memory of why and by whom now unclear.

"But don't you worry about her. You focus on getting better. We're moving you out of intensive care in the morning," the nurse said with a smile.

**

Duncan sat bolt upright in bed, his room barely illuminated by the small nightlight over his dresser.

Did he imagine it? The noise he'd heard just now?

"Hello?" he said inquisitively.

He stared between the dresser and the wall, at the darkest of shadows cast by the faint glow of the nightlight and saw nothing. This was where the shadow man used to come from. But the more time passed, the more he questioned it all. Was it real or had the man from the shadows been a figment of his wild imagination all along?

Duncan picked up the action figure on his bed and examined it. This one, his new favorite was half man, half rhinoceros. It had the torso of a muscle-bound man, powerful grey legs that had cloven feet. His head was a misshapen blend of human and rhinoceros features with a pair of giant horns on his snout.

Duncan flopped back down with a sigh of frustration. The shadow man was real, this he knew but he couldn't understand why he had abandoned him.

***

The nurse smiled as she pushed a supply cart past the cop guarding the door of the hospital room.

"Where's Bruce?" she inquired, referring to the cop that had been on guard duty the last few days.

"He had an appointment," the replacement cop stated.

"Is he coming back today?" the nurse inquired.

"I don't think so," the balding cop replied. "He wasn't feeling well."

"He seemed fine to me," the nurse said as she leaned against the cart. "More than fine," she added with a smile. "Tell him I'll take care of him if he's sick."

"I'll be sure to do that," the cop replied dryly.

"Thanks," the nurse said with a cheeky grin as she walked off with a little extra bounce in her step while pushing her cart.

"You have a nice day, ma'am," the cop added as he watched her walk away.

***

The cop guarding the door glanced up and down the quiet hallway. Satisfied that no one was watching, he hitched up his ill-fitting pants as he entered the room.

From outside the closed door, the voices could be heard in the hallway.

"Carl. I thought I recognized your voice," Fingers said.

"The boss sent me to tie up loose ends," the man in the

cop uniform replied.

"Of course she did, gotcha," Fingers replied.

Two loud consecutive gunshots echoed through the closed door and down the empty hallway, a third gunshot a few seconds later. This was followed by the sound of a body crumpling to the floor and then the hallway went quiet.

CHAPTER 37

AT A LITTLE PAST 1 AM in the dim light of a single lamp illuminating her bedroom, a fully dressed Robyn glanced at her phone, assuming she knew who the text was from.

"You awake?" is all it read.

Thomas obviously couldn't sleep either.

"I'm sorry about your grandfather," Robyn texted.

"Thanks. My mom hasn't stopped crying since we found out."

Robyn replied with a sad, teary eyed emoji as her phone rang.

"Hey," she said as she picked up the call.

"I didn't tell you. That dog they saw, the one that dug up the bodies. That was my grandfather's dog, Bert."

"You serious?" Robyn replied.

"He went missing after my grandfather disappeared. They think that's why he dug them up. He was looking for my grandfather."

"That's amazing."

"My dad thinks they may put him down if we can't find him first, so I've been leaving food near my grandfather's old house."

"Is it working?"

"He's eating it, that much I know. I think he's starting to trust me again."

"That's good, I think," Robyn replied.

"Hey, I'm sorry they didn't find Sun-Yun."

"Me too. At least then I'd know," Robyn replied. "It's weird because they found an old woman wearing her clothes. They said the dental records matched and she even had that leather bracelet. The one with the heart charm I gave her a few years ago, but it was an old woman. It can't be her."

"I don't know. Maybe we should be glad they didn't find her in one of those holes," Thomas said. "I don't know how to feel about it."

"Yeah, I had assumed they'd find her in there somewhere but after four days, I think they've found all the bodies there was to find."

" I heard they've only identified half the bodies."

"Rumor is, Lizzy was there," Robyn said. "She was my little brother's age."

Truth was, Robyn didn't know for sure how old she was but her point was that she was a kid and they had found her buried in a shallow grave in the park, the horror of which she couldn't get over.

Robyn sat up and crossed her legs as she spoke on the phone. From under the bed, crawled a large black cat. It turned and hoped onto the bed and flopped down directly in front of the teenager's legs as it began to purr. Robyn petted the stray cat they had taken in, a feeling of calm washing over her as she did.

"Are you making new posters?" Thomas asked. "For the ones they didn't find?"

"Not right away," Robyn replied. "The cops asked me not to and my dad is mad at me for making the other ones."

"Mad?"

"Well he's mad that I didn't ask for permission."

"He probably would have said no if you had," Thomas

stated.

"Maybe," Robyn replied. "I already remade the posters with the ones that haven't been found."

"Already?"

"Yeah but I'm not printing them right away so if something changes, I'll just modify the poster."

"I suppose," Thomas replied.

"I'm going to wait until the cops are done in the park and they're sure they've found all the bodies."

"I don't know about you but I'm never setting foot in that park ever again."

"Time will tell," Robyn replied. "If they don't find Sun-Yun, I may go do some digging of my own, once the cops are done."

Odessa stood, stretched and climbed onto Robyn's lap and curled up as it purred loudly.

"I can't believe you'd go in there again. After everything that happened," Thomas stated.

"Well it's going to be a while before the cops are done there. Besides, the dark doesn't bother me anymore," Robyn replied as she scratched Odessa behind the ear.

"You can't cure phobias," Thomas insisted. "Unless you were bullshitting me."

"I can't explain it," Robyn said. "It's as if I feel safe in the dark now."

"You're weird," Thomas replied with humor in his voice.

"Thanks," Robyn said, laughing.

***

Odessa rolled on her back and lay still, getting belly rubs from the young girl she would come visit occasionally for a while, until she felt she could move on.

AUTHOR'S NOTE

I often say characters are created out of need. You don't create a plumber if you need an archeologist. Indiana Jones and Toilet of Doom just doesn't have the same ring to it. For me, usually there's a story idea first and then the characters needed to make said story happen are developed. But this book was an exception as the character of Lucinda Mayweather came first and I knew what she would be from the very beginning. A fearless woman gifted with special abilities that allowed her to carve her path through life with ease. Until she bit off more than she could chew, that is. And while I didn't have her all figured out yet, I knew she was someone who would only care about herself. So, she began taking shape before I started writing the actual story.

Now with that said, if she was going to take what she wanted from the vulnerable, then that would leave a path of victims behind. From that idea came Robyn Skidmoore, whom I knew would be a teenager with a younger brother, parents, and a fairly normal existence. So far. Although circumstances of what was happening around her would soon change that.

From this idea, I wrote the second scene from the first chapter. This was the very first scene written in this novel. The prologue and what would become the first scene were added much later. But from the first scene written, I now had a story idea and the concept blossomed into the book that you've just finished reading.

Story ideas and developing them come easy enough for me. But writing them in a captivating way, keeping the story intriguing and entertaining throughout is the hard part of a craft I'll never perfect.

As for the book's title. Well, if you read it before reading this note, you'll understand how picking a title can be difficult to do with a tale that has a lot going on. So, I did what I often do which is to focus on the setting for a title.

Now something else I always like to mention in the author's note is the book cover itself. I sometimes wonder why large publishing houses put out so many different covers for the one title. Are they trying to trick people into buying multiple copies of the same book?

I recall at a young age, collecting Conan the Barbarian comic books and knowing if I had a back issue from the cover alone. A sort of photographic memory you could say. Which makes me also think that perhaps they want collectors to buy different versions, a bit like is done with some comic books these days. And I'm sure there are people who would do this. But for me, the cover is important, and I've mostly gotten my own ideas or collaborated on the ideas for most books that bear my name. I do have an artistic eye and so usually have ideas for this. But with that said, sometimes you have to realize that you're working with certain skillsets that might not fit what I was imagining this time. My friend and sometimes co-writer Angella Cormier has done most of the work on our covers up to now. She does fantastic work and always surpasses all my expectations, especially on my novel Poplar Falls: the Death of Charlie Baker. For that one, I knew what I wanted but didn't have the ability to make this one myself like I had done with the anthology Sleepless Nights. So,

I enlisted her skills to take a mundane photo and turn it into a book cover. What she created was stunning imagery which blew my socks off.

But that brings me to the cover for Maple Springs and my point about certain skillsets not being a good fit. I was debating something darker for this book and was toying with a few ideas. And while surfing pages on social media, I came across an artist from Montreal Quebec named François Vaillancourt. I was amazed by his work and instantly thought I would love to have this artist illustrate something from my writings for a book cover. Of course, I didn't think an artist of his caliber would work with a little-known author like myself. But I was delighted to learn that Francois, while extremely talented, wasn't beyond my reach after all. He explained his process and I knew I wanted to work with him for this book cover.

He read an early draft of the book and proposed some ideas. I found this quite fascinating as after having read this book yourself, you probably realize there is a lot of imagery one could draw inspiration from in this novel. We used a toned-down version of one of his concept ideas for the back cover. But of the three images he'd proposed, the horned ape was the winner for me. And I'm hoping it inspired curiosity and forewarned you as it was meant to, of the darkness contained in the pages of this labor of twisted love. With that said, even if the book was filled with creepy darkness, pure selfish evil and many characters you wouldn't want to meet in real life, I sincerely hope you enjoyed the tale as much as I loved writing it.

Until next time, be well.
Pierre C. Arseneault

ABOUT THE AUTHOR

The youngest of eleven children, Pierre C. Arseneault grew up in the small town of Rogersville, New Brunswick, Canada. As a cartoonist, Pierre was published in over a dozen newspapers. As an author, he has written solo and in collaboration.

Dark Tales for Dark Nights (2013)
Sleepless Nights (2014)
Oakwood Island (2016)
Poplar Falls – The Death of Charlie Baker (2019)
Oakwood Island - The Awakening (2020)
Maple Springs (2022)

Additional short stories were published in the following multi-authored anthologies:

Autumn Paths (2021)
Winter Paths (2022)

Pierre currently lives in the outskirts of his hometown again, near Rogersville in New Brunswick, Canada.